PRAISE FOR DAVE RUDDEN

'Scary and funny – my two favourites. Dave Rudden is more than a rising star, he is a shooting star'

Eoin Colfer

'[*Knights of the Borrowed Dark*] is action-packed, atmospheric and powerfully imagined. But it is most notable for writerly wit and unexpected turns of phrase . . . this is engaging storytelling for any age'

Sunday Times

'Dave Rudden writes brilliantly: his sentences are full of surprises, his ideas are shiny and fluid or sharp and shocking'

Times Educational Supplement

'Rudden is an author to watch. *Knights of the Borrowed Dark* is a pacy, entertaining read, but it has heart too'

Guardian

To Donovan, for handing me that TARDIS key.

BBC CHILDREN'S BOOKS

UK | USA | Canada | Ireland | Australia
India | New Zealand | South Africa

BBC Children's Books are published by Puffin Books,
part of the Penguin Random House group of companies
whose addresses can be found at global.penguinrandomhouse.com.

www.penguin.co.uk   www.puffin.co.uk   www.ladybird.co.uk

First published 2018

001

Written by Dave Rudden
Illustrated by Alexis Snell
Copyright © BBC, 2018

Set in 12/19pt Baskerville MT Std
Typeset by Jouve (UK), Milton Keynes
Printed and bound in Great Britain by Clays Ltd, Elcograf S.p.A.

A CIP catalogue record for this book is available from the British Library

ISBN: 978-1-405-93827-3

All correspondence to:
BBC Children's Books
Penguin Random House Children's
80 Strand, London WC2R 0RL

TWELVE
ANGELS WEEPING

DAVE RUDDEN

Illustrated by Alexis Snell

PUFFIN

CONTENTS

INTRODUCTION
HALFWAY INTO THE DARK

Everywhere in the universe, on every planet that has existed or will exist, there is a winter.

On the planet of Karenina, winter lasts for exactly nine seconds – just a flutter of shadow across the sky. Cabatori's moons have been locked in winter for a million years, and summer is a story told to children when the winds start to howl. There are worlds trapped in orbit round dying suns where winter is eternal and everlasting, and axially locked worlds where winter is a country with a border and a gift shop on the way out.

Everywhere has a winter, and everywhere there's a winter people celebrate reaching halfway. On some worlds there are festivals. On others there are songs, counting each day like a gift. Candles are lit, presents are exchanged, decorations are fashioned from paper or glass or frozen methane depending on the atmosphere.

Most of all, there are stories, because you don't need light to tell stories. Stories are a light in themselves.

Everywhere humans have gone they have carried that light. That is why the Twelve Cities of Gehanna have a Christmas, though the world itself is parched and dead. That is why the Ninth Cyber-Legion crush tinsel under their footsteps on war-torn Agrippina, recording the bright colours without knowing what they mean. For seven Sontarans, Christmas is camouflage. For four Zygons, it's a distraction. For a little girl in Dublin in 1966 it's the day she realises she's outgrowing her world, and in a university on the moon it's the day where a woman forgets to be afraid. And remembers. And forgets.

Christmas is a story, one of thousands told across centuries, like reflections in a shop window, different and similar and personal and gigantic, finding their own place in the cosmos like meteors, like stars.

In London in the nineteenth century, a Silurian chooses a present for her love.

In a tower of glass, there is a mantle that is crown and coffin both.

At the end of the universe, there is a trail of Christmas lights a million miles long, draped across the void like a lure.

We all have our talismans when the cold creeps in. We all have our customs when the sun begins to fade. But every light casts a shadow, and the brighter the shine the deeper the shade.

To get halfway out of the dark you have to enter it in the first place, and that's when the song becomes a countdown. Like a timer. Like a bomb.

Twelve days. Twelve stories.

Every light casts a shadow.

And every story needs a villain.

THE WEEPING
ANGELS
GREY MATTER

N o one knew which came first, the sickness or the storm, but one thing was clear: the planet of Gehanna was drowning in dust.

For three weeks, an unknown epidemic had eaten city after city, as a blizzard of grit thickened the air and veiled the sky. From his study high in the Basilica of Wellness, Chief Medical Officer Perinne should have been able to see the entirety of City One – its golden domes, its slender minarets – but now there was nothing but shifting, swirling grey.

Sometimes Perinne thought he could see faces in it.

It was the first time such a storm had besieged the Twelve Cities, just as it was the first time disease had laid them low. Gehanna was the definition of a controlled environment: a parched rock uninhabited by even the tiniest of life-forms, the perfect location for medical research. Everything on the planet was meticulously managed, from the great orbital engines that provided a suitably neutral atmosphere to the sterile gowns that had become Gehannan civilian dress.

But this was something new, something never before recorded in the towering diagnostic engines in the basilica's heart. Perinne had done everything he could – instigated quarantine, deployed troops, grounded all flights and cancelled all travel (though by that point the storm was doing that anyway) – and yet, somehow, the plague still managed to spread.

City Twelve had fallen in a single night, and then City Eleven, exploding into riots as infected and healthy alike tried to escape. City Ten had left a simple goodbye message repeating on its comm servers, like a guest politely excusing themselves from a party, and then they had gone dark as well.

No storm ever displayed such thinking, whispering spite – finding its way under nails, down shirts, into the gap between eyelid and eye. No plague had ever acted with such accelerated virulence, erasing city after city like footprints in a sandstorm.

By the time City Four fell, Perinne's servers had groaned under the weight of requests and demands and pleas for help, and now City One was all that remained. The relative silence was almost a relief.

'Sir?' The voice was thin, scraped raw by static from the infernal blizzard. It got everywhere, eroding communications and fuzzing signals, the way the plague numbed the nerves. He shook off the thought. There were enough superstitious doctors in his wards already, thinking the two were somehow connected, despite all their exhaustive tests.

Data, not sentiment. Only data mattered.

'Screen One, display communications.'

The Chief Medical Officer's desk was clustered with screens, like the multi-faceted eye of a fly. Most displayed the medical data of every last surviving person on Gehanna – a list that had shortened dramatically in the past eleven days – but one displayed a figure hunched against the storm, the face anonymous beneath the white curve of a salus-mask.

Salus-masks were a requisite of employment on Gehanna. Why risk exposure diagnosing a patient when they could automatically send their diagnostics straight to you? Perinne could see his own mask, identical to Lieutenant Rozz's, half-reflected in the screen: the wide red lenses, the sweeping nose with its bio-filter and built-in chem-scrubbers, and the narrow, downturned mouth grille surrounded by delicate crimson circuitry like smears of wine.

Inside each salus-mask was the most sophisticated bioware of the thirty-fourth century. All were connected directly to the wearer's synapses, and fed information directly to the basilica's diagnostic engines and the team of scientists interpreting the data.

And to Perinne, of course. That was his privilege as Chief Medical Officer.

'Lieutenant Rozz, are we ready to seal the basilica?'

The figure on the screen did not show any surprise at being recognised. Perinne didn't need to see Lieutenant Rozz's face, when his own mask was telling him exactly how much Vitamin D she was missing from her diet, and what day her heart would eventually give out. He knew it was her.

This was also how he knew, after all other communication had failed, that each city had fallen. He'd seen it, in the corner of his eye.

'Yes, sir. We've stripped every hospital and clinic in the records you provided. You were right about the noble houses as well. They'd been stockpiling.'

So had Perinne. Files on those citizens with a tendency towards addiction. Profiles of obsessive personalities, and those who planned for crises almost as well as Perinne himself. All relevant. All useful. Gehanna was a controlled environment. It was *his* environment, and there could be no secrets from the man trying to keep them all safe.

'Good. I am triggering Seraphim in four minutes. Anything not inside the basilica stays outside.'

'But, sir . . .'

Perinne watched with interest as the lieutenant's heart rate rose. A sign of infection?

'Not all the teams have returned. Some reported resistance. From the infected.'

'They came in contact with plague carriers?' Perinne snapped. 'That is directly against orders!'

He leaned back into his soft leather chair. How was he to keep the basilica – Gehanna – safe if his orders were disobeyed? He'd seen how fast the plague moved. All their safety protocols, all their quarantines – nothing had slowed its advance.

That was why he had shut City One. That was why he'd refused any requests for aid. He'd told them to do as he did – wall off their cities, preserve what could be preserved – and yet they had insisted on trying to help the infected, securing their own ruin in the process.

In the corner of his eye, Screen 12 flickered. The one screen he had never reassigned. *This is your fault*, he told it, as he had done many times while his world died around him. *If only I'd got you to work . . .*

'Sir, we're still in contact with them. They will be back here in –'

'No. Wait for them if you like, but we will be sealing the basilica in three and a half minutes. Where you are when that happens is up to you.'

A spike in adrenaline betrayed the calm in Lieutenant Rozz's voice. 'Understood, sir.'

Chief Medical Officer Perinne nodded to himself, satisfied behind his own salus-mask, and made a note to schedule Lieutenant Rozz and her entire platoon for extra decontamination, just to be sure.

'CAUTION.'

Deep inside the basilica, machinery began to grind.

'CAUTION.'

Systems that had lain dormant since the founding of Gehanna flickered slowly to life.

'CAUTION.'

The basilica was a knot of rounded towers, surrounded at the base by bulbous hospital centres and dormitoria. City One huddled close to it, but now signals pulsed to long-embedded munitions, demolishing the nearest buildings with precise blasts. When the dust cleared – as far as it could clear in the choked and heavy air – there was a barren, sterile gap between city and hospital.

'ENTRANCE TO THE BASILICA OF WELLNESS IS NOW FORBIDDEN.'

Speakers blared the warning, as a rising shield of ionised light vaporised the dust, wrapping the tower in a blanket of pure, clean air. Gates fell. Shutters slammed down over windows, and portholes slid open to admit the long barrels of automated cannons. These cannons, shiny-black and never fired, began to pan back and forth, purring with sensors.

'Seraphim Protocol now in effect.'

The dust swirled like spooked birds, and then quietly descended once again.

'Ladies and gentlemen, the doctors are in!'

Dutiful laughter rang out around the dining hall, tinny through 1,500 salus-masks. The data these masks had collected had been invaluable to Perinne in choosing who, of the great and good of Gehannan society, would be offered sanctuary here in the basilica's halls. The same was true of the guards here – it was no coincidence that the loyal and dutiful Lieutenant Rozz had been given warning of the protocol being activated, while other, more troublesome soldiers had been ordered to range further afield.

Caution. Always, always, caution. And now, with Seraphim engaged, Perinne could at last be sure that they were safe.

'My friends, we now reside behind the most complex and comprehensive quarantine technology known to humankind.'

The commissary was a massive sprawl of gilt and granite, artfully arranged flowers almost hiding the sharp scent of bleach. There were no seasons on Gehanna, but the original settlers had brought their midwinter festival with them, hanging it like tinsel on an arbitrary date, and in accordance with the rules Perinne had bestowed a modest budget towards decorations. Strands of red had been draped over the doorways and steel-shuttered windows, hanging across the painted white like the elegant circuitry of a salus-mask.

Porters had moved all the tables to the walls, leaving only Perinne's massive chair at the head of the hall. It was pleasingly reminiscent of a throne.

'The Seraphim Protocol renders the basilica a fortress on a molecular level, guarded against every illness the human race has ever encountered by both cutting-edge human technology and the innovations of alien races.'

No rise in heart rate. No readable excitement. *No matter.* Of course they didn't understand. How could they?

'Only here will we find the root of the Plague Cinereal. Only here, surrounded by Gehanna's finest minds –'

None of which (bar himself) were actually present at this little celebration, as Perinne had practically chained them to their desks until a cure was found, but there was no harm in making these hangers-on feel part of the club.

'– will the cure be found for the illness lurking outside our gates.'

There was the jump in heart rate. Their salus-masks recorded it, and his salus-mask played the data as a stream of symbols across his retinas. They all stared at him, faces identical above their finery, while he read each of them more completely than they could ever know themselves.

'In that case . . .'

Magentress Sapphix of the Golor Dynasty had raised her hand, and Perinne blinked at the interruption.

Sapphix. Hadn't Perinne heard that Golor's finances were struggling? This brief thought opened a cascade of figures: bad decisions, shrinking funds, all recorded dutifully by the basilica. The smile he gave the Magentress was indulgent, with just the faintest touch of commiseration.

'Yes, Magentress?'

She looked at him through the red gleam of lenses. 'Can we take off the masks?'

In his long years of study, Perinne had researched all types of toxin. There was a lab deep within the basilica where thousands of the most dangerous chemicals in the universe were analysed and experimented upon, taken apart and put back together so that cures might be found. But it was only as he watched city after city die that Perinne had realised that doubt was the most dangerous disease of all. Doubt made people avoid their doctor. Doubt made people forgo their meds.

The other cities had doubted his wisdom and died for it. Chief Medical Officer Perinne would suffer no doubt here.

'Oh, absolutely, my dear!'

Sapphix lifted gloved hands to her mask.

'Though that does mean immediate expulsion from the basilica.'

Her fingers froze on the mask's clasp.

'And I'm afraid the perimeter defences are automated. To keep away the infected, you understand. Though it is only a . . . five-hundred-metre dash?'

'Four hundred,' Lieutenant Rozz said, from the back.

'Four-hundred-metre dash to the city.' The Magentress's vitals blinked across his vision. 'Someone as healthy as you should definitely make it to the infected zone. And, I must say, in the interests of science, if you wore your mask while doing so it would provide us with *very* interesting data.'

The Magentress's hand fell. 'I . . . Never mind.'

Perinne clapped his gloved hands. 'Excellent!'

Porters began to enter, bearing platters of festive, nutritionist-approved food. Jaunty traditional music began to leak tinnily from the intercom.

'Do not worry, my friends! While we – *I* – work on curing the mysterious and deadly plague that threatens us all, you should revel! Be merry! Be assured, your fate is in good . . .' He trailed off as his eyes fell on one of the great pillars.

No one had so much glanced in its direction, but Chief Medical Officer Perinne knew every single inch of the basilica. He knew its systems. He knew its capabilities. He knew how much food was in its stores and how many rounds in its defensive cannons. He knew it like he knew the human body – and, like the human body, the presence of foreign objects came as a nasty surprise.

He knew, for example, that the foyer had never had a phone box.

'Hello,' came a voice by his ear. 'I'm the Doctor.'

*

There wasn't a protocol in place to decontaminate people who arrived during Seraphim lockdown. It had never happened before. After Chief Medical Officer Perinne had got over his shock – a process aided greatly by watching the intruder get dragged away – some improvisation had taken place.

'How long has it been now?'

Relocating to his study had not hurt, either. He had his salus-mask. He had his screens. What more did he need?

'Three hours and forty-five minutes, sir.'

Magne-scrubs. Chemical peels. Lung-scrapes. All manner of invasive instruments had been applied to the intruder and, while sympathy didn't show up on salus-mask data, Perinne could hear it in Lieutenant Rozz's voice all the same.

Perinne's smile rubbed at the edges of his mask. 'Then I trust he is ready to talk?'

'He's . . . he's singing, sir.'

'What? Screen One, display decontamination cell.'

A lined face, a thundercloud of grey hair and an expression that was less a smile than a baring of the teeth. The stranger stood in a shower of scalding chemicals, yelling some unintelligible song at the top of his lungs, his deep-set eyes seemingly bypassing the camera entirely to stare directly into Perinne's.

'We had to halt the automated psychological examination because he upset the computer,' Lieutenant Rozz said.

This is ridic—

Perinne activated the intercom.

'Who are you? Why are you here? How did you get in?'

The stranger stopped singing, and glared up at the camera silently. Glaring seemed to be his default expression. Perinne had a separate screen speed-running through the footage they'd already captured. Three hours and forty-five minutes of rigorous examination, and this person's expression had never changed: weathered and ferocious, like a statue of some old general that had endured centuries of storm.

'All terrible questions,' the stranger retorted. 'And, if anyone tries to put one of those masks on me again, I will snap it in half. Where did you get them anyway? There's Derullian tech in there, Mondasian, it's a pick 'n' mix —'

'This is a research hospital,' Perinne said, flushing. *Nobody* spoke to him like that! At least not when wearing a salus-mask. Even the mouthiest patient went silent when Perinne started detailing all the illnesses they might have. 'We use every piece of technology we can get our hands on to combat disease – alien or otherwise.'

Doubt is the most dangerous disease. Perinne took a deep breath to steady his voice. He couldn't let his soldiers, his doctors, his *interns* see any sign of weakness. It had to be fortified against, vaccinated against like the toxins in his lab far below.

Screen 12 flickered like a mote of dust in the corner of his vision, like a scrape on his cornea that wouldn't heal. If only he had been able to . . . Then they could have been really, truly safe.

Seraphim Protocol. Only he knew that name for the lie it was.

I tried. That was all he could do.

'Very good,' the Doctor growled. He had an odd accent. Consonants kept disappearing, only to reappear and ambush Perinne in unexpected places. 'That's it right there. *That* is what a doctor does. They use everything at their disposal. Which leads me to my next question. The most important question.'

Perinne's heart rate stuttered unhelpfully across his vision. 'What are you –'

'This is a hospital, yes? The whole planet? That's why you colonised it. Chosen for its sterility, its lack of natural pathogens. A clean Petri dish. You make cures here. You help sick people. That's what you do.'

There were four other doctors outside the stranger's decontamination cell. Six guards in the corridors outside. They were all listening as closely as Perinne. He could see it on his screens.

'And?'

'So why are your doors closed?'

Heart-rate spikes across the board. Perinne made a note of each and every one.

'There is a disease –'

'I know there is. And you're a doctor. This is a hospital. You should be groaning at the seams.'

'We are studying –'

'You should be *treating*. You should be out there trying to find –'

'That's what the other cities did!' Perinne was shaking now. Sweat was fogging the inside of his mask. 'And they died! There are valuable medical professionals here, and –'

'Doctors,' the stranger rumbled. 'There are doctors here, and you closed your doors. Now, tell me about the disease. Symptoms. Who –'

'Not until you explain who you are,' Perinne snapped. 'Not until you tell us how you got in here. What you want.' This wasn't how things were supposed to go. He had sealed off the basilica to have time to think, to figure out what was happening to his world, not to be attacked.

'Now you're asking me questions I've already answered! Easy knowing I don't charge by the hour. As for how I managed to get in . . .' He laughed then, and it was somehow worse than his snarl. 'I'm like a virus. There's no keeping me out.'

'This place was designed to keep viruses out,' Perinne retorted. 'So why come here? Why are you putting all of us in danger? You could have brought the plague in with you. You could have trapped us all in here with it.' His voice had risen higher and higher. A rash of lights spun across his vision – his own vitals in distress.

'Oh yes, the most depressing bit of this whole farce,' the Doctor replied. 'And, believe me, that is a category with stiff competition. *You* would ask me that. *You* would question why I'd show up on a planet that was drowning in plague.'

He leaned forward, and in those deep-set, dark eyes Perinne saw dead worlds and dying lights and an ancient, ageless fury that was at once utterly alien and jarringly familiar. He'd seen that same look in the eyes of the battlefield medics who transferred to Gehanna to work somewhere they weren't getting shot at, before they inevitably got cabin fever and transferred out again.

It wasn't anger. Anger was specific. This was *frustration*, and it emanated from this stranger like radiation from a dying star.

'I'm a doctor,' he said simply. 'I came here to help.'

*

The Plague Cinereal.

It began in the lungs. Or in the heart. Or in the eyes, the liver, the brain, the hands. It grew in the limb you used the most, or festered in a cut you didn't realise you had, or one day it was simply there, twisted through you like ivy, as if it had been there long before you were born and would be there long after you were dead.

Like dust. Like the stones under your feet.

Numbness. Lethargy. Stiffness. Thickening, flaking skin. Loss of feeling in extremities. Paranoia. Tumours on the spine. Paralysis. Death.

'I'm missing something,' the Doctor murmured, as he scrolled through page upon page of reports. They hadn't let him out of his cell, but there had been too many eyes on Perinne to deny that another doctor could only help. He'd grudgingly allowed him access to the basilica's diagnostic systems, projecting data on to the white walls of the Doctor's cell in red and blue and sickly green.

'This is all the notes we have,' the Chief Medical Officer said over the intercom. He had dismissed his staff, telling himself that it was because they couldn't neglect their own work in favour of listening to a madman – and not because he didn't want them listening to a madman who might know more than him.

Bad for morale. He was in charge. He made the decisions. The chain of command had to stand.

'The salus-masks provide a constant link to every single human on the planet,' Perinne said, trying unsuccessfully to keep the pride from his voice. 'Tracking the plague's progress was simple, but as for how it started and who it targets . . .'

'City Twelve fell in a *night*? An entire city?'

'Yes.'

The Doctor scrubbed a hand through his wiry hair, the light of a million cases reflected in his eyes. 'But diseases start somewhere. A vector, a patient zero, a contaminant – they don't just appear everywhere across a city all at once. That's not how diseases *work*.'

'The disease doesn't behave like a disease should.' A flurry of keys being pressed, then all of Perinne's carefully assembled theories began to flash across the Doctor's cell. 'Normally the weak and elderly fall first, but here older sufferers held out for hours while young and strong patients fell immediately. Those already suffering from illnesses resisted longer than the healthy, except when they didn't. There's no pattern. There's no reason.'

'Yes there is,' the Doctor muttered. 'You just don't know what it is yet. And this storm isn't right, either. The whole planet's climate-controlled. How is –'

'We thought of that,' Perinne countered. 'The atmospheric engines are working perfectly. Or they were before we lost communications. We've tested the dust.'

'And?'

'And it's dust. No bacteria or viruses. It's just plain marble dust –'

The Doctor stopped scrolling. 'Marble?'

'Yes.'

'Marble dust. Here?'

'Yes.'

The Doctor's voice was the quietest Perinne had heard it. 'I need all of the examination records carried out on the infected. I need pictures. Why are there no pictures?'

'Are you insane?' Perinne snapped. 'We lost eleven cities in as many nights! I quarantined City One as soon as I could, and the basilica soon after that. We have the salus-masks –'

'Salus-masks. Yes. You keep saying. But masks look outwards,' the Doctor said. 'And hide what's right in front of your face. Can someone, anyone, show me a picture of what a late-stage case looks like?'

'You have to understand,' Perinne said. The corner of his eye was itching, and he fought the urge to take off his mask and scratch it. 'The other cities were lost causes. We had to close our gates, and even that didn't stop the plague. Our only chance was sealing ourselves off.'

Had the figure on Screen 12 moved? *No.* It couldn't have. Perinne's buyer had been very specific, and if there was one thing the Chief Medical Officer knew how to do, it was follow the instructions on the box.

He'd so hoped to incorporate it into Seraphim. The perfect defence against disease. Against everything. And instead it had just stood there and mocked him. The act of observing something was to change it – that was what he had learned in university – and yet, no matter how much he observed it, it never changed at all.

'That's. Not. What. We. Do.' The words came pained through clenched teeth. 'That's why you haven't figured this out yet. Because you haven't stared a single patient in the eye. As soon as it seemed as though you were losing control, you closed your eyes and pretended it wasn't happening. As if it was a problem. A puzzle. Not *people.*'

The Doctor looked suddenly old. Old and drained, as if more than germs had been scrubbed away.

'Except, if I'm right, they're all still out there. All your sick. All your waiting patients. I imagine this hospital has defences, yes? In case the sick people try to see a doctor?'

'Yes,' Perinne whispered. 'But why –'

Something was unfolding in his head. A realisation, like all the times – and there had been many – when he had wanted a patient to live, wanted something to turn out to be nothing, and felt that terrible powerlessness that was the lot of a doctor.

'And those defences have cameras? Automated cameras. On all the time. Right?' the Doctor said. 'That's why *you* haven't seen them yet. Those cameras are the only thing keeping everyone here safe.'

'Doctor,' Perinne said. It was very nearly a plea. 'I don't understand.'

'Marble dust,' the Doctor repeated. 'You thought your people were dying, but the salus-masks stopped recording data because what was underneath was no longer human. The tumours. The stiffening skin. It's not death. It's a transformation.'

'What do you –'

'They're not tumours,' the Doctor said. 'They're wings.'

It was the night of the festival. Perinne only realised because the city's festive lights were on an automated timer and, between the plague and the riots and the shutting of the basilica, nobody had thought to turn them off.

Music pounded through the basilica as the revellers tried to remember what it was like to be outside, or to forget what was actually outside, or both. Perinne was alone in his study, staring out through the exterior camera feeds. Through grainy night vision, he could see the bubble of clear, clean air generated by the shield, and beyond that the circle of flattened rubble that had once been clustered homes.

Everything after that was just grey, shot through with the red festive lights, like the dying thoughts of an ailing brain.

Everything I have done, I have done for the best.

The cameras were a Caballian design; engineered to read every type of energy a living body could produce. The cannons were Sontaran scrap a predecessor had lovingly restored. Every improvement that could be made had been made – cost and danger be damned.

Don't turn those cameras off.

'I haven't done anything wrong.'

He'd turned Screen 10 to the commissary, where the great and good of Gehanna danced and feasted still. Someone had draped tinsel over the camera, a red blur like an inflamed vein.

City Eleven had eaten itself in its desperation to flee. He'd watched it, abstract data disappearing from his screens like midwinter lights going out one by one.

They're the only thing keeping everyone here safe.

City Ten had simply said goodbye.

'I did what I could to save what I can.'

City Nine had triggered its self-destruct mechanisms, painting the horizon red with nuclear flame.

They're wings.

The Chief Medical Officer of City Eight, screaming down the comms at him. City Seven pleading, and Six swearing revenge. Five cursing him to his dying day.

Perinne's finger hovered over the camera controls, the dust a shroud over empty ground.

Four had prayed, a whole city chanting as one. Three had tried to reach out to the nearest inhabited world, messages Perinne's quarantine had blocked. Two had said nothing at all.

All your waiting patients.

He turned the cameras off, and then back on. The system rebooted with a petulant hum, screens going dark, then bright again . . .

To reveal the sick of City One.

What had once been bare ground was now crowded with motionless figures, flushed red by the flickering festive lights. They stood amid the ruins of the homes they had owned. They crouched on fallen rubble. Some were frozen, undignified, mid-step, others stretched in feline sprints. Some crowded in huddles as if taking shelter, and some stood lonely as tombstones, as if silently mourning themselves.

And every pale, gaunt figure, without exception, was wearing a salus-mask.

'Sir?'

It was a long time before Perinne could make himself respond.

'Lieutenant Rozz?'

'Sir, the Doctor's escaped. We need to –'

'Open fire,' Perinne whispered.

'Sir . . .'

'The basilica defences. Prepare to repel invaders. There's . . . there's . . .'

A pause.

'But, sir, the sensors are reporting no life-forms out there. Did you hear what I said? The prisoner – he's escaped. The cameras in his cell shut off momentarily, and when they came back on he was gone. Sir? Sir, are you there?'

Perinne was already running.

The Doctor was waiting for him in the commissary.

Around him, the revellers danced and swayed, a room built for thousands now pathetically vacant but for the last colonists of a dying world. The wine was gone, the plates scattered, and the music crackled through speakers that were only ever meant to direct doctors to those they were trying to save.

None of the revellers turned as the Chief Medical Officer entered, their masks gleaming in the soft blue lights. Some swayed alone to the music, others turning in slow circles, clinging to each other as if they had lost everything beyond what they could hold with their own two hands.

And above them sat the Doctor, in Perinne's seat, pale and washed out, like a ghost at a feast.

'You saw them,' was all that he said.

'What . . . what are they?'

'You know what they are,' the Doctor said. 'You've always known what they are, because you have one downstairs. You have a Weeping Angel. Here. Once I stopped looking at the sick and started looking at your systems, I found it. You were torturing it.'

'I bought it,' Perinne whispered. 'I buy alien technology all the time. We were . . . we were researching it.'

The frustration. The secret behind that motionless face, the secret it wouldn't give up, no matter how many knives Perinne blunted on its skin.

Seraphim Protocol. He'd taken a hammer to it in the end.

'I didn't ask you if you took *notes*,' the Doctor snarled. 'I asked you what you *did*. I should have known from the name – you wanted to figure out how it quantum-locked. You wanted to reverse-engineer how they freeze when observed and use it for this place –'

'More time,' Perinne said. 'That's all. A doctor must save what he can.'

'No. A doctor saves *all* he can. He never stops looking. Never stops fighting. You never even started.'

His voice was rising, and the revellers had turned to watch. Perinne had designed the masks himself. How could there be such accusation in their eyes?

'The image of an Angel becomes an Angel,' the Doctor said simply. 'It's their way of getting their own back on a universe that freezes them in place. Meet their eyes, and they can get into your head, change you from the inside out. And you did nothing *but* look at it, through a mask connected to the brain of every other person on the planet.

'There's your plague, *doctor.* The image of an Angel becomes an Angel, and this image went viral. It took City Twelve from you in one night. And then City Eleven, and City Ten. Angels love a countdown. They like scaring people.'

The music had stopped. Sweat was pouring into Perinne's eyes, fuzzing his vitals and the heart rates of everyone he had tried to save. Everything had gone very still. The revellers seemed like a painting, a tableau, something from an old story. No one tried to run. *Where would they go?*

'That's what the storm is,' the Doctor said, stalking down the hall. For a moment, Perinne thought the Doctor was going to strike him, but instead he just brushed past him on the way to that strange blue box. 'Marble dust. The exhaled breath of a million Angels. Dust, and rage at what you did.'

He looked around at the majesty of the basilica, the opulence and the gilt.

'You're not safe. You were never safe. It was just saving you till last.'

Perinne blinked sweat from his eyes, and in that moment every reveller took off their masks.

There was Lieutenant Rozz, her features pale and dusty white, and a hundred interns whose names he'd never bothered to learn, grinning with mouths of sharp and shapeless teeth. And the Magentress, and his secretary, and a thousand others, all staring up at him with empty marble eyes.

The data feed in his salus-mask struggled and went silent. Even his own heart rate was just a flickering ghost.

'Listen very carefully,' the Doctor said, his eyes angry and wide. 'We're going to get you to the TARDIS. We're going to figure out a way to reverse this, and save you, and –'

Not a single reveller had moved. All were silent. All were still. And yet . . . he could feel their gazes boring into him, pupil-less and malevolent. There was a terrible, strained *need* about them, a compacted, living menace in their every lifeless limb.

'No,' Perinne said.

'I know you're afraid,' the Doctor whispered, 'but we have to *move*. One foot in front of the other. You've been doing it your whole life. Just don't blink, and we'll –'

'No,' the Chief Medical Officer said. 'I'm patient zero. Aren't I? The infection started with me. If you take me out of here, it'll spread. They're probably counting on it.'

'I'm not leaving you, Perinne.'

There was that frustration again, lining his face, and Perinne could see that it came from *caring*, a kindness so potent and far-reaching that it was very nearly an illness in itself. They had only just met, and Perinne had spent most of that time inflicting chemical scrubs on him. And still the Doctor was ready to risk his life for his.

'They won't let me leave,' Perinne said, and there was no fear in his tone. 'You know they won't. I have an Angel in my head, and the second I get into your . . . TARDIS, it's going to come out. Is that what you want? How many more people die if what's behind this mask comes out? Or I could stay here, and the infection stops with me.'

Perinne could do it. He could end the plague. It was almost ironic – he could finally achieve the quarantine. He was just going to be on the wrong side.

'Perinne, *please.*'

Perinne raised a hand to the edge of his mask. The Doctor watched it like it was a snake.

'I won't inflict this on the universe,' Perinne said. 'I'm a doctor too. Now go.'

'I'm sorry,' the Doctor said, and the pain in his eyes told Perinne that something of Gehanna had entered him all the same, that he was going to carry remorse with him wherever he went. 'I'm so sorry.'

He disappeared into his blue box and, with a grinding of hidden gears, the TARDIS faded away. When it was gone Chief Medical Officer Perinne was alone, with the patients he had failed. He stared at the Angels for as long as he was able . . . and then blinked. When his eyes opened again, the box had gone, and so had the Angels.

All but one.

Half its face was missing. One of its wings. He had thought . . . he had thought he would find living tissue underneath. Something he could learn from. Something he could use.

It was holding a mirror in its claws.

Perinne stared into it with an Angel's eyes, and felt the dust swirl in.

ICE WARRIORS

RED PLANET

This is how the Cage works.

It is rickety, because it is of Sycorax make, and the Sycorax are galactic scavengers – chieftains of rubbish, masters of mongrel tech. It might once have been the hull from a cargo freighter, or the shielding from a dozen battle tanks, or a hundred something elses, but whatever it *was* it is now the Cage.

The Sycorax are superstitious. They have a firm belief that when something is broken down or dismantled – or stolen, as is the case with almost everything the Sycorax acquire – it becomes new. Theft is a baptism, a transformation. This may be an elaborate justification for their crimes, to make piracy into a form of prayer, but that doesn't matter to them, and it doesn't matter to Kyrss.

When they stole him, they transformed him too.

The Cage is fifteen metres wide and as perfect a circle as jagged, fused debris can make. There are raised areas, and lowered areas, and areas that have been fitted with long retractable spikes and the hidden nozzles of flamethrowers. If the Cage was a planet – a child's drawing of a planet, just a horizontal circle – then it would be at each pole that the huge gates sit, carved of the same repurposed scrap.

The lifting of these gates is a tortured affair, thick chains straining in a series of slow jerks, but when they descend they come down as thundering fast as a guillotine.

They have slammed behind Kyrss now.

Above the metal ramparts of the Cage, the gathered Sycorax hoot and yell, slamming their long, curved blades against their corrugated-iron seats. They are hunched and grimy as vultures, chattering as wagers are made and money exchanged. The gleaming exposed bone of their skulls gives them the impression of being helmeted, though not a single one of them has ever seen honest war. They are pirates, raiders, murderers and thieves, and contempt for them rises through Kyrss, into his shoulder and down his arm to lift the great cleaving blade that is the only metal he is allowed. He slams it, just once, against his chest.

The scales there hum with the impact, and silence spreads out across the Cage.

Again. There is a constant bruise dappling his barrelled chest.

Again, and the gate on the other side of the arena begins to rise.

Leela of the Sevateem had seen a lot of incredible things during her time as the Doctor's companion. Plucked from her tribe, she had seen false gods toppled, incredible metropolises explored, even Old Earth, the long-lost spawning-ground of her ancestors. However, in all their travels, all the peril and the wonder, she had never seen anything as spectacularly ugly as what lay before her now.

'The fighting pits of the Sycorax!' the Doctor exclaimed, as their captors shoved them out of the tunnel mouth and into a great cavern dotted with hastily dug pits and rickety towers scabbed by mud. There were deeper holes, too, glowing fiery red, and above them a massive dome of stone that stretched away as if ashamed of what lay below.

'You know this place?' Leela said.

They had been captured by these clicking, cockroachy things almost as soon as they had left the TARDIS, and it stung the tribeswoman's honour that she hadn't had so much as a chance to retaliate. Fancy laser guns still needed two working arms to use them, and the second that one of them let down their guard –

'Of course I know this place,' the Doctor said huffily, gathering up his scarf so it wouldn't trail in the mud. 'Those are the fighting pits. And those –' he pointed at the bone-helmed guards with their dried-meat faces and wide rodent eyes – 'are the Sycorax. Self-explanatory, really. Are you paying attention at all?'

'I was paying attention when you told me we were going to look at a storm,' Leela muttered. 'And you don't find storms underground. Do you, Doctor?'

'Not just any storm, my dear,' the Doctor said, grinning cheerily. 'The Great Desolatrix, a cosmic storm of unparalleled magnitude and ferocity. You know how . . .' He thought for a moment. 'You know how Christmas lights, no matter how neatly you put them away, always end up in an impossible tangle that takes a month and most of your sanity to unpick?'

'What's Christmas?'

'Ah.' The Doctor's smile wilted. 'Well, that's what the Great Desolatrix is doing to space, Leela. Space and time all snarled up together, whole civilisations cut off, entire patches of the universe rendered inhospitable. It's been boiling away for five hundred years, displacing whole cultures, devouring fleets –'

'And you thought you'd take a look? Storms are storms, Doctor,' Leela said exasperatedly. 'You take shelter. You don't *do* anything. Sometimes there's nothing to be done.'

That made his smile disappear. 'I don't think I believe that at all,' he said.

The guards forced them on, marching them through the muck and morass of an industrial wasteland. Ramshackle buildings formed a sort of strange township beneath the stone sky, the narrow, squalid streets populated by hostages clad only in rags and bruises, with Sycorax overseers glaring down from walkways. There were ships too –lumpen stone things with gaping engine cones parked haphazardly on stretches of bare ground, the mud underneath scorched to glass by take-off. Leela was no expert in space travel, and, though the Doctor fiercely denied it, there was no way she'd ever believe the TARDIS didn't run on magic, but the engines looked barely capable of ignition, let alone flight.

'They're leaving,' she said, after they and their escort had been halted to allow another heavily laden procession to squeeze by. 'These creatures and their slaves. They're evacuating this place.'

'It's an asteroid,' the Doctor mused. 'This whole base is a rogue planetoid. Probably some sort of waypoint for roving bands of pirates. Now, with the Desolatrix closing off this quadrant of space, they're abandoning it.'

Even as he spoke, the ground rumbled. Leela had grown up on a jungle world. She was used to the earth being the earth, and the sky being the sky, and both being as solid as each other, but now the whole asteroid shook like a toy held in the hands of a child. Ahead of them, an emaciated Draconian staggered and fell to one knee, the crate in his hands spilling its contents into the mud. His overseer didn't even blink, raising his rifle and shooting the lizard-man down.

'And I think you might be wrong, Leela.'

'Wrong?' the tribeswoman hissed. She had seen it too, and it had clenched her hands into fists. The casual *cruelty* of it. The disdain. In an instant, she'd slipped two of the venomous Janis thorns she carried into her hand. The closest guard had his head turned away. All she had to do was –

The Doctor caught her hand, neatly avoiding the thorns. 'No, Leela.'

She whirled on him, expertly breaking his grip. 'I'm not just standing there and watching, Doctor! It's dishonourable! These people need our –'

'Yes,' the Doctor said. Around them, the guards had noticed the delay. Already they were trading growling barks, their weapons rising in their hands. 'And I want to help them too. But honour's no good if it gets you killed. Marry it to reason, Leela. Because –'

She glared at him with undisguised fury. 'Because *what*?'

'Because they've shot nine prisoners since we entered the cavern. Because Sycorax don't preserve things when they can just steal more. Because there might not be much of the asteroid left when the storm hits, and there are far more Sycorax and captives than there are ships, which leads me to think that they aren't taking their slaves with them.'

And with that he spun, lightning fast, graceful despite the muck, to throw back his head and yell, 'I am a warrior of great renown! Puissant, you might say, if you haven't said that word in a while and happen to know what it means. In short, a terrible foe for any alien to face. Markedly terrible. A nightmare in battle. Evacuation work detail would be a complete waste of my murderous, hyper-violent nature. You should put us in the –'

Caught by surprise, the guards exchanged glances. Sycorax overseers were looking over too, and even the slaves had raised their heads, staring at the Time Lord with dull, exhausted eyes. They were all looking at the Doctor, actually, which in Leela's opinion was a severe tactical error.

With an expert front kick, she doubled the nearest Sycorax guard in two, before hooking his rifle with the toe of her boot. He went down, the gun went up and, with what Leela would have called a parade-ground spin had she any idea or interest in what a parade ground was, she caught it out of the air, reversed it in her hands, and executed its former owner with a single, precise shot.

'Fighting pits,' the Doctor finished. 'You should put us in the fighting pits.'

On the fourth strike of steel against Kyrss's chest, the beast attacks.

It seeps out under the half-opened gate like blood from a wound, a howling flood of living oil lit from within by a lurid map of glowing veins. The floor of the Cage is dirty and rusted, but everything this creature rolls across is left bright and sparkling and clean, as if scoured by a tongue.

It howls, and the Sycorax howl too, in glee or recognition or both. Kyrss does not watch the other bouts or listen to the chatter of his fellow prisoners, but maybe this particular creature is a champion, or a much-feared predator, or something the Sycorax revere as a bloodthirsty god.

It comes at Kyrss unstoppably fast, but the warrior just stands there, stock-still on a ridge of curved steel pocked and scarred by a thousand dirty fights. The creature's bulk seems to swell as it advances, a flash-flood of black and dirty white ready to drown Kyrss in darkness and death.

Drown. Kyrss comes from a dry world. Water holds no fear for him.

At the last second, he lifts his sword. It is huge, and ceremonial, and there are gaps in its hilt where power cells and energy conductors were once installed. The Sycorax stole them, as they stole everything else. He blames them more than he blames the storm. The storm killed his people, but the Sycorax should have killed him.

The beast rears like a tsunami. The audience howls.

Kyrss sweeps his blade in a single, economical arc . . . right in front of the flamethrower sensors built into the ridge.

The world ignites.

The beast flares up like a bonfire, suddenly surrounded by a shimmering caul of superheated air. Parts of it separate off, flaking away as if trying to escape. The Cage fills with the acrid stench of burning flesh. Lights play across Kyrss's expressionless face as the creature's nervous system flashes through distressed colours before finally going dark.

Perhaps it was a prisoner. Perhaps it was an exile. Perhaps, like Kyrss, it was the last of its kind and its death represents the universe becoming that little bit smaller, that little bit less diverse.

The Sycorax stare silently.

And then they begin to cheer.

Money changes hands. A fight breaks out between three different gamblers as they argue over whether the flamethrower killing the alien means Kyrss won or not. Laser weapons are loosed at the ceiling like fireworks.

The Ice Warrior ignores it all and, hefting his sword over his shoulder, strides slowly back to his gate.

They were put in the fighting pits.

The gladiators' chambers were cramped, shabbily buttressed with slabs more rust than steel, tight with the sound of machinery and suffering. In the outer passages, prisoners simply slept where they had fallen from injury and exhaustion. Fodder-slaves: those who were pushed out into the arena to die in battle against carnivorous beasts and panels of Sycorax riflemen to get the audience's blood up.

Leela felt their pain and misery as sharply as the bruises she'd sustained during their recapture. *I will avenge you*, she promised inwardly to the ones she thought were living and the ones she knew were dead. *I swear it.*

The inner passages were reserved for those who had lived through a handful of battles. They seemed more lucid, their wary looks reserved for each other. The trembling

of the storm-lashed asteroid seemed not to trouble them
at all.

The true gladiators were kept beneath the Cage.

The chamber was low and round, with earthen ramps
leading up to two enormous gates. Dirty iron formed its roof,
and through gouges and ventilation holes Leela could make
out the massive structure above them: an arena red with rust
and stains of blood. Coming off the chamber were four
smaller caves, their entrances hidden by torn and flimsy
lengths of cloth.

The Sycorax guards, with their weapons firmly aimed at
Leela's head, motioned for her and the Doctor to step inside,
then pressed a button on a small remote. There was nothing
flimsy about the portcullis that fell over the exit as they did.

'Right,' Leela said, whirling on the Doctor. 'What now?'

'Now you fight.' One of the curtains had been lazily
twitched aside, and a lithe creature stepped out, her tawny fur
streaked with grey and separated by scars.

The Doctor peered through the gloom. 'A Catkind?
What is a Catkind doing all the way out here?'

Bright feline eyes gleamed, the pupils long and slender as
the metal claws sheathing her fingers. 'Same thing you are.
Fighting.' She examined them with the disinterested hostility
that only a cat could summon. 'You want advice?'

'Always,' the Doctor said.

The alien extended a long talon, pointing at the curtain opposite theirs. 'In there. Rutan. Do not fight.'

'I try not to,' the Doctor said. 'What –'

The Catkind's finger swung ninety degrees. 'In there. Nimon. Do not fight.'

'Your faith in us is staggering –'

The talon stabbed again. 'In there. Kyrss. *Do not fight.*'

The Doctor's eyes narrowed. 'Kyrss? That's an Ice Warrior name. What is an Ice Warrior doing here, in this sector of space?'

The Catkind shook her head like an interrupted tutor. 'Focus.' The claw rested delicately on her thin chest. 'I am Bathast. Do not fight.'

Leela frowned. 'Then who are we supposed to fight?'

'Each other?' the Catkind offered, before twitching the curtain back into place.

And then they were alone, the Doctor wearing that genially bewildered look he always had when death was imminent, and Leela, as always, trying to figure out a practical way to survive. She scanned the chamber for possible exits, sighed, then crouched down and held the pose for a moment, before rising again and repeating the movement.

'There's something off,' the Doctor said to himself when
she had done five. 'Not the Sycorax and the prisoners and the
fighting pits – that's par for the course with these grotty little
raider bands. But something doesn't feel right. Unless . . .' he
said, as she hit number fifteen. 'The Great Diaspora of the Ice
Warriors! The Abandonment of Mars! Eleven great world-ships
went out, and all contact with them was lost due to the storm.
How *tragic*. How *interesting*. How – Leela, what are you doing?'

Leela looked up. 'Stretching, Doctor.'

'Whatever for?'

'Because,' she said, lightly rolling to her feet, 'while
you're busy making deductions about why the people trying
to kill us are killing us, I will be killing them right back. I'm
sure this lost fleet is very exciting, but –'

The siren was not loud. It transcended sound, rattling
Leela's lungs against her ribs and spiking her ears with lances
of pain. It pealed off four beats, then two, earth-shattering but
mercifully short, and the Catkind reappeared, a look of
consternation on her whiskered face.

'What's that, friend?' the Doctor said brightly. 'Dinner?'

'The Cage,' Bathast hissed. 'Have to fight Kyrss. Will die
now. Pity. Wanted to go home.'

The resignation in her voice made Leela want to spit, or
cry, or punch something, but then another curtain was jerked

aside, and she suddenly forgot to be anything but intimidated. The creature that emerged was a mountain of green-white scales, fully half Leela's height again. Immense muscles warred for space with every heavy step, and his bare breast was corrugated with fat, pale worms of scar tissue and patches of ridged, devastated flesh. One arm looked chewed, as if it had once held some fierce animal at bay.

'Kyrss,' Bathast said softly.

The Ice Warrior nodded his blunt reptilian head, and reached over to pick up what Leela had thought was some sort of support strut for the roof, but now realised was actually a great two-handed blade. Kyrss lifted it as if it was nothing – and then a small man stepped directly in his way.

'Hello,' the Doctor said. 'Aren't you a long way from home, High Marshal?'

Glittering red eyes beheld the Time Lord.

Leela tensed, though the thought of him confronting this creature was thoroughly laughable, but the Ice Warrior simply made to step round the Time Lord.

The Doctor once again stepped in his way.

Somewhere in the distance machinery was grinding. It set Leela's teeth on edge. She looked around for the source, but she couldn't discern it.

'That's a High Marshal's sword. Missing its power converters, obviously, but that's Sycorax for you, isn't it? You're of the Great Diaspora. A captain of a world-ship, out to find a brand-new homeland for your fierce and honourable people. How did you end up here?'

The Ice Warrior did not respond, stepping round the Doctor once more.

Yet again, the Time Lord stepped in his way.

The machinery was growing louder, a growl like continents being ground for scrap.

The Doctor took a deep breath. 'Where are your people, Kyrss?'

The Ice Warrior bared his teeth, and that growl suddenly became an awful lot louder. *Oh*, Leela thought. The sound was coming from him.

'You remember advice?' Bathast said. 'Nobody ever remembers advice.'

'The world-ships vanished,' the Doctor said, and Leela could barely hear him over the predator's tectonic snarl. 'They vanished into the storm. I always meant to find out what happened to them. Is that why you're here? With your blade dimmed and your heart laid low? What happened, Kyrss?'

The Ice Warrior's voice was deep and dangerous as an earthquake. Leela felt it, thrumming bone-deep. 'I led my people into the storm.'

'He's never spoken before,' Bathast whispered. 'A hundred fights. A hundred kills. Weeks of fighting, and he has never spoken.'

'Yes,' Leela said. 'The Doctor is just that annoying.'

'I was supposed to bring them to safety,' Kyrss rumbled. 'Instead I brought them death. I lost the other ships in the storm. And my ship, it crashed. And . . .'

'You were the only survivor,' the Doctor said quietly.

'I didn't even *die* with my people!' Kyrss roared, the sound a physical blow that sent them all staggering back. 'I woke to find these scavengers picking the ship's bones, and I tried to contact the rest of the fleet but there was no reply. I was alone. I *am* alone.'

'But you can't be sure,' the Doctor said. 'Are you going to just give up? Spend the rest of your days entertaining Sycorax with your blood? If I was the last of my people, I would never stop looking for them! Where's the *honour* in that?'

'I held the bridge for seven days,' the Ice Warrior said, and now his voice was quiet, as if all his fight had gone. 'On a broken world-ship, its deck canted, its engines bleeding out, I planted my feet and I said, "*This* – this is my Mars," and I did not sleep, and I slew all who sought to claim it, while the failing computers searched for any sign that my people lived. Seven days. Every minute fighting. Every minute awake. Do not speak to me of honour, human. My honour died with my people, and I did not have the good grace to die with it.'

With one clawed hand, he picked the Doctor up and put him, not ungently, to one side. Above them, the Cage gate began to open.

'Well,' Bathast said. 'It was a good try.'

'Everybody stop,' the Doctor snapped. 'I have a plan. An excellent plan. We just need to find the armoury, release the prisoners, arm them, then take the evacuation ships for ourselves.'

'And how do we do that?' Leela asked.

'I'm not sure,' the Doctor admitted. 'I'm working backwards from the solution. Bathast, can I count on you and the other gladiators? The prisoners will need leaders, and you're the cream of the fighters.'

'People have tried,' Bathast said gloomily. 'I must go fight Kyrss and die now.'

The chains had pulled taut. The gate was rising, and the Ice Warrior stood in front of it, like the titanic statue of some forgotten god. Leela could hear whoops and howls above the grind of the gates – the cheers of a blood-maddened crowd.

'Besides,' the Catkind said. 'You need remote to open portcullis.'

'Like this one?' the Doctor said, holding up a small metal square. 'I nabbed it from that nice guard you assaulted, Leela. You remember. When he was retrieving his gun?'

Leela did remember, despite the head injury. 'So then we just need to –'

'No.'

The Ice Warrior had his back to them.

'I will not run. My honour is stained enough. I will not run from what I deserve –'

Leela had seen this before. In her tribe, there were warriors who had lost everything, warriors who sought death because the weight of living was too much. The 'sleeping'. That was what they were called. Those who sleepwalked through life, just looking for the blade that would end it all.

'Then I challenge you.' The asteroid shook as if it agreed. 'On your honour, Ice Warrior.' Leela's voice was calm. 'I'll give you the death you need.'

'Leela!' the Doctor hissed. 'What are you doing? I don't know if you've noticed, but he is quite a large –'

'You need Bathast to show you where the armoury is,' Leela said, her mind falling into that calm, still place that always preceded combat. 'So I will buy you that time.'

'Child,' Kyrss rumbled. 'If this is some ploy to make me come with you, I cannot. I will not.'

'No ploy,' the tribeswoman said flatly. 'Just honour. If that's all you have left.'

'Leela,' the Doctor snapped. 'Wait!'

But she was already running towards the lifted gate. After a moment, the Ice Warrior lumbered after her.

'Save me from honour,' the Doctor growled to himself, before turning to Bathast. 'Will you at least help me now?'

The skinny Catkind's shoulders sagged. The scars on her hide stood out more than ever, white against tawny gold.

'Please!' the Doctor said. 'She took your place!'

'People have tried,' Bathast purred sadly, and padded back to her cell.

'Bathast, no!'

The curtain was tugged back into place.

Leela of the Sevateem steps out into the blinding lights. The Cage is a rolling wasteland of jagged steel, misshapen and cruel as a Sycorax face. Kyrss, his eyes slits against the blazing torches, stands beside her.

In a booth high above the arena, a raider with a circlet of gold speaks into a battered microphone, his voice amplified by towers of fat, sparking speakers. He might be explaining the rules, or shouting odds, or praying – Leela has no idea – but, when his speech finishes with a roar, a great cheer rises up to meet him. It sounds like the coming of a storm.

They could be evacuating, she thinks, as she and her opponent walk to opposite ends of the Cage. They *should* be evacuating. Somewhere out there, a universe-shredding tempest is bearing down upon them, and instead they are here, hungry for blood, for one last show before the end of the world.

'You don't have to do this,' she calls, and though her voice is nearly swallowed by the audience, she knows Kyrss hears her.

His only response is to pound that massive blade just once against his chest.

The Sycorax go silent.

The fight begins.

'Honour,' the Doctor hissed as he crept down the passageway, the word a curse.

Getting out of the gladiators' chamber had been easy, Sycorax raiders not generally being the type to set regular patrols, but that had merely left him wandering a warren of identical tunnels, hoping to run into something that would help. What *didn't* help was the knowledge that, as unreliable and magpie-distractable as these pirates were, the one place that was guaranteed to be defended – not least from their own soldiers – was the armoury.

'I swear by the laws that hold the universe together,' the Doctor muttered, ducking into a side chamber as a pair of raiders trotted by, 'I am going to find the first human and Ice Warrior responsible for this obsession with grandstanding and bang their heads together.'

Another corridor, another set of dank barracks and mouldering food stores. Somewhere in the distance, the Doctor could hear the vibrations of the storm – or maybe that was the crowd watching his companion fight the pinnacle of Martian military might. He broke into a jog, turning a corner and trying to keep some sort of mental map in his head. Such *idiocy*. It made him want to –

There was a *click*.

'Hello,' the Doctor said cordially to both the rifle and the surprised-looking Sycorax holding it. 'Would you like a jelly baby?'

She expects him to be slow. It nearly kills her.

All that muscle, that numb, defeated torpidity – but his stillness is that of a reptile, going from motionless to movement in the blinding beat of a cold-blooded heart. His blade comes thrumming at waist-height, and it is all she can do to vault across it, landing hard on her side. He doesn't stop, doesn't relent, using his weight like a centrifuge to redirect that massive blade up and then down, inexorable as a clock hand.

She scrapes her skin raw rolling out of the way, and the whole Cage leaps as the blade hits.

'You don't,' she gasps, 'have to –'

The rest of her words are lost in the panting rush to avoid another swing, and then a thundering charge. She scrambles up a wrought-iron slope, the hoots and cackles of the audience in her ears, turning just in time to somersault over the Ice Warrior's shoulder, the scales grainy and iron-hard under her fingers.

His frustrated bellow shakes the air, and Leela's hand goes to her waist, where her pouch of Janis thorns lies. A nick, a single puncture in his eye or the soft flesh of his throat, and even an Ice Warrior would go down.

But she can't. He might have given up, but she has not.

'You don't have to do this,' she repeats, as the crowd yells and her hands bleed and the behemoth turns with his massive blade. 'And you know that. That's why you're doing this – because you're looking for a way out.'

He comes at her again, and Leela leaps to meet him.

*

'Now, let me explain again.' The Doctor held up a jelly baby. 'You see this yellow one?'

There were eight Sycorax now, which was not an improvement over one, but nobody had started shooting either, so it all balanced out. They were sitting cross-legged in front of him, a jelly baby in each of their grimy hands.

Sycorax loved gambling. The thought of venturing a small amount of capital and receiving a large amount of capital was practically holy to the mind of a pirate, and there was nothing a gambler loved more than a system.

The Doctor's hand reached into the paper bag. Eight pairs of eyes followed it.

'Now, what colour is going to come out next?'

A chorus of barks. The Doctor grinned. 'Very good. Probability theory. How likely a thing is to happen based on how many times it has happened before. Who here has bet on Kyrss?'

They all raised their hand.

'Ah. But the thing is, at some point, since he's won so often, he has to lose. And, when he does, everyone who's bet against him becomes rich!'

Frowns creased their rodent faces.

'Not that I *want* him to lose,' the Doctor said hurriedly. 'Because you've already placed bets.'

Hands were moving towards rifles. Teeth were suddenly bared, flashing white in the tunnel's gloom.

'No, no,' the Doctor said. 'It isn't my fault. It's the *system* —'

The lead Sycorax leaped to his feet, and then abruptly froze as a low growl wafted through the chamber, the kind of noise reminiscent of prehistory, and predators, and what happened when one went alone into the red of nature beyond the fire's light.

Bathast dropped from the ceiling, claws shining bright.

'Do not fight,' she hissed.

'This isn't about honour,' Leela snaps as the Ice Warrior comes for her, his every step tolling the Cage like a bell. 'This is about *rage*. This is about you wanting to spill blood, because you think you've failed.'

At the last moment, she dives, an inch ahead of that blurring blade. Kyrss snarls, switching grips with practised skill, whipping the sword in a tight and vicious arc. She feels the wind of it snap her hair back against her skull. There is no such thing as a grazing wound in this duel. One blow and she will die. He will break her in two without even slowing down.

She has to slow him down instead.

'Honour is about living for more than yourself,' she gasps, staggering backwards from a brutal downward slice. 'But it must be married to reason, or you're just wasting a life that could save someone else's when the time is right.'

'My people are dead,' Kyrss says, and she doesn't know which is worse – the resignation in his voice or the fact that he isn't out of breath *at all*. 'There is no one left to save. My life, my death, they are meaningless now. I fight because my body will not lie down and die. That is all.'

'You *have* lain down and died,' Leela counters. 'It's just that your heart's still beating.'

Kyrss howls, a long, drawn-out sound of loss and pain. There is some sort of commotion in the corner of Leela's eye, Sycorax shoving and pushing each other, but she can't – won't – take her eyes off the Ice Warrior before her. Her own honour demands it.

'Honour isn't a cheat,' she whispers. 'It isn't an excuse. It demands we keep going, even when all seems lost. It only demands we spend our lives when the greatest gain can be made. This isn't about your honour. It's about you wanting to be punished for failing your people, when the real failure is giving up on them.'

'There are no other battles if my people are gone.' The blade comes up again. 'Now send me to them.' He takes a deep breath. 'Please.'

'Hello?'

The voice crackles from the speakers.

Leela freezes. The Sycorax look around in confusion, and all flinch when the entire Cage rattles with a resounding, echoing clang.

Kyrss has dropped his sword.

'Hello? Can anyone hear us? This is High Marshal Creyass of World-Ship Three calling for aid. We have lost contact with the lead vessel of the flotilla and –'

In a lifetime of war, no blow has ever struck High Marshal Kyrss of the Ice Warriors so thoroughly as that voice. Borne on a tide of static, reaching out across an immeasurable distance, the voice is thin and reedy, but unmistakably Martian.

'This is World-Ship Six. We are damaged, but holding. Is there anyone else out there?'

'World-Ship Four here. The storm . . . the storm . . . We are . . .'

Messages pour from the speakers, an overlapping chorus louder than any cheer that has ever echoed around the Cage. Sycorax snarl uneasily, turn in their seats – there is nothing more unnerving to their craven hearts than the thought of being outnumbered – and Kyrss looks up to the announcer's booth, where a dishevelled human is holding a whirring screwdriver to the speakers' controls.

'Sorry about the quality,' he says. 'But last time you looked for them it was in a damaged ship. The asteroid's long-range comms are in better shape.' He grimaces. 'For the most part. Hello, Leela!'

The tribeswoman waves.

'Now,' the Doctor says. 'Duck.'

Kyrss and Leela frown. 'What?'

One side of the Cage explodes. The metal buttresses and the seats resting above them lift away with a deafening roar and detonation of light. The entire asteroid seems to shake, cracks racing through the ground, pitching Sycorax and debris through the air. Chains split with thunderous cracks, and suddenly there are prisoners – former prisoners – swarming up through the gate and firing on their captors.

Leela is already running. After a moment, Kyrss runs with her.

The Doctor, it seemed, had been busy.

'Oh, nothing too complicated, Leela, my dear,' he said, as they sprinted towards the TARDIS. 'The gladiators took the armoury – very difficult to find, by the way; there should be maps, like a shopping centre – and I hacked the asteroid's long-range comms.'

'Very good, Doctor,' Leela said. 'I'm glad you added new goals while I was fighting for my life.'

Nerves twanging, she suddenly flung him headlong into a side chamber as a squad of Sycorax soldiers appeared, firing wildly. The pulse blasts whirred over Leela's head to impact harmlessly on Kyrss's thick hide.

The Ice Warrior turned and let out a long, low hiss.

The Sycorax fled.

'Good. Excellent. Marvellous,' the Doctor said. 'Now, if you could just repeat that trick another hundred times . . .'

'They are getting reinforcements,' the Ice Warrior said.

Distantly, they could hear explosions and cries, the sounds of the asteroid tearing itself apart. The freed gladiators were leading attacks on the hangar bays and furnace pits, fighting for ships or hunting down overseers. The Doctor had tried to impress on them the danger of the storm outside, offering them sanctuary in the TARDIS, but only Bathast and Kyrss had taken him up on it. The rest, it seemed, were far more concerned with revenge.

'The TARDIS isn't far,' the Doctor yelled, as the high whine of pulse fire warred with the hyena-chatter of carbine blasts and the thudding roar of grenade launchers.

'How far is not far?' Bathast snapped, loosing a spray of light from the carbine in her paws back down the passageway. Answering fire chipped shards from the walls around them. 'They're right behind us!'

'Yes, I am aware!' the Doctor snapped back. The rate of fire was increasing, the tunnel behind filling with enraged raiders taking potshots. Fire sizzled off Kyrss's hide and he snarled, that huge blade rising in his fist. The Sycorax were becoming bolder, less afraid of the gladiators' superior skill, and the minute that heavier weapons were brought to bear . . .

Leela turned the corner and there it was: the box that the Doctor insisted was technology but that she knew in her heart was magic, bright and blue and shining in the grim darkness of the tunnel. The Doctor let out a delighted laugh to see it, but the mirth died on his face when he saw the dirty iron disc bolted to its door.

'No. *Nonononono.*'

'What is it?' Leela asked.

'A clinch-lock,' the Doctor explained, passing his sonic screwdriver over it. 'Raider tech. Must have been worried a rival clan might steal it. I can get it off, but it will take a couple of minutes.'

'We don't have minutes!' Bathast snapped.

Kyrss's expression was caught somewhere between rage and fierce yearning. Leela could understand how he felt – he had fought for so long with no hope, but now hope was right on the other side of a locked wooden door.

And then she saw the frustration melt away.

'I will give you time.'

'What?' the Doctor and Bathast said together, but Leela realised it before either of them. *Honour. Sacrifice.* A chance to save his people. That was all the High Marshal had ever wanted.

'A good death,' she whispered.

'You can save them?' Kyrss said to the Doctor. 'You can lead them out of the storm?'

The Doctor stared at him for a long moment, while the gathering Sycorax snarled and pulse fire scorched the air and the asteroid shook as if tearing itself apart.

'Yes,' he said finally, then reached for Kyrss's sword. The Ice Warrior flinched, but the Doctor opened his hand and held out two small square components, their edges trailing wires. The High Marshal's eyes widened.

'The power couplings for your sword,' the Doctor explained. 'I found them in the armoury. And if we just . . .'

He clicked them into the gaps in the hilt of the Ice Warrior's massive blade. A low whirr trembled the circuitry-inlaid steel, and Kyrss bared his fangs and growled right back.

'Goodbye, Doctor.' He turned to Leela. 'Thank you for reminding me who I am.'

Bathast was shaking, fur bristling, gun spitting fire in her paw. She never took her eyes from the massing raiders still firing on them, but the anger in her voice was directed at Kyrss. 'Why are you doing this? We can escape! Do not . . . do not fight.'

The High Marshal simply shook his head.

'Where do you get it?' the Doctor said wonderingly. 'This iron. This unerring, unstoppable will? Where does it come from?'

'Mars,' Kyrss said simply, and turned back the way they had come.

The asteroid is lost. The Sycorax know it. This is not a decree passed down by the notoriously rickety command structure of raider clans; it is something they simply know, deep as the shaking of the storm, in the way bullies and monsters know when the tables have turned. The knowledge has infected the warriors chasing the gladiators, driven them into a vicious, petty rage. This was *their* place. *Their* home. *Their* world of iniquity and cruelty, a place where they could feel secure in their bleak and rodent hearts.

There must be a hundred of them now, pressed tight as termites in the passageway, and so bestially vexed at the thought of losing what they have that they have entered into an entirely un-Sycorax-like system of co-operation, sharing ammunition, passing spent cartridges back down the line. They clog the tunnel like sewage, slavering at the thought of tearing apart those who have wronged them and fighting over the bloody shreds.

Kyrss hits them like a meteor.

The blade of a High Marshal is embedded with energy converters and conduction circuits that turn kinetic energy into heat. The impact of each air molecule on the edge of the blade is registered, stored and converted into flickers of lurid green flame. By the time Kyrss hits the Sycorax line, he is a glowing sun.

The air ignites. Raiders howl. The weight of the Ice Warrior actually pushes the entire company of raiders back, like an irresistible flow of water dislodging a blockage in a pipe. Pulse fire from the Sycorax explodes, causing more casualties among their own ranks than injuring Kyrss, but he feels the kiss of flame across his back all the same.

He swings. He slays. *Mars.* The snarl is silent, because he needs every dram of oxygen to sweep that flaming blade, but the word is not for these cursed raiders anyway. *Mars*. It is solely for him.

Mars. Unforgiving and cold, and dry as ancient bones, but so beautiful it takes the breath from your lungs. *Mars*. The majesty of Olympus Mons. *Mars*. The dawn flaring out over the Cydonian Highlands, turning ochre to blazing red.

He *is* Mars. He can feel it now. His waist is the hemisphere, turning unstoppably to scythe his blade left and right. His shoulders are the highlands, scored by the passage of a thousand brutal storms. Energy whips slither across his back, leaving canals of riven flesh as deep as those that cross his world. Blood sluices the air around him. Some of it is Sycorax. More of it is his.

Mars.

His people will be safe. They will find a new home. That is all he wants. All he wishes to fight for. All he wishes to die for.

Mars.

Kyrss is going home.

TIME LORDS

CELESTIAL INTERVENTION –
A GALLIFREYAN NOIR

'What kind of colour's blue, anyway?'

The boy comes through my door like he has a grudge against it, smoke-eyed and pale, with a predator's smile. There's a ratty old chair in the corner of my office that I save for special occasions, like employment or sleep, and he falls into it with a boneless, theatrical slump, fingering the diamonds in his ear.

I count carats. He counts wrinkles. There is an impressive number of both.

'Nothing against it myself,' I say, without taking my feet off my desk. With certain clients you've got to go easy, let them talk around the point until they get there of their own accord. There is a manic sort of fright to this kid, beneath his gems and his grin, and if I spook him they'll both walk right out of the door.

'I've been robbed,' he says. 'Something's been stolen, and I want you to find out who took it. Why it was taken. Everything you can.'

'I'm not Celestial Intervention any more,' I say, as if he needs the hint. The retirement certificate on the wall could have told him that, and the dead flies in my inbox could have verified it. *That* was an open-and-shut case – the first this office had seen in a while.

The client has a cute brow. It doesn't deserve the furrow he puts in it. 'But you used to be, right?'

The Celestial Intervention Agency is my old outfit, the guys the Time Lord top brass call when they need the universe changed to their advantage. Cross the President of Gallifrey or any of their cronies and the agency won't just ice you; they'll read your future and change your past so you never existed in the first place. They're Gallifrey's dirty right hook, the sock in the jaw you don't see coming until they've settled their timeline in the black and yours in the red.

'I don't work there any more.'

'Can't or won't, Detective Maris?'

Can't. 'Won't. It's a young woman's game. And it's just Maris now. No detective about it.'

'I tried the Celestial Intervention Agency,' he says, smoothing down robes carefully devoid of any identifying insignia – no Gallifreyan house colours, no party lines. He has dressed for the occasion. Clients often do, hiding anything that might identify who they are out in the world, either out of shame at hiring a private eye or because they want to keep their lives from getting mixed up in the case – as if their lives aren't always at the heart of it. 'They told me it wasn't their "jurisdiction". They *laughed* at me. Said it was small fry. "Who'd steal a Type Forty TARDIS?" they said. "How'd he even get it to fly?"'

His lip wobbles, and I wobble too. Saying no to angry is easy; saying no to sad is something else. A single beam of sunlight slinks in the window, painting my skin a rich brown but failing to bring any colour to his. Dust motes spin when I breathe. The client's breath barely disturbs the air at all.

'*Small fry*. What's a guy got to do to be taken seriously around here?'

I snort, before I can help it. Taking things seriously is not the Time Lords' problem. Serious is in our blood. Some genius connected a couple of wires sometime in the past and suddenly we had all of time and space at our command. And, boy, did we command – to the point where half of us are too afraid to do anything in case we *do* something, while the other half change the passage of time like changing a suit of clothes.

'All right,' I say. 'I'm not promising anything, but I'll hear you out. So someone stole your TARDIS?'

The smile comes back, like a clear sky through clouds. 'You know the TARDIS repair shop on the Boulevard of Grand Milieu?' He doesn't wait for me to nod. 'There was a Type Forty there. A real piece of junk. And then someone ran off with it. Two someones, actually – an old guy and his granddaughter.'

'They got names?'

'He calls himself the Doctor.'

There's that old Gallifreyan arrogance again. Never enough to go with the name you were given; people have to go for titles. Gives me a headache.

'And this was your TARDIS?'

What is *that*? Anger? A sudden jolt of rage on that pretty young face? Whatever it is, it doesn't faze me. I've seen worse.

'Not going to tell me, hmm? Or . . . is the girl your squeeze? She run off on you and you want to know where they've gone?'

Silence.

I sigh. 'I'll tell you upfront, kid. I'm not in the business of tracking down girls when I don't know why boys are after them. Maybe she doesn't want you to find her.'

He shakes his head. 'It's not that. I don't care about her. I want to know where he's going. Can you do that?'

I shrug. 'Don't know. Universe is a big place. And I haven't said I'm taking the case.'

'You'll take it,' the boy says, and that smile breaks out again, bright as a noonday sun.

'You sound mighty confident.' I turn away to pour myself a drink from the glazed bottle on the shelf. 'Why's that?'

'Because you're small fry too.'

I'm pretty sure I had a clever retort. Yeah. I know I did. But business has been slow and I've got slower. When I turn back round, the boy is gone.

Five minutes and two glasses later, I pull out the chugging little potential engine that was my unofficial retirement gift from the agency. Nothing compared to what they have down at head office. This is a field model, the kind I used to take out on dark jobs in dirty weather. A potential engine searches back and forth along someone's timeline and reads the direction their lives might take. Time travel, in a way, except all it does is observe, plotting a map of all the routes you might take, all the turns your life could take.

You'd think it would be impossible, rendering the entire potential of someone's life down into a few lines on paper. Mostly, though, it's depressingly easy. People don't have as many options as you'd think, and they have the courage to choose even fewer. The agency mostly uses them to see which timeline a criminal got caught in, then make sure that's the one that comes to pass.

And, before you say it, I know. Feels like cheating. But that's the CIA for you. They're fixers, and fixers don't care about fair.

Potential engine whirring, I ease myself out of my chair and slip on my battered old long-coat, the low-brimmed hat I'd picked up on Metaxis, I think. Or Nastalar. Some wild place light-years to the left, where things still matter, where events are still left up to chance.

Small fry, I think.

The search will take a couple of hours. More than enough time to go for a walk.

Gallifrey. The Shining Star of the Seven Systems. The jewel of the Kasterborous constellation. Home to a cosmos-spanning empire that's reigned for a million million years. The top spires are a nice place to rule the universe from – or so I hear. From where I'm standing, they just look like a good excuse to ignore what's under your feet.

If you can go anywhere and do anything, you don't bother doing anything about a place like the Lower Len where nobody's discovering new dimensions or how to split the chronum. They could fix it, the highborns, the Great

Houses of Gallifrey. They could make this world a paradise for everyone, instead of for just those who can afford it. But despite all the power we have, and all the time in the world, we'd rather climb alone than pull the next guy up.

The Lower Len clusters around the great spires like dogs looking for scraps, a collection of motley domes and walkways half-chewed by rust. The sunlight that scorches the rest of Gallifrey barely touches down here, and that's how everyone likes it.

Step into the wrong alleyway and you'll wake up with a headache, no memories and a set of stitches where your past used to be. There are bootleg futures on sale, variant timelines as easy to slip into as a tailored suit, and rogue chameleon circuits turned predatory and strange ready to mimic anyone you like for assassination and revenge. The only time travel you can count on here in the Lower Len is from one day to the next, and even that's no guarantee.

There are levels to the TARDIS repair facility. It's a huge cylindrical tower, stretching all the way up to the red and gold sky. I head low, to where they keep the old relics like the Type 40s. It's the only place an old relic like me might get some answers. There's a service entry at the end of the boulevard, and I find the door unlocked under my hand.

Inside is a room so bright-lit and polished that it almost makes up for what's outside. I see dismantled TARDISes, their chameleon circuits inert so they just look like ancient rockets from the first days of space travel. I won't lie and say a pang of sadness doesn't touch my hearts. There's nothing quite like piloting a TARDIS. I hear the ones they fly these days are even more advanced than in my day, with Type 45s and even Type 50s that can take human form. Talking to a TARDIS – actually speaking to one – would nearly make you consider going back to work.

But I've already got a job to do, and I drag my focus back to it as a twitchy little squirrel of a man lifts his head out of the dismantled console of a Type 58.

'Clastivas.'

He flinches when he sees me. The wrinkles in the corner of his eyes smooth out, re-wrinkle, smooth out again. Occupational hazard of spending a few centuries elbow-deep in time vortexes – your own timestream gets a little hinky.

'Maris,' the squirrel says, nose twitching. 'Hey! I haven't seen you since that whole mix-up about . . . '

'About you working on TARDISes without a licence,' I say. 'I remember.'

His hands go to his pockets. 'I got my papers, Maris. Want to –'

'Not in a reading mood. I'm more interested in numbers,' I say. 'Like forty. Type Forty, to be exact.'

He scowls. 'I already spoke to a couple of CIA snakes about it.'

I frown. Had the client lied? Did he want a little insurance in case the real police weren't able to find something? Or was the agency just covering itself by taking a cursory look?

'They didn't seem to care too much. I know it was just a beat-up old thing, but they're sensitive machines.' His eyes narrow. I can see the cogs turning. 'In fact, that Type Forty was an antique. It was a relic. I'm pretty sure I should be given some kind of compensation.'

I fold my arms. 'I see you're good with numbers too. Let's try this one. How do you feel about Eleven Sixty-Five Dash Beta Four?'

His face scrunches up.

'Too big for you? Let me clarify. That's the statute that says that all TARDISes under repair should be time-clamped so that, I don't know, some old geezer called the Doctor can't run off with one. These sensitive, incredibly important, highly dangerous machines, which you apparently just let walk out of the door.'

That lights a fire. He starts backing up, waving his arms.

'Whoa! Whoa! The Bureau of TARDIS Assignation could confiscate my licence for that!'

'Feels like you should have taken that into consideration,' I say idly, that old CIA steel slinking into my voice. 'Feels like you should try and be helpful now.'

He sighs. I have him over a barrel and he knows it. Funny how the old skills never leave you.

'Look,' he says, eyes twitching all over as if trying to escape from his head. 'I swear I did have it clamped, and those things don't come off easy. You need your repair licence code, and they're government mandated. He couldn't have hacked it.'

I'm not impressed. 'Well the TARDIS didn't do it itself, did it?'

'I . . . No, of course not,' he says. 'But there's something not right about all this. The CIA spooks. I've met CIA. They're dogged, relentless, but they don't . . .'

My eyes narrow. 'Go on?'

Clastivas throws up his hands. 'Well, they've got it sewn up, don't they? They ain't in no rush. With those timeline readers I heard about, and those fancy human-form TARDISes, they don't –' he sighs – 'they're in no rush, see?'

I did. I couldn't argue, either.

'But these two – they had a badge, but there was something hungry about them. Something mean. And they didn't care one bit about the TARDIS. They just wanted the Doctor. It was like it was personal. And that's not the weirdest thing.'

'Oh?'

Clastivas leans in conspiratorially.

'I asked around a little about the Doctor. We repair guys stick together. The Doctor didn't need to steal a TARDIS at all,' Clastivas says. 'He already –'

His gaze flicks over my shoulder, but I know a trick when I see one. My mouth opens, and then, as I hear the tread behind me and something roughly the weight of a class-G planet crashes down on my head, I think maybe I don't know a trick after all.

I wake in the trash, and deserve it.

It's hard to know whether the liquid oozing down my ear is blood, and how I feel about it if it isn't. Someone must have thrown out a bunch of clock parts, because whatever's in this refuse bag is digging into my spine like it's trying to make it tick. Maybe I could just stay here. Think for a little while. Someone might throw out something to drink.

'Hey! Get out of my trash!'

Figures.

The smell of disused maki-soup cartons and old caboo sauce follows me out of the alley and back round the block to the service entry. I can tell by the smeary challenge of keeping on my feet that I probably have a concussion, and I can tell by the fact I'm still alive that I wasn't the one they were after.

The door's still unlocked. Inside, I find the lights off, the TARDISes looming out of the shadows like disapproving mothers. *If you could talk*, I think, but they're in no state to be helpful.

The repairman isn't looking too healthy himself. He's slumped over a console, his face shocked, a little petulant, as if being killed has really ruined his schedule. *Well*, I think, *it's doing mine no favours either.*

'Hello?'

'Kit, that you?'

'Maris? Long time.'

'As long or short as you want it to be – isn't that the company line?'

'Ha, um, yeah. Hey, speaking of, we're missing a potential engine down here. You haven't seen –'

'Sorry, Kit. I'm just calling to give you a heads-up. A murder. Down in the TARDIS repair shop on the Boulevard of Grand Milieu.'

'Wait, what? How did –'

'Yeah. Might be connected to the theft of that Type Forty TARDIS.'

'What theft?'

'Right, right. I get it. Can't share ongoing cases with the plebs, even if this pleb used to be your superior officer. Just get down there.'

'Maris, I genuinely don't – Maris? Maris, you there?'

I go home to get my gun. Slim little piece, a meta-calibre Magnetar pistol with modes for both energy rounds and solid slug. In the CIA we had vortex clips, hand-moulded paradox shells, personalised space–time catastrophes (which, honestly, were one piece of tech I was glad to leave behind).

It's no wonder the Time Lords have atrophied. We've got the CIA out there treating history like a game where you can press the reset button whenever you want. And yeah, I get it, sometimes you need a hand on the wheel, a guiding eye, but when you have a hammer suddenly everything starts looking like a nail. To the agency, you're either a fixer or a problem. There's no third category. There's no mystery.

I like a little mystery, me. Call it a flaw.

I take a moment outside of my office to listen, just in case whoever blapped me on the skull has found my address and is looking to make another impression. I guess I've taken the case now. Or the case has taken me. Either way, an irritating little man is dead, and thoroughly enough that no regenerations kicked in. There's tech that can do that. I used to have tech that could do that.

There's something not right about all this.

You're not wrong, buddy.

But maybe my luck is changing. There's nothing in my office besides the potential engine, which is making the sick sort of spluttering noise that means it's out of paper, but that doesn't make any sense because most potential maps come out at about a page, two at the most. I've got a couple of hundred pages turning the floor of my office into a snowfield.

I pick one up.

```
The Doctor. Born to the House of
Lungbarrow, created by their Loom
as per the decree of Rassilon . . .
```

High-born. Of course. I lay it down, pick up another.

```
The Doctor. Born to a human mother
and Time Lord father on the Holiday
of Otherstide under the sign of
Crossed Computers, the symbol of
the maternity service . . .
```

I find three more birth notices, all in that typical poetic Gallifreyan style, and not a single one of them seems to agree with any of the others. The Doctor attended the Time Lord Academy for twenty years. No, centuries. No, he was expelled. No, he was involved in a riot just two days ago and is currently wanted for interfering in non-time-travel-capable species' development, except that another sheet tells me he was never trained to fly a TARDIS at all.

Printing resumes when I reload the printer. I dig through the sheets to find some sort of steady ground, but nothing tracks and nothing follows and I read until the sun goes down and the ache at the back of my head has migrated to right behind my eyes.

They aren't lies. I ran with experts in misdirection and fakery for longer than I like to think about, and I know the difference between what's real and what isn't. They're all real, except they can't be, except they are. Pages of Doctors slip through my fingers, and I can't seem to find where his story ends or even begins.

The potential engine complains. I reload it again, and as I do I get that butterfly flutter against my brain that is the birthright of the Time Lords. It's not just the TARDISes. We and time are linked, like animals sensing storms, and I sense a storm now, the timestream snapping back and forth like washing on a line.

Some of the sheets are blank now, but had writing on them when I picked them up. I pick a handful of the closest, and put them in a bag, before grabbing my hat and my gun.

I was never much for reading, anyway.

The Time Lord Academy is my first stop. It'd be easier if nobody had heard of the Doctor, but it seems like everyone on campus has. He graduated with flying colours. He scraped through with fifty-one per cent. He got expelled for political leanings, and there's a warrant for his arrest, except that I can't find any record of it in my notes, except when I can.

Again that feeling, like moths under my skin, fighting to be free.

He is a doctor. He isn't a doctor. He has a degree in cheesemaking. He studied higher-dimensional physics at Time Lord University, which doesn't exist, and he got officially sanctioned by the university's chancellor for trapping a lecturer in a time loop.

I walk, and I ask questions, but the more I ask the more I find. I hear he has a brother, some government stooge, but nothing I do turns up a name, and then the records tell me he doesn't have one at all. Sometimes there's a family. Sometimes there's a wife.

I can't even find his real name.

When I was in the CIA I erased lives. I changed history – Gallifrey's for the better, and mine for the worse, and I always wondered what it felt like from the inside when unseen hands shaped the story of you. Now I know. It feels like a current, like kicking for the surface only sends me further down.

It has to be them. The knowledge drives pins of rage into my aching head. The sheer scale of the cover-up, my flummoxed potential engine, the billowing probabilities that don't make any sense – it has to be them. This is Gallifrey. They're messing with this Doctor's life, changing it, turning it into chaos. It'd make you feel sorry for the guy. It'd almost make you take his side.

'Detective Maris. Have you found who he is yet?'

'You're the one who hired me. You tell me. Who is this guy? I checked the newscasts and there's no mention of a theft at all. It's like it's been undone. Or it didn't happen. What's so special about this Doctor that the CIA would –'

'Just tell me where he's going, Maris. That's what I'm paying you for. Tell me how to track him down.'

*

When I return to my office, the door is ajar, and my gun noses it open the rest of the way.

Everything's as it was. The potential engine is still going, the pages now ankle-deep, and on every single one of them I see the Doctor. On some he is old and hawkish, with a glint in his eye that might be mischief or a great, enduring irritation. On others I see bright colours – though my potential engine only prints in black and white – and a grin big enough to swallow the world. One is smeared with ink as if the engine choked while printing it, and the only detail I can make out are eyes full of wild and dark potential.

I wade through the blizzard of back-stories and ask myself why an agency so dedicated to control, so fat and happy with their own superiority would manipulate someone like this. What are they making?

Who are you?

My rooting around has uncovered other pages, and one of them catches my eye. There's a smudge on it, just a faint little curve. *A footprint.*

That's when the chronal mine goes off.

It feels like I have all the time in the world to watch it happen – though, of course, that's the dilation effect and in reality I have no time at all. Chronal mines: a nasty little CIA trick. They're compressed knots of time on a hair trigger, just waiting for you to step on them so they can catastrophically age everything within three metres.

The moment and the explosion expand, pages spinning upwards like leaves in a gale, and I see the story on them change. Maybe it's the mine. Maybe it's the potential engine. Maybe it's both, but suddenly the ink crawls and shimmers under the weight of all the choices yet to be made. The lives of the Doctor run together.

I see a hero. I see a changeling. I see a warrior. I see a god. I see faces change, and hearts break. The pages tear as futures writhe and on some there is fear and on others hope, and on a thousand more I see a world of green and blue and I *know* that's where he's headed, where he'll go a million times, where he'll go as long as they'll have him and sometimes a little bit more.

Man, but that TARDIS can move.

And then the explosion reaches me, inevitable as an avalanche, and the blast wave moves me too.

'Oh, good. You didn't kill her.'

'Hmm. Never been congratulated for that before. Not sure if I like it.'

It's too nice a room to be tied to a chair in. Old High Gallifreyan etchings, tapestries in gold and silk. I see myself in the polished wall opposite; the swathe of deeper wrinkles across my cheek where the chronal mine grazed me, and then two high-born brats flutter into my field of vision like a pair of preening crows: dark-eyed, milk-skinned, so alike they could be brother and sister. Fancy robes. Academy accents. The most preoccupying detail, however, is my pistol in the young man's hand.

'You should make a habit of it,' I croak, sitting up in the chair as much as my restraints will allow. 'I hear it's good for you.'

The boy gestures idly with the gun. I'm put in mind of snakes, of things that need to lie out in the sun for a long time before they'll give a damn about anything but themselves.

'Nobody talks to me like that,' he says, and cocks the pistol.

'I have evidence to the contrary,' I say, and the girl smiles. She's prim like a scientist, and I can see she's good at counting because I could fling myself forward, chair and all, and land just half an inch out of reach.

'Oh, stop,' she says. 'I like her. She's playing with you, because she knows it amuses me. Which means I might take her side.'

His smile deepens like an abyss, like a bright and happy child who isn't at all used to not getting what he wants. The most dangerous kind.

'Funny,' he says. 'Smart as she is, does she think taking your side is the best idea?'

'No,' I say, eyes still on the gun. 'But I think you'll do what you want, no matter what I say. That's the side you're on. But *she'll* care about what I know. Am I right?'

They don't say anything.

Finally, the girl shakes her head. 'You have me, at least. Put away the gun. She's tied up.'

'I like how she looks at it,' the other kid says. There's nothing healthy about him. Pewter, washed-out skin, and the beginnings of a goatee, which is the clearest sign of an evil man. Dealing with psychopaths is a balancing act: they want to be looked at, but challenging them sets them off.

'What do I call you?'

She shrugged. 'We're not here for *your* questions.'

'No,' I say. 'We're here for the Doctor, aren't we?'

There. A tremble in the gun.

'Where is he?' the boy snaps, and the girl raises a hand.

'She's about to tell us. Aren't you?'

'First tell me why you're looking for him. Is it your TARDIS he stole?'

They look at each other and grin.

'A Type Forty?'

'Us?'

'Marvellous.'

'The idea.'

'All right, all right,' I say. 'Quit the comedy routine. If he didn't steal it from you, then why are you chasing him down? Because someone's messing with his timeline, and you two aren't CIA.'

'How do you know that?' the girl says languidly.

Because we have psych evaluations, I think. 'Because you're asking me instead of using agency resources.' *Not that a potential engine would help.* 'And his timeline is changing too much for me to say. You're not catching him now –'

My pistol bucks in the boy's hand. *Energy round*, I think, because I can smell the oxidised stink in the air. *Yes, definitely an energy round*, I think again, because the alternative is thinking about the fact that the shot just removed the top half of my ear. There's no pain, not yet, but I sense that an appointment has been made for the future.

'I wish I could help you,' I lie, 'but I'm afraid I've got nothing. Less than nothing, in fact. I know he's gone, but I don't know where to. And the CIA are messing with his timeline so much that even this moment might get rewritten. Maybe you should get moving – it might take you a long time to catch up with him, especially if you spend your time setting bombs and laying out repairmen.'

'What a pity,' the girl says. 'You really don't know anything. The mine was us –'

'I wanted to see if I could build one,' the boy interrupts.

'But the CIA don't have a clue who the Doctor is. We hacked their communications network a long time ago –'

'And made some badges,' the boy interrupts again. 'Never know when they might come in handy.'

'And they have no record of the theft of a rickety old TARDIS. As for the repairman, we interrogated him but we didn't kill him.'

'Only because you wouldn't let me.' The boy pouts, and the girl shoots him a withering look.

Confusion washes over me. *The potential engine. His timeline.* 'Then who did?'

The girl just looks at me, and I realise I was wrong. The boy isn't the insane one. He's just the one who wears it like a heart on his sleeve. She's the one who looked at everything sanity had to offer, and wrote it a polite and reasoned rejection. He had no chance to be right in the head, but she had every chance – and, as I outlive my usefulness, I realise I have no chance at all.

'Thank you for your help, detective,' the girl says, and the boy gives me his most brilliant smile yet, then shoots me in the head.

It's like someone let off another chronal mine. Time seems to slow enough for me to see the bolt gather in the gut of the gun, climb the throat and launch right at me . . .

Only to fizzle out against empty air.

The boy's eyes widen. He fires again, and again, and even the girl is turning, smile frigid and glassy, but the bolts ricochet away. Again I feel that flutter, that strangeness, time flowing around me, but this time it's not my senses.

It's a TARDIS.

Walls materialise around me, and I see the shocked faces of the Doctor's friends fade and vanish, and I find myself in a control room, bare and blank as if the pilot has not yet stamped their personality upon it. The ever-present light that suffuses a TARDIS isn't there either – instead, the corners are lost in shadow, piled with darkness as if the timeship is losing its internal structure.

Or its temper.

That's when it clicks. What Clastivas said. What the client wanted. The lack of a console or a pilot here, and that blue box going further and faster than any TARDIS before it.

What kind of a colour is blue, anyway?

'You can come out now,' I say, settling back into the chair, and the client stalks from the darkness of the control room, still in those anonymous robes, his predator's smile long gone. He doesn't bother with the diamonds this time, and his eyes are the same inky shade as the shadows in the corner of my eye.

'Why can't you find him? You were supposed to *find* him.'

'You never went to the CIA,' I say calmly. 'How could you?'

Anger, like a cloud crossing the sky, a literal darkening, a fade.

'They wouldn't have helped me. And then, when you went to Clastivas, I thought he was going to tell you –'

'And you tried to cover your tracks.'

'I just want to know why he took it. Why he took a stupid, useless old Type Forty with a broken chameleon circuit –' the boy's outline flickers, really flickers, like a hologram, like a life hit by a chronal mine, and he turns to me with tears in his eyes – 'instead of me.'

He swallows. 'Unassigned TARDISes are time-clamped. Do you know what that means? It means our ability to perceive the timestream is taken away. Do you know what that's like? Going from all of time and space being ours to see to being blind and deaf and unable to move?' His voice hardens. 'That's what Clastivas, or someone like him, would have done when my owner disappeared. That's what was stolen from me, Maris. The universe. Everything. And I'm going to find him, and get it back.'

'No,' I said mildly. 'No, you're not.'

The whole TARDIS shakes. Its voice comes from everywhere, a raging, lonely god.

'WHY NOT?'

Howling pages. Changing faces. A potential engine struggling to keep up.

'Because I thought the CIA were messing with his timeline. I thought only they had that power. I thought . . . I thought they had everything sewn up. A Time Lord boot on the neck of the universe.'

I can't help it. I smile. 'But it's him. He's a traveller, and he's going to keep travelling, no matter what any of us do. He's going to run so far and so fast that no one – not you, or me, or the mightiest civilisation in the universe – is ever going to stop him. He's too big to fit into you. He's too big for Gallifrey. No wonder he –'

Before I can get the word out, the TARDIS is gone, dematerialising around me with that same terrifying finesse. I'm suddenly sitting in my office, pages settling to the floor in the dimensional backwash. I always thought we piloted them . . . but maybe we're just holding them back.

I want to hope he finds the Doctor. But I don't. That man and that Type 40 were made for each other.

The office hasn't changed. It's still dusty and grey, and my old retirement certificate has fallen off the wall. That's okay. Maybe I haven't retired after all. In the agency, you're either a fixer or a problem. I quit being one. Glad to see there's someone out there being the other.

CYBERMEN

GHOST IN THE MACHINE

The Ninth Cyber-Legion march on the planet of Hȳf, and 9.9P-VIV marches with them.

Hȳf is a monochrome world, bleak as a blueprint, with long, stretching wastelands of black and grey and dirty, dusty white. The only colour comes from the sky, and even that is an anomaly. Hȳf has been wreathed in a constant storm for as long as it has had a weather system, but that was until today and the coming of eighteen thousand, four hundred and twenty-seven troop carriers. So many fat silver ships descending upon the planet have compressed the atmosphere, squeezing the clouds into a mist that hangs low over the chalk wastes below.

Today, Hȳf is experiencing its first blue sky in a hundred million years.

9.9P-VIV marches. Chalk dust has stained the lower half of its body and puffs outwards with every step. The moisture in the air has glued dust to its shoulders, now flakily drying in the heat from the long barrel of 9.9P's arm-blaster.

9.9P has been firing since landfall, fourteen hours and twenty-five minutes ago, pausing every thirty-five seconds to avoid overheating. The sound of its weapon is high and drawn-out, painful to organic ears. The noise is a new design feature. It will be tested here on Hȳf by 9.9P and its fellow Cybermen, and then the Cyber-Controller will decide if it should be incorporated into the standard build.

The Racnoss hate the sound. It drives them insane. They scream when they hear it, flinging themselves into the frenzy of blaster-fire the Cybermen are pouring forth from their blasters and from huge track-mounted cannons. The silver warriors march in neat, regimented lines stretching as far as the eye can see, and the monstrous scarlet arachnids pour from their warrens to meet them, swarming so tightly that it is like being assaulted by a single organism, a thrashing wall of red the length of a horizon. There are so many that the targeting system built into 9.9P's faceplate cannot fix on a single target. Instead, it simply picks out single details of the horde: scurrying legs, talons, black glittering eyes.

The Racnoss are not compatible with Cyber-conversion. This may be because they are too non-standard in form, or because they have a slavish devotion to their Empress that cannot be suppressed by lobotomy or implants. Perhaps it is because it is proving difficult to capture a live Racnoss for experimentation. In the fourteen hours and twenty-six minutes since the invasion force landed, 9.9P has seen the crimson arachnoids ignore life-threatening wounds to bring down Cybermen. It has seen Racnoss tear themselves to shreds just to get close enough to strike, driven by an unstoppable biological impulse, like salmon dying to get upstream.

And they *are* dying. 9.9P has recently been upgraded to a Primus operating system. It now has higher function, independence and authority. It has nine other units in its cohort, and a privileged connection to the Cyberiad – the system link between every Cyberman – so it can direct those units to the benefit of the Legion.

For this invasion, the Cyber-Controller has even granted access to the progress of every other Primus unit on Hȳf. 9.9P is aware that the Racnoss are crumbling. It can see the kill-tallies each Primus unit and their cohort are dutifully recording, just as they can see 9.9P's. This knowledge, this access, is a gift from the Cyber-Controller.

They are winning. The Cyber-Controller wishes them to know this.

9.9P does not know why the Racnoss are incompatible with Cyber-conversion. It does not know why the Cybermen are invading Hȳf at all. What it does know is that a two-second pause in firing every thirty-five seconds is sufficient to prevent overheating. It knows through the Cyberiad that its pauses are accounted for through the fire of other units. There is no respite for the Racnoss, no weakness or hesitation they may exploit.

This is efficiency.

9.9P's targeting system is a simple blue crosshair in the centre of its vision. It clicks and whirrs over snarling mouths, stabbing claws and –

9.9P-VIV's arm-blaster abruptly ceases fire.

The Cybermen around it have not ceased firing. Racnoss explode. They shrivel. They burn. They come apart in tatters of red.

9.9P is still not firing, though its arm-blaster is functional and overheating had not reached critical levels. It is not firing because there is a girl in the middle of the Racnoss swarm.

She is shivering. Hȳf's temperature is not lethal for humans, but nor is it optimal, and she is not dressed for this cold chalk world. A fine coating of dust has stolen the colour from her clothes and her cheeks; the strong winds have plastered her hair to her skull. She stands in a writhing tide of Racnoss like a child hip-deep in a river, and though 9.9P's crosshair centres on her, its sensor system does not or cannot explain why she is there.

A Racnoss rises behind her, howling, its claws splayed wide –

And 9.9P's cannon stutters once more to life, splattering the Racnoss to chitinous shards and rubbery entrails. Another falls. Another. The Cyberiad informs 9.9P that its rhythm is now off, and the surrounding units have to shift their own firing rates to compensate.

Somewhere behind, a cannon volley turns a wide stretch of the Racnoss line into a smoking crater. Arachnids stumble, fall, snap at each other in confusion, and 9.9P automatically orders its cohort to take advantage of the disarray and schedule a pause in fire.

When it looks back to where the girl was standing, she is gone.

Orders are given, and 9.9P obeys.

The Cyberiad directs it and its cohort back to their troop carrier. It does not make 9.9P aware whether the battle for Hȳf is finished, or lost, or won, but the Primus unit notes that some troop carriers have been marked by claws and great sprays of fluid.

The Cybermen leave the surface of Hȳf behind.

The transit is short. Storms are returning to the sky. Two of 9.9P's cohort were damaged prior to take-off, and the turbulence as the carriers leave the atmosphere seems to disable their systems completely. The carriers ease themselves into the hangar bays of the Cyber-Legion's great battleships, jets spluttering, and gleaming robots the size of housecats dart forward to repair them.

Undamaged Cybermen return to hibernation cradles, and those in need of repair march to the Forges – a honeycomb of chambers deep in each battleship's heart. As a Primus unit, 9.9P is given priority, and it quickly finds a sterile white repair cell, studded with sensors as black as Racnoss eyes. The sensors scan for imperfections, pouring blue light into every crack of 9.9P's form. It obediently raises its left arm so the prototype arm-blaster can be assessed, then staggers as clamps disengage and remove the forearm, lifting it away into the walls of the Forge. For a tenth of a second, 9.9P registers the loss of a limb as an attack before correcting itself.

It does not enquire as to whether the new arm-blaster will become part of the standard design. Another forearm is not forthcoming, so it lowers its stump to its side. The scanners deactivate – all but one directly at eye level, which flashes brighter than ever before. Cybermen cannot be blinded, but all detail is lost in the sudden glare.

++ *9.9P-VIV.* ++

The Cyber-Controller's voice is not a voice. It arrives in 9.9P's head as if from everywhere – as audio, as data, as a scrolling line of text across its targeting system. It is the first time the unit has ever been addressed by the Cyber-Controller directly.

++ *UNSCHEDULED PAUSE IN FIRING AT 0014.27.14 OF CAMPAIGN. CAUSE SOUGHT.* ++

It is not a question, and even if it was 9.9P realises suddenly that it does not have an answer. It does not know why it ceased firing. Before it can fully reflect on this, the Cyber-Controller accesses its memories directly. Through the dazzling blue of the scanner light, 9.9P sees the moment replayed. It sees arachnids come apart under laser-fire. It sees chitin flake and jaws shatter, claws snap and chalk burn, and above all waits to see the glitch its systems were unable to explain.

++ *NO CAUSE FOUND.* ++

++ *Query* ++ the unit vocalises, a dry bark of sound it did not intend to make.

The Cyber-Controller does not acknowledge the vocalisation, but the image is frozen, then rewound, then played again. It sees the monochrome plains of Hȳf, the raging crimson horde . . .

There is no girl. At fourteen hours and twenty-seven minutes of the campaign, the crosshairs hang on empty air.

The planet Agrippina, of the Tiberian Spiral, is a world suitable for Cyber-conversion. It is so suitable, and the resistance from its human inhabitants so great, that two Cyber-Legions have come together to claim it. The flagships of the Ninth and Eleventh Cyber-Legions have taken residence over each of Agrippina's poles, and the great spinning cylinders can be seen from the surface like new moons. A thin trail of silver connects each ship to the planet.

Troop carriers flow back and forth between the planet's surface and the flagships. The battle is fierce, and already there are thousands of units needing repair. The Forges are working to capacity. Units are restored to function and immediately redeployed.

9.9P has been returned and repaired twice since first making landfall three days and four hours ago.

Even now, striding through the flames of Agrippina's capital, it has already sustained more damage than on Hȳf.

There is a notch from a sniper round in its head frame. The casing on its left leg has been cracked. A unit of guerrilla fighters ambushed its cohort with flamethrowers and, though both the weapons and the ambush proved ineffective, the flames tarnished the bright silver of 9.9P's body to the dull grey of an old kettle.

Agrippina's capital is a city of pillars and domes in a style that the Cyberiad informs 9.9P is 'Greco-Roman'. It does not offer any further information as to what those words mean. Agrippina is halfway through its winter cycle, and the Cybermen have invaded during some kind of human celebration. Metallic strands have been hung in windows. Trees have been groomed to arrow points and hung with paper stars.

The Cyber-Controller has given the order to destroy these where possible, because humans are weak and rely on morale.

Primus units have been installed with an understanding of morale. It is an algorithm – one of many at play in this war. Cybermen do not possess morale, and therefore will fight to the last unit if their Cyber-Controller so wishes, or retreat if their losses become untenable.

Conservation of resources is everything to a race that cannot breed.

The Cyber-Controller is committing and recommitting its forces. This tells 9.9P that the victory here is worth the expenditure – or that human expenditure *is* the victory.

Not all the carriers returning to orbit are transporting damaged Cybermen.

The government district of Agrippina's capital is a collection of concentric streets linked by a tangle of alleyways, each one seeming to contain endless humans wielding singing pulsar rifles. It takes concentrated pulsar-fire to disable a Cyberman, but occasionally there is also the coughing roar of antique anti-Cyber-guns, stockpiled from the many times Agrippinan flesh has faced Cyberman steel.

9.9P's left arm now ends in a standard-issue gauntlet, and it hefts a massive blaster rifle that would take two humans to lift. This is the second blaster rifle it has wielded today. The first was detonated by a sniper round, the resulting explosion removing 9.9P's chest plate and the lower half of its face.

Further memory of the incident was removed after being deemed deleterious to efficiency.

Agrippina sounds different from Hȳf. There are long silences between clashes, broken only by distant explosions or scuffling, crackling firefights. It is snowing, and specks of white hang in the air like ash. This battle is not as simple, not as geometric as on Hȳf; here, Cybermen fight in clusters, street by street, cohort by cohort. They file down avenues, blockade archways – straight lines in a city of curves – and everywhere humans try to stop them.

9.9P is being ambushed. Pulsar rounds are *spang*-ing and *prakk*-ing off its metal skin, diminishing the little shine it still possesses. The humans fire and fall back, fire and fall back, one step ahead of the marching silver horde. They know the city because it's their home. There is an organic, desperate speed about them that the Cybermen are unable to match. Three times, 9.9P's cohort have overrun a barricade only to find the soldiers already gone. Now the Cybermen are half a kilometre out of position, trying to keep up.

The humans grin fiercely as they fight, though judging from the elevated heart rate and adrenaline indicated by 9.9P's targeting system, this is likely a psychological response to extreme terror.

Primus units are advanced, but they are incapable of feeling something as complicated – as *human* – as frustration. However, 9.9P is aware of how many of its cohort have now been permanently disabled. It understands that if this continues, key strategic objectives will not be achieved within the Cyber-Controller's projections. This is taking longer than it should. It is . . . inefficient.

9.9P is also aware that this is not solely its fault. It has deduced this from the mis-alignment of its newly issued faceplate. The component was installed after only three alignment checks instead of the standard six – a deviation in protocol requiring Cyber-Controller approval. Its targeting system is from a previous build: a square of red instead of blue crosshairs.

Expenditure and victory. The algorithm is swinging back and forth like a blade.

The battle rages. Marble burns. The whole front of a building comes away under laser-fire, and a human soldier suddenly deprived of cover yelps and flings himself backwards, rounds cooking the air. 9.9P swivels to track him, blaster rifle raised –

And suddenly there is another human there, hair tucked messily into an Agrippinan military-service cap. Her skin is pink, her nose an upturned sprig half-hidden beneath a scarf. She is dressed like the Agrippinan folk heroes featured so prominently on propaganda posters – the ones with slogans such as 'UPGRA-DEAD' and 'STEEL ISN'T REAL'; slogans meant to remind the humans of Agrippina that they cannot reason with or save Cyber-converted humans. The Cybermen will not recognise those they once knew or loved.

The posters are, technically, incorrect. The truth is that all Cybermen are equipped with sophisticated sensors capable of recognising individual humans who may be injured, useful or dangerous. There are pictures of these dangerous humans – galleries of those who have thwarted the Legion stored in the Cyberiad.

9.9P-VIV knows that this is the girl it encountered on Hȳf.

She is unarmed. Laser-fire whips and snaps by her. The long coat she is wearing dances in the thermal eddies from so much energy discharge, and she is staring directly at 9.9P, her eyes bright and hard as coins.

Once again, the unit ceases fire. It has a sudden urge to shake its head like a human or a dog, except that doing so would not clear its vision and indeed might make the mis-alignment issue more pronounced. It does not know why it has ceased fire. It accesses the Cyberiad – that system which has always provided all the information it has ever needed – and no answers can be found.

The girl cannot be here. It is a mathematical, logical impossibility. For a moment, 9.9P can focus on nothing else and, at that same instant, the algorithm of battle changes once again.

The humans have a positron cannon.

There is no sound analogous to that of a firing positron cannon. Its beam tears molecules apart, splitting the world with light brighter than the skin of a star. The dust-hazed Agrippinan boulevard turns into a searing negative of itself, then a line of yellow slices six Cybermen into pieces. Before the rest of the cohort can turn to face this new attack, the beam lashes out again, bisecting five more.

9.9P recalls the humans' smiles, and briefly considers the fact that the soldiers' retreat may have been a trap.

Cybermen do not panic; they are incapable of it. Panic is an instinct deleterious to victory. However, like any computer system, a Cyberman can be overwhelmed when the input of data is too high or the parameters of the problem it is trying to solve change too rapidly.

There are protocols for dealing with sudden shifts in battle – enemy reinforcements, unprecedented technology, catastrophic failure in the chain of command. These situations are why Primus units were developed: to innovate and react, instead of waiting for orders from above; to capture that organic sense of speed.

9.9P should be responding now.

But the girl is advancing, ignoring the laser-fire searing the air. Human soldiers run and fight and fall around her, firing wildly from their pulsar rifles. Celebratory lights pop and crackle underfoot. Multiple impacts fizzle out against the kettle greyness of 9.9P's skin, and it marches forward too, blaster rifle hanging forgotten from one hand.

The positron cannon turns the world inside out, separating Cyberman heads from bodies, torsos from limbs, and 9.9P-VIV's cohort requests orders. 9.9P is Primus, but they are not. They need direction.

Her eyes are blue, and bright, and cold. She is *staring* at 9.9P and, though its sensors are fully capable of distinguishing one human from another, it is unable to identify the emotion on her face.

But it knows the girl looks horrified.

This deduction does not come from 9.9P's sensors.

9.9P does not know where this deduction comes from.

She raises her right hand. 9.9P's left gauntlet, replaced just three days ago for the invasion of Agrippina, spasms in involuntary response –

And the positron beam passes through her to cut the Cyberman in half.

++ *TEST ACTIVATION OF DAMAGED UNIT.* ++

9.9P wakes in stages.

First comes the connection to the Cyberiad, and this unit's place in it. It is unaware how other legions name their units, or if they name them at all, but the Ninth Legion's naming protocols are clear and simple and efficient. This unit is the Primus unit of the Ninth Cohort of the Ninth Division of the Ninth Cyber-Legion. It is 9.9P-VIV. It knows this.

It knows it cannot move. That is according to protocol. Units must know their place in the Cyberiad before movement will be granted, because units that wake without knowing their place often act in ways that are deleterious to efficiency.

Visual sensors activate. 9.9P is no longer on Agrippina. It is in the Forges. White walls surround it. Outside its cell is the vast and busy hum of repair. Unable to vocalise, 9.9P data-blurts instead: ++ *Connection to Cyberiad achieved.* ++

There is no response.

++ *Connection to Cyberiad achieved. Connection to body can now be established.* ++

Though the Cyberiad has many directories that are inaccessible to Primus units, and many that are not visible at all, the connection between unit and network is always clear. 9.9P knows that its query has been recorded. It knows that it has been heard.

++ *This unit is experiencing a malfunction. Access to physical function required.* ++

9.9P attempts to move but is unsuccessful.

++ *Query.* ++

The door to the repair cell opens. Standing just beyond, bright against the smoky darkness of the Forges' great vats, is a towering silver figure. 9.9P's sensors note where their designs are similar, and note where they are not. This new unit's torso is finished in black – a dead, deep black like the space between stars. The fingers of its gauntlets bristle with connectors and data-spikes, so that it may connect with and monitor the systems it controls.

And it has a brain – an exposed brain, pink and wet in a skull casing of glass.

++ *RESPONSE.* ++

The Cyber-Controller's voice booms from inset speakers. It is modulated to strike terror into organic hearts, and for a moment 9.9P feels a dull metal shadow of that fear.

It is the Cyber-Controller. Here. Speaking to a Primus unit.

This is irregular.

++ *CYBER-LEGION IS TRAVELLING TO NEW WORLD. ACCESS TO PHYSICAL FUNCTION UNNECESSARY.* ++

That is a logical explanation. Cybermen do not need food. Their bodies do not require exercise. Resting in a hibernation cradle is the most efficient use of transit time between worlds. However, access to physical systems is not usually denied in case quick re-activation is required.

9.9P dares a logical query.

++ *Query. Why is physical function denied?* ++

The Cyber-Controller does not reply.

The unit blurts again, though it is sure the Cyber-Controller's systems are functioning.

++ *Query. Is physical function denied due to this unit not designating orders during positronic assault?* ++

The Cyber-Controller's brain glistens, a wet and living gleam. 9.9P is aware – as all Cybermen are aware – that, beneath upgrades and efficiency protocols and the majesty of the Cyberiad, there was once organic matter. It is . . . the heart of them. For a moment, 9.9P is reminded of the celebratory trees on Agrippina – organic things, sharpened to a purpose.

++ *Query. Is physical function denied because this unit did not fire on the girl?* ++

9.9P had acted in a fashion deleterious to efficiency. Deleterious to victory. It had acted outside its function. The girl had raised her hand, and its hand had moved in response.

++ *Query. Is this a punishment?* ++

The Cyber-Controller steps into the cell and the floor trembles a little under its weight. 9.9P can see its own reflection in its master's polished torso, and begins to understand.

++ UNIT IS NOT DENIED PHYSICAL FUNCTION. PHYSICAL FUNCTION IS IMPOSSIBLE. ++

9.9P's head still exists, cradled in the repair-cell clamps. However, that is all that remains. That is why attempts to connect to its body have failed. Those connections and that body no longer exist.

++ QUERY ++ the Cyber-Controller barks. *++ INDICATE HUMAN. ++*

The Cyber-Controller does not move, and yet, within the Cyberiad, 9.9P suddenly feels its mind gripped as if in a vice. Its memories are accessed, appearing bright and spectacular: the domed city, the hanging stars and . . . as before, an inexplicable gap.

It cannot see the girl.

The girl was there.

The girl is not there now.

9.9P's data blurt is simple*: ++ Unit designation 9.9P-VIV requests full disassembly and component scan. ++*

The Cyber-Controller responds immediately: *++ ERROR LOCATED. ++*

Cybermen cannot feel relief, but each unit is programmed with survival protocols. The error has been found. Optimal behaviours will be regained. This is efficiency. This is the way things should be.

++ UNIT HAS STATED DESIGNATION INCORRECTLY. UNIT DESIGNATION HAS CHANGED. UNIT DID NOT OPERATE EFFICIENTLY AS PRIMUS UNIT. FURTHERMORE, OVER 80 PER CENT OF UNIT DESIGNATED 9.9P-VIV HAS BEEN DESTROYED. PREVIOUS DESIGNATION NOW INACCURATE. YOU ARE NO LONGER 9.9P-VIV. ++

Cybermen do not panic.

++ Query. What is unit's new designation? ++

They are incapable of panic.

++ ASSESSMENT OF DAMAGED UNIT COMPLETE. ++

Panic is an instinct deleterious to victory.

++ Repeat query. What is unit's new designation? ++

However, like any computer system, they can be overwhelmed when the input of data is too high or the parameters of the problem they are trying to solve change too rapidly.

++ TEST ACTIVATION CONCLUDED. ++

++ Wait – ++

The Cybermen march on Delastrio. They march on Xexos. They march on Aaster and Batraxi and Niami Majora Quintus. They drop like silver rain on the green meadows of

Tagarn and punch like bullets through the atmosphere of
Quell. They face Judoon and Slitheen and Daleks and most of
all humans, because humanity is exceedingly Cyber-
compatible and infests the stars like mice.

The unit once designated 9.9P-VIV is assigned a new
body, sleeker than the last, with no exposed cabling and a
slim blaster on its wrist. Previous weaknesses with its model
have been identified and compensated for with gold filters,
remote detonation capabilities and a bonding lacquer for its
limbs that is more efficient at deflecting positron-fire.

Its internal power system gleams cold and blue from its
chest – a design feature that is often interpreted as a weakness
by enemies but is intended to draw fire to what is actually the
strongest, most reinforced area of the design.

The unit is no longer designated Primus, though it still
serves in the Ninth Cohort of the Ninth Division of the Ninth
Cyber-Legion. All new components were installed with the
standard six alignment checks. Its targeting system has been
upgraded, and now two rotating blue circles fill its vision,
feeding the Cyberiad with data.

But it still sees the girl. On Barranos IV, it sees her in the
aftermath of an orbital bombardment where an entire city
was fused to glass, and where somehow the lethal-to-humans
temperatures do not affect her. On the shrine world of

Cadogan, where the indestructible Vault of Ages prevents the Cyber-Legions from bringing their full numbers to bear, she wears the dress of a dowager duchess. She scowls through C-goggles on the night planet of Praxes. She is the last to board the refugee ships of Houndstooth, only a step ahead of the silver horde. She hangs from the rigging of a sky galleon above Drowning Vale, even as Cyber-fire sends the boat into the molten green sea.

Sometimes she is speaking, though no words can be heard.

Other times she simply glares.

After each instance, the unit once designated 9.9P-VIV submits itself to the Forges for full diagnostics, but no fault can be detected. Eventually, its requests are denied. They are inefficient, a waste of resources when there is no damage to be found.

It loses an arm to the acid gods of Erodas. A Dalek electronic counter-measure pod fries the circuits in its automotive systems, requiring them to be stripped out. A hard round from a Tallax chattergun dents the edge of its left eyehole so that the notch there becomes more pronounced, like a clearance hole or a tear. Each time, the damage is mended. The component is replaced.

Each time it sees the girl, its hand spasms and its rate of fire falters, and no explanation can be found.

Until New Cadmus.

New Cadmus is a space station – a fist of iridium hanging in space that dwarfs even the flagship of the Ninth Cyber-Legion. Cybermen march into troop carriers or stand silently waiting on teleportation pads to be transported to the space station. Teleportation technology is rarely used because of the vast expenditure of energy required – an expenditure the Cyber-Controller must have deemed necessary on this occasion.

There is something or someone on New Cadmus that the Cyber-Controller desperately wants.

There is also resistance. Soldiers with the initials N.C. stitched on their breasts fire upon Cybermen from gantries, roll grenades through air vents, and blow airlocks so units are dragged out into space.

The unit once designated 9.9P fights its way through corridors, down stairwells and across hangar bays. A map of the space station has been made available to all units through the Cyberiad, marked with the target the Cyber-Controller wishes them to destroy. This target is not static. It disappears and reappears. Cohorts suffer heavy losses to conquer one area, then are commanded to abandon the hard-won ground in favour of assaulting another.

No Cyberman questions this. They march as indicated, then march again when the orders change.

It is in the thirty-fourth minute of the conflict that 9.9P sees the girl. It has been waiting to see her. It has sustained damage because of this expectation – in this battle and in others. This is inefficient, and yet damage allows it access to the Forges, where it can ask for further diagnostic checks and try to locate the error that is leading it to see the girl.

Through the Cyberiad, the Cyber-Controller informs the Cybermen that their tactics should change. They split into groups of three or four, flooding the station and trying to lock down their target. 9.9P and eight other Cybermen come across a loading bay littered with lifters and crates.

A group of defenders are using the lifters as cover, filling the air with blaster-fire while two humans dressed unlike the others kneel over a console. 9.9P's auditory receptors pick up the words 'Cadmus Engine' and upload them to the Cyberiad in case they are relevant.

It is no longer Primus. Such things are no longer for it to understand.

The defenders have faced Cybermen before. They focus their fire on one unit at a time, concentrating their lasers on one of 9.9P's brethren until its casing cracks and ignites. The remaining eight advance nonetheless, wrist-blasters spitting blue.

And the girl is standing there, framed by fire from both sides. She is unarmed. She is never armed – not on any of the worlds where 9.9P has seen her. She is dressed in the tunic and breeches of a New Cadmus guard, but those details are irrelevant. She is different on every planet and every battle and yet she is always the same.

9.9P's targeting system focuses entirely on her. It is many times more advanced than on Hȳf, and yet completely unable to deliver any information beyond the fact that she is inarguably, unstoppably there.

Except that she *cannot* be. She has not been. Every piece of 9.9P has been taken apart and examined. Every part has been upgraded. Every component replaced. Even its name has been dismantled. It is not the same Cyberman any more.

She is an error. She is deleterious to victory.

Its wrist-blaster has also been upgraded, and now only requires a one-second gap in fire to prevent overheating. 9.9P takes advantage of this, firing again and again and again. Another of its cohort goes down in a flurry of light. There are clashing orders being uploaded to the Cyberiad. The Cadmus Engine is activating, or deactivating, or set to explode. 9.9P does not have the clearance to know what is true and what is false.

The girl is standing there. She is just standing there and, unbidden, 9.9P's vocaliser activates for the first time in months. Units are rarely required to vocalise, though it is known that vocalising can have an intimidating effect in battle. Communication through the Cyberiad is far more efficient. A feature that has lain dormant for so long needs a moment to reactivate.

The girl's teeth bare in a snarl, fierce as the laser-fire turning the air to flame.

The unit's targeting systems lock, fail, lock again.

'YOU.'

The word is hoarse with static. 9.9P's wrist-blaster floods the air with light, and soldiers dive and duck for cover. The girl is screaming at it now, and its auditory sensors stretch to catch her words, but nothing of her voice can be heard.

She is an error.

'WILL.'

An error. An error. An error.

'BE.'

9.9P -VIV's wrist-blaster is shrieking, as if the sound can stop the girl where laser-fire cannot.

'DELETED.'

The wrist-blaster overheats and explodes, taking 9.9P with it.

++ *Query.* ++

'Doctor? Doctor, what are you doing? We've no time –'

'Never quite true, Peri. Now, this is interesting.'

'What's interesting? Leave it alone – it tried to kill us!'

++ *Query.* ++

'I don't think it did, actually. It fired, yes, but every single shot missed.'

'Good! The way it was roaring at us . . .'

'Well, that's the most tragic thing, isn't it?'

'What is?'

++ *Query.* ++

'It wasn't talking to us, Peri. They never are. Well, the posh ones are – the Leaders, Controllers. But the rank and file – all that "delete, delete" business? They're talking to the human inside them. The bit they can't get rid of, no matter what they replace. They're talking to themselves.'

++ *Is this a punishme–* ++

THE SILENCE

STUDENT BODIES

[CASE FILE 1098722 – ABDUCTION/HOMICIDE:
CLAIRE, DONOVAN. AGE TWENTY-SEVEN.]

[The following document is a complete transcript of a series of recordings related to the disappearance of Luna University PhD student Donovan Claire. These files were transmitted in their original audio format to Claire's thesis supervisor, Professor Emmeline North (see Case File 1098721 – Abduction/Homicide: North, Emmeline) on Christmas Day, 25 December, in the year 5124.]

[As some of the recordings appear in non-chronological order, dates have been added to provide clarity but, for reasons that will become clear, the transcript is presented exactly as recorded. Beyond a limited audio scrub for quality purposes and attempts to describe background noise, no editing has taken place. The original recordings may be accessed

through the Lunar Security Forces database (clearance Gamma or above).]

[Recording begins: 25 December 5124, 11 p.m.]

    [Transcriber's note: The subject here is female, young, vocal pattern matched from the Luna University database to PhD student Donovan Claire and henceforth referred to as CLAIRE.*]*

    CLAIRE: Yesterday in Aje IV's Commercial District a man fell from a balcony and never hit the ground.

    Today is Christmas Day.

    [Recording ends.]

[New recording begins: 20 December 5124, 1.15 p.m.]

    CLAIRE: The last shuttles are leaving. Can you hear them? There's a sort of *mwop* noise when they pass through the atmospheric shields. Like someone has placed a huge thumb in an equally huge mouth and popped an air bubble. Which is basically what happens, I guess. It's just funny that it sounds so human.

    Professor North tells us not to humanise space. 'Cosmic cartographers must be rational.' The human brain is meant to look for patterns, but you can't rely on space to be that kind – sorry, ordered. Biological, logical, emotional – these systems can't be applied to the cosmos, and if we imagine they can we'll waste months expecting comets to come back because we miss them, or gravity to have a sense of humour.

North smiles when she says it, though.

Hang on. There goes another shuttle. I'll see if I can get a recording –

[creak of bedsprings, footsteps, sound of window shutter being pulled open, recording is briefly lost to high winds and engine-roar]

CLAIRE: You get that? I'll listen back later. See, the reason I mention it is because you can't hear the pop of the shields when you're inside the shuttle. The shuttles are all about fifty years old, and the engine casings are held in place by glue and goodwill, so mostly you're trying not to get sick as your shuttle struggles to drag itself out of the atmosphere. That *mwop* noise is something you can only hear from the ground. That's why I like it.

It's the sound of being left behind in peace.

Luna U officially closed a week ago, which means every student who can leave has left. The exams are over, the shuttles are departing – *mwop*, there goes another one – and the cleaner droids have been deployed in a futile attempt to clear away the wreckage of a thousand end-of-year dorm parties before January term starts and all the back-to-school parties kick off.

And yes, there's staff members, and yes, there's admin staff, and yes, there's the occasional undergrad from a colony

too far away to go home to, but *effectively* I have the whole of
Luna University all to myself.

[muffled footsteps, possibly dancing]

CLAIRE: Granted, I am going to spend the whole
holiday working, obviously. I have six months left until I hand
in. Every spare second counts. I'd be wrapping with one hand
and writing with the other, if I had anyone to buy presents for.
But you have to enjoy the little things when you're finishing a
PhD. The *minuscule* things – things that aren't word counts or
supervisor spats or teaching fees or the simmering worry that
someone half a galaxy away is going to accidentally discover
the same thing I've spent three years and a hundred thousand
words discovering.

Okay. Do not think about that. Think about the things
you can control – like the entire PhD study room in the
library, because everyone else has gone home like fools and
there'll be no queue for coffee.

I am as a god, for the next two weeks. Donovan out.

[Recording ends.]

[New recording begins: 20 December 5124, 3 p.m.]

*[footsteps, echoes indicating stone floor, background hum of
fluorescent lights]*

CLAIRE: I should probably explain why I'm doing this. Not that anyone else but me is ever going to hear it, because I'm here to study maps and not whether someone can die of embarrassment, but just for the sake of posterity I should explain why I'm recording my voice into a microbead.

Everyone says the last six months of your PhD is hell. You stress and you worry and you lose touch with people and you end up so obsessively focused on handing the thing in that you barely notice a significant chapter of your life coming to an end.

I don't want to forget Luna U. Not a detail. Not an inch. The college gave us these little microbeads for recording lectures, and the mic is actually *really* good, and I already kind of talk to myself so I might as well make it official. Although I'll keep the coursework talk to a minimum – my personal computer's already groaning with hundreds of hours of lectures – and I'll just concentrate on describing things. Emotions. How it feels to be here, because in six months I won't be.

[footsteps stop]

CLAIRE: So. Luna University. What do I say? I'm in the Cosmic Cartography campus – 'Map Out Your Future!' – which is situated on the lunar highland of . . . Okay, sorry, you can get all that from the brochure. What you need to know is that Luna U is *big*. I think it covers a third of the moon's surface, and the CC campus is just a small part of that – all these little basalt squares clinging onto the highland cliffs for dear life.

There's an artificial atmosphere and gravity controls, so everything feels like Earth – I know, I was disappointed too – and the air sort of tastes a little electric from the shield holding it in, so sometimes you get a little shock when you're brushing your teeth.

[footsteps resume]

CLAIRE: Over there is the Archaeology campus, and over there is the . . . Actually, I don't know what that is. I have been walking along this corridor every day for three years and I don't know what that tower is. See – these recordings are important.

This is what I can see right now. This corridor is long and low, and there are veins of zinc in the stone so it looks like it's cracking even though I know it's not. Outside of the windows is the Moon, just like it looks in pictures – this dusty grey curve rippled and wrinkled with craters – and, even though we're on the wrong side of the moon to see Earth, it's still beautiful because the stars are out. They're always out – they're like undergrads that way – and their light bends in the atmospheric shield so they blur like your eyes are full of tears.

I wish I could tell you about what was over there, but exploration is for people who don't have deadlines. I've been here three years and I can tell you where all the stellar geography books are, but everything else might as well be the dark side of the galaxy.

There is nobody around. Obviously. If there was, I wouldn't be talking to myself. Oh, the glory of the holiday season. Everyone's off at home with their families . . .

[rummaging, rustling]

[Transcriber's note: Audio here has been scrubbed and boosted due to CLAIRE *lowering her voice. No other manipulation or editing has taken place.]*

CLAIRE: Come on, card. Where are you?

[voice returns to normal volume]

CLAIRE: And this is the library. I'll take some pictures before I go, add them to this. Wait. No I won't. A slideshow with narration? You'd know I was in academia. Basically, picture a drill. That's what our library looks like. A spiral dug into the earth, lined with shelves that go down for nearly a mile. It's all dark basalt as well, just like the corridors, and the zinc cracks have got wider, like the wounds have started to bleed.

And now I've creeped myself out. The chairs are nice!
Very brightly coloured. And . . .

[footsteps speed up, sound of door creaking open]

CLAIRE: Nobody here. You should see the private study
room during term-time. Nobody does turf war like a doctoral
student. There are fights over power outlets and elbow space.
And there are seat-snatchers. I've genuinely come back from a
mere four hours in the shelves looking for *Orpenesque Cosmology:
A primer* only to find that someone has neatly stacked all my
stuff on the floor and hopped into my seat.

But now it's empty.

[voice rises]

CLAIRE: It's empty.

It's empty.

[repetition of phrase due to echo]

[laughter]

CLAIRE: Okay. I need to do some work. On this table.
Ooh. Maybe I'll pull over *another* table. And put up my feet.
And . . . Oh, maybe I'll even . . .

*[Transcriber's note: CLAIRE was in possession of a Hawking
Mark 9 personal computer with wrist-attachment and inbuilt holo-
projector. This device has not been located by investigative teams, and
robbery is not suspected, as the model was several years out of date. The
Hawking Mark 9 is henceforth referred to as COMPUTER.]*

CLAIRE: Computer, engage projector.

COMPUTER: Projector engaged.

CLAIRE: There is a special circle of academic hell reserved for people who engage their computer's projectors in public. It's like people who play music at the back of the shuttle. But am I in public when there's no one else around? That's a question for people who study philosophy.

Computer, show me Rogue Planet Route Donovan Claire A.

[whirring sound believed to be engagement of holo-projector]

CLAIRE: Hello, universe.

Okay. Back-story. In six months, barring meteor strike, total event collapse or nervous breakdown, I am going to be Doctor Donovan Claire, CCES. My thesis is titled 'Lost Bodies: A plotting of rogue exoplanets in Stellar Region IIIOBI'.

I know what you're thinking. Yes, I am a hit at parties.

And, you know what? I realise that I promised to keep the coursework chat to a minimum, but Professor North says the most useful skill a PhD student can have is to be able to explain their dissertation without a flipchart or a nervous breakdown, so here goes.

Rogue planets are planets that don't orbit suns the way regular planets do. Instead, they just swing freely through space or orbit the galactic centre on an arc so big that each of their 'years' is a full millennium. Some used to be part of a solar system, until their star collapsed or something knocked them out of their own orbit. Some never had homes at all and have just been spinning alone since the birth of the universe.

'Orphan planets'. That's what some people call them. I don't like that name. It's too sad. Not . . . majestic enough.

Computer, track planet designated Donovan Claire B4.

COMPUTER: Tracking planet designated Donovan Claire B4.

CLAIRE: I'm studying a little planet that nobody has ever bothered naming. It's just a chunk of titanium and dust circling the Milky Way. But I have a theory that it didn't always do that, because space only looks sedate and dignified. To our lifespans, space seems as unchanging as a photograph, but on a scale of aeons it's a Petri dish humming with life.

I have a theory that this planet used to belong to something. That something existed, and then it didn't, and poor little Donovan Claire B4 and the eleven other planets I've been tracking have been falling away through the universe ever since.

Wait.

Sorry. *Sorry.* Got spooked for a second. Thought there was a —

[voice rises]

CLAIRE: Hello? Is anyone there?

[voice returns to normal volume]

CLAIRE: Probably just a cleaner droid. They freaked me out a little when I first got here. I mean, imagine you're the designer of a cleaner droid. Why would you make it this elongated bone-white plastic man? Why not like a . . . cute little . . . rabbit or something? I don't know. I am not a robot designer. We are not supposed to be humanising things.

But you could have given them faces.

I'm over it now, though. There's only so many times you can be spooked by something holding a feather duster. After a while, you stop noticing them at all.

Wait. Why am I thinking about cleaner droids? *Focus.*

Computer, zoom into –

[Transcriber's note: Despite best efforts to identify the following sound, no match in any database has been found. The closest comparison that can be made is to a human death-rattle. This particular sound is henceforth referred to as 'unidentified audio'.]

[unidentified audio]

CLAIRE: Wait.

Sorry. *Sorry.* Got spooked for a second. Thought there was a –

[voice rises]

CLAIRE: Hello? Is anyone there?

[voice returns to normal volume]

CLAIRE: Probably just a cleaner droid. They freaked me out a little when I first got here. I mean, imagine you're the designer of a cleaner droid. Why would you make it this elongated bone-white plastic man? Why not like a . . . cute little . . . dog or something? I don't know. I don't design robots. And humanising things is bad.

But you could have given them faces.

Wait. Why am I thinking about cleaner droids? *Focus.*

Computer, zoom into –

[Transcriber's note: What may appear here to be a loop in the recording is in fact Donovan Claire having a second startled reaction, with no apparent recollection of the first.]

[unidentified audio]

CLAIRE: Oh, my god. Oh, my god. What are you? What –

[Recording ends.]

[New recording begins: 25 December 5124, 11.05 p.m.]

CLAIRE: They're like spiders – that specific terror that only spiders create. The jump-start movement that means you don't notice them when they're moving, only when they're suddenly, terrifyingly close.

And the realisation becomes a black hole. You forget where you are. Who you are. You only know that they are suddenly within striking distance, and you never even knew they were there.

Yesterday in the Horsehead Nebula three ancient civilisations froze to death, unable to ever remember being warm. Their sun had vanished. Even the memory of it had . . .

Today is Christmas Day.

[Recording ends.]

[New recording begins: 20 December 5124, 3.20 p.m.]

CLAIRE: Please, don't hurt me. Please –

[Transcriber's note: At this point in the audio file, an extremely loud siren is triggered. This correlates with a recorded triggering of the fire alarm in the library at Luna University on 20 December 5124 at 3.20 p.m.]

CLAIRE: Is that the fire alarm? Did someone set off the fire alarm? This is typical.

[siren continues, sound of papers being gathered]

CLAIRE: And now I feel bad, because maybe it's a real fire. And *now* I feel silly for feeling bad because, honestly, how often is the fire alarm going off in a university actually a fire, and how often is it a prank?

[hurried, echoing footsteps, siren continues]

CLAIRE: I bet someone's done research on that. I should do research on that. Wait. What am I saying? Ugh. I'll come back tomorrow. It was just really nice to have the place to myself.

[Recording ends.]

[New recording begins: 21 December 5124, 4.50 p.m.]

CLAIRE: The fire alarm was River Song. Of *course* it was River Song.

Generally we doctoral students keep to ourselves. I barely even see the other students studying cosmic cartography, and when I do the conversation revolves around the handful of things people studying the same subject always talk about. Namely, whether we want to kill our supervisors, whether they want to kill us, and how we are ever going to get jobs.

But even I've heard about River Song.

River Song, who teleported half of the Dean's office into the lower atmosphere in an attempt to snag a look at term papers. River Song, who keeps putting in funding requests for an expedition to Dalek space to 'see what they're up to'. River Song, who broke into the Academy of Time Travel to steal an antique vortex manipulator so she could contact her future self for essay topics, and managed to avoid expulsion by positing that you couldn't plagiarise yourself.

She's beautiful, if you like that sort of thing. Immensely irritating if you're trying to get any kind of work done at all.

We've never *actually* met, but she irritates me all the same. After her little caper at the Academy of Time Travel, they stopped taking one in ten archive requests and started taking one in every million, so *my* request to *peek* at a relic Time Lord star map was denied. And everyone's off-world visit permits got withdrawn after she stole a shuttle to go play cards with Silurian corsairs.

She's broken eighteen laws of Luna U, thirteen bylaws and started six brawls in the three years she's been here. I'd love to know what she's studying that gives her the time. Actually, no. I'd just love to know why nobody's actually kicked her out.

It's like she has a guardian angel.

[soft music playing]

CLAIRE: The library was closed today. Apparently *someone* discharged a home-made alpha meson blaster in the foyer yesterday, and now all the sprinklers have to be recalibrated in case they go off and ruin 300 years' worth of accumulated books. I'm sitting in my dorm trying to access the library's star maps on a connection really only designed for phone calls home and I could *spit*.

I was going to spend today listening to the audio files I've been recording, but I didn't get enough done yesterday and now I'm behind and I hope by the time I do get to listen to these recordings I'm a professor and she's . . . Well, not flunked out. That's too mean. But I hope she's stuck somewhere *really inconvenient*.

God, I can't even curse someone properly.

Donovan out.

[Recording ends.]

[New recording begins: 25 December 5124, 11.30 p.m.]

CLAIRE: Cosmic cartography works in one of two ways. The first is simple: you simply look for the object you wish to observe in the sky. You look for the shape of it. You look for the space it occupies in space.

This is the easiest way, but it is also flawed, because we can only see as well as we can see. We are limited by our instruments.

Today, the Twenty-ninth Sontaran Battlefleet disappeared. None of the many enemies of the Sontaran Empire will claim responsibility for the victory. Indeed, none of them will remember engaging the battlefleet at all. As if even the memories have drained away, like water through a cracked glass.

Today. Today is . . .

[Recording ends.]

*

[New recording begins: 21 December 5124, 9.46 p.m.]

CLAIRE: That doesn't make any sense. Computer, check connection with library star maps.

COMPUTER: Connection established.

CLAIRE: No, this must be an old map. That's not right.

COMPUTER: Map last updated this morning at 11 a.m. December twenty-first, 5124.

CLAIRE: But it can't have been. This map must be older, or a mistake or . . . B4 is missing, computer. The planet is missing.

[whirring of computer]

COMPUTER: Clarify?

CLAIRE: The planet, computer. The *planet*! Sorry. Sorry, computer. I didn't mean to raise my . . .

[silence for four seconds]

CLAIRE: Computer, where is the planet designated B4? The planet I've been looking at every day for three years. Where has it gone? It's not showing up on the star map.

COMPUTER: Searching.

CLAIRE: So, other me who's listening to this, you and I are going to laugh about this at some point in the future, but my star map is wrong. The star map I've laboriously put together from satellite proximity scans and unclassified military data and shipping routes and the star maps of every sentient race within fifty light-years. You know, my life's work.

It's wrong.

I'm missing a planet.

My planet. It's gone. And planets *do* get destroyed, but there's a sign left behind – debris or whatever. A planet doesn't just vanish. Not overnight. Not without a trace. Not like it just . . . fell out of the universe. The computer must be malfunc–

COMPUTER: No malfunction detected.

CLAIRE: Okay. Okay, breathe, Donovan. There's an explanation. Oh, god. Of course there's an explanation. Oh, god. This is like shutting down your computer and forgetting to save your work, except that it's not 500 words of an essay. It's a hundred-trillion-ton lump of rock that's just *gone*.

No. It's not gone. The professor always says that if you can't see something it's your fault, not the universe's. Professor North always stays over the holidays too. She probably has access to better maps, maybe even some classified data . . . I'm sure this has happened to her before. I bet it happens all the time! Nothing's wrong, and the library will open again soon, and it's probably a connection problem because I'm trying to access the maps from here and . . . and . . .

[Transcriber's note: The audio file continues recording, but only captures faint, distressed breathing. It is the opinion of this transcriber that CLAIRE suffered a mild panic attack at this time.]

CLAIRE: River Song, I hope you end up somewhere really, *really* inconvenient. Donovan out.

[Recording ends.]

[New recording begins: 25 December 5124, 11.31 p.m.]

CLAIRE: Sometimes the thing you wish to study is not there. Sometimes it has vanished, or moved, and maybe you worry that it was never there in the first place.

Consider the detection of dark matter in the earliest years of the Stellar Age. In the twentieth century, it was theorised that dark matter existed – a type of matter that was invisible to every sensor available at that time. The only evidence for its existence was the effect it had on everything else.

Sometimes you cannot observe what you wish to observe. Sometimes you observe everything around it, the gap where it should be, and that gives you the clues you need.

[Recording ends.]

[New recording begins: 22 December 5124, 1.28 p.m.]

[two pairs of footsteps, one growing louder as it nears CLAIRE's microbead]

[Transcriber's note: Though a name is given by the second speaker here, no record or matching vocal pattern can be found in the Luna University database. This speaker is therefore henceforth referred to as UNKNOWN FEMALE.*]*

UNKNOWN FEMALE: Can I help you?

CLAIRE: I'm looking for Professor North.

[both pairs of footsteps stop]

UNKNOWN FEMALE: Administrative leave, I'm afraid. I'm her replacement. Professor Kovarian.

CLAIRE: Oh. Okay.

UNKNOWN FEMALE: Can I help you with something? Helping students is my job. I'm very . . . maternal like that.

CLAIRE: No, I just, um . . . Maybe you can help me. I was wondering, did you have any access to . . . I was wondering if you had access to better star maps than the doctorate students. I'm doing my PhD on rogue planets –

UNKNOWN FEMALE: Oh, you're North's little orphan girl! The scholarship waif. She told me about you. Oh dear. Spending Christmas *working*. That's no Christmas at all.

[Transcriber's note: CLAIRE*'s response here is too quiet to be picked up by her microbead.]*

UNKNOWN FEMALE: What was that?

CLAIRE: Yes, I said. Yes, I'm . . . Look, sometimes Professor North loaned us her clearance for pre-approved data. Nothing important, just little things. I've lost . . .

UNKNOWN FEMALE: Lost what?

CLAIRE: The planet I'm studying. I've lost it. It's disappeared off the star maps I have access to.

UNKNOWN FEMALE: Where?

CLAIRE: Well, I –

UNKNOWN FEMALE: *Where?*

CLAIRE: Stellar Region IIIOBI. Designated planet B4. It's probably just a glitch. It can't just have –

UNKNOWN FEMALE: The cracks are spreading. I didn't think –

CLAIRE: What?

UNKNOWN FEMALE: Oh, nothing. I wouldn't worry about this, Ms Claire. It's a glitch. A mistake. I'm sure one of the technicians will be back after the holidays to fix everything. You just – What is that? On your lapel?

CLAIRE: It's a microbead. I use it for –

UNKNOWN FEMALE: You're recording this?

CLAIRE: We're . . . we're encouraged to. Professor North –

UNKNOWN FEMALE: Is no longer here. And I'm afraid you'll have to hand that over. You can't simply record staff and students without –

CLAIRE: Isn't that an eye drive?

UNKNOWN FEMALE: What?

CLAIRE: Your eye patch. I've read about them before. It's an eye drive. Records audio and visual directly in the brain. It *is* an eye drive, isn't it? Have you just been recording me?

UNKNOWN FEMALE: I am staff, you little wretch. And I will be having a word with your supervisor.

CLAIRE: Oh, that would be Professor North.

UNKNOWN FEMALE: Ah.

CLAIRE: When did you say she'd be coming back? After Christmas?

UNKNOWN FEMALE: I didn't say, as a matter of fact. Well. Maybe you should be running along.

[UNKNOWN FEMALE's footsteps resume]

CLAIRE: *[voice lowered]* Oh, god. I can't believe I just did that. Oh, god.

UNKNOWN FEMALE: *[distant]* Oh, and, Ms Claire? Don't worry about your little planet. Things go missing all the time.

[Recording ends.]

*

[New recording begins: 23 December 5124, 3.17 a.m.]

CLAIRE: There's something in my room.

Oh, god.

Oh, god.

I went to the bathroom. It's . . . stupid o'clock and I couldn't sleep and I went to the bathroom and there's something in my room. I can see its shadow on the wall. Long and thin. Like a spider. It's like a spider, just standing still, the shape of a person but *wrong*, stretched out and waiting . . .

It's blocking my computer's wrist-attachment. There's no signal. I've lived in this room for three years and I've never so much as lost coverage. It's doing it. It's doing this.

I'm going to die.

This is how I die.

It can't not know I'm here. The bathroom light is on – oh, god – and it's just standing there. It's just standing there waiting and I don't want to die in my bathroom six months before I hand in. I don't want to disappear. I don't want to disappear and be forgotten –

[sound of door banging open]

Please, please don't kill me please I'm sorry I'll stop I'll stop I won't ask any more questions I won't investigate I'll forget B4 I will I will oh, god, what are you –

[unidentified audio]

[Recording ends.]

[New recording begins: 23 December 5124, 9.40 a.m.]

CLAIRE: I think I'm stressed out. I woke up last night just standing in my bathroom, staring off into space. That is not normal, even for a PhD student. I even had the mic recording, as if I was taking notes.

Now *that* is an audio file I'm never listening to. God, the embarrassment. I haven't been able to bring myself to listen to any of them, actually. I've been feeling . . .

I sent some mails last night. I don't know – the way that Kovarian spoke to me, I got so mad, and so I decided that I couldn't be the only person out there looking at my little rogue planet. It has cultural significance for four races on nearby worlds, and there are commercial shipping companies that have to navigate round it all the time. They actually encourage people to send in information, because they use it to improve their routes.

I wonder if they're hiring.

But it took me the longest time to actually send those mails. I felt sick, doing it. Not like a panic attack, but as if my whole body was rebelling against me, muscle to muscle, bone against bone . . .

There was a game they used to play in the orphanage. We'd go down to the tracks, and two of the bravest kids would lie on their backs with those cheap little video harnesses on their chests, and let the trains pass over them, just a few inches above their faces. I have no idea how they did it . . . and I could always see, as the other kids egged them on, that they had their eyes closed, as if they didn't know why they were doing it either.

That's what it felt like, sending those mails. Like I was watching someone do something incredibly dangerous, something that would get them killed.

Sorry. All these recordings were supposed to be about Luna U, not me slowly losing my mind. I think I've been on my own too much recently.

There was a firefight in the shuttle bay last night. River Song *again*. I heard two janitors talking about it. She'd been yelling about things following her, but couldn't tell the security anything about them, and then flatly denied she'd ever said anything. Which is what criminals do, I guess.

But it left me feeling . . . uneasy.

She was sitting outside the Dean's office this morning when I walked by. They'd taken her gun, but just left her there. That can't be safe, right? For anybody?

She looked really confused. I found myself nearly wanting to go and sit with her. That's how weird I'm feeling. I'd probably end up being dragged along as her accomplice for something.

I can't believe I'm the accomplice in my own fantasy.

Okay. I am going to get some sleep, and hopefully the mails I sent out requesting other viewpoints will help. That's what Professor North always says. If your eyes are wrong, find other eyes.

Donovan Claire, Space Detective. Accomplice to nobody.

I need sleep.

[Recording ends.]

[New recording begins: 23 December 5124, 10.50 p.m.]

CLAIRE: This isn't right. This isn't right. I'm seeing things. I have to be seeing things. I can't sleep. I keep jerking awake like someone's knocking on the door.

[unidentified audio]

CLAIRE: Hello? Is anyone there?

[unidentified audio]

CLAIRE: Hello? Is anyone there?

[unidentified audio]

CLAIRE: Hello, is anyone there?

COMPUTER: Message received.

CLAIRE: One of the shipping companies. They've replied. Oh, thank god. Okay. Find me my planet so I can sleep. Find me –

No. *No.* They don't have any record of it. They don't have any record of a planet they've been navigating round for the last thirty years! I've ordered charts off them before – they *know* it's there. Are they lying? Why would they lie? Nobody cares enough about that planet to lie, and nobody cares enough about my PhD to lie to me.

Computer, search for mail related to planet designated B4.

COMPUTER: Term not found.

CLAIRE: What?

COMPUTER: Term not found.

CLAIRE: No. *Nononono.* Computer, search again.

COMPUTER: Term not found.

CLAIRE: Computer, open doctorate file one.

COMPUTER: Doctorate file opened.

CLAIRE: Search for term 'Planet B4'.

COMPUTER: Term not found.

CLAIRE: Computer, open doctorate backup file one and search for same term.

COMPUTER: Term not found.

CLAIRE: Computer, open doctorate backup files one through forty and search for term.

COMPUTER: Term not fo–

[unidentified audio]

[Recording ends.]

[New recording begins: 25 December 5124, 11.45 p.m.]

CLAIRE: I am an observer. That is what I wanted to be. I wanted to see where distant things were. Maybe that is why I can see the things that are going missing. Or maybe it is that I am distant, and maybe we do not notice the dangers that are closest to us. Like spiders. Like memories fading away.

The physicist Heisenberg is often quoted as saying that one cannot observe something without changing it. This quote is incorrect. What Heisenberg actually said was that the more you know about an object's position, the less you know about its momentum.

It's Christmas Day. I know it is Christmas Day. And I . . .

[Recording ends.]

[New recording begins: 24 December 5124, 3.05 a.m.]

CLAIRE: I remember. I remember now.

This is what they do. This is how it works. You see them and you forget. And then you see them and you forget. And then you see them and you forget. And then you see them.

This is what I see.

There is a Silent standing outside of my window.

There is a Silent standing in the corridor.

The courtyard outside is full of them, swaying like reeds, like drowned men at the bottom of rivers, like candles on the graves of the dead. They watch me. They all watch me.

I have left myself notes, which they take. I have fashioned clues, which they steal. They are here because there are cracks in time that are eating worlds, or because they caused them, or because they worship them, or because they hate them. I do not know. Or I do know and I have forgotten.

I am Donovan Claire, but I am also the Donovan Claire who does not know her life is bricked up with the bulbous white heads of things she cannot see.

I envy her, and that when she knows what I know they will kill her.

[Recording ends.]

[New recording begins: 24 December 5124, 6.15 p.m.]
   CLAIRE: Hi.

[Transcriber's note: The second speaker here is female, age thirty-four, vocal pattern matched from the Luna University database to student River Song and henceforth referred to as SONG. *For River Song's full criminal record, please access the Lunar Security Services database.]*

SONG: Hello. Staying over Christmas too? We should have gone for drinks. Or stolen something. How are you doing?

CLAIRE: Good. I think. Yeah. Feeling a little . . . I'm fine. Holiday blues. You?

SONG: Bored. Very bored. I'm studying archaeology –

CLAIRE: Sorry, you study *archaeology*?

SONG: Yes. Why?

CLAIRE: Nothing.

SONG: Hmm . . . Well, all it's doing is reminding me that there are places I'd much rather be. You know?

CLAIRE: Um . . .

SONG: Hey, is that a microbead?

CLAIRE: Yeah. It's an audio diary. For my last six months.

SONG: Diaries are cool. I traded mine for some lipstick. Been meaning to start another one . . .

CLAIRE: For *lipstick*?

SONG: It's special lipstick. Hey, you've been recording for a while?

CLAIRE: Yeah. I mean, I thought I hadn't done that much, but it's really mounting up. I haven't even looked back over –

SONG: Can I listen?

[Recording ends.]

[New recording begins: 24 December 5124, 11.30 p.m.]

SONG: Stop crying. It's going to be okay.

CLAIRE: Easy for you to say. You're not going *insane*. That's me. That's me in that audio! That's me talking about things in my room and things in my head, and I'm just here to . . . I'm just here to . . .

[sobbing]

CLAIRE: I just wanted to do my PhD. That's all. I just wanted to look at planets and make things . . . easier for people who wanted to go places.

SONG: I know. I know. And I'm sorry. Hey, is your microbead on?

CLAIRE: What? Why?

SONG: Because I'm going to take a look out of your window. And I want us to remember what I see.

[unidentified audio]

SONG: We should go. Now.

[Recording ends.]

[New recording begins: 24 December 5124, 11.40 p.m.]

[running footsteps]

SONG: Run!

[unidentified audio]

CLAIRE: There! To your right!

[sound of energy weapon discharge]

[Transcriber's note: Database match indicates the energy weapon is a Luna University Security Forces Hand Cannon. Check for stolen pieces?]

SONG: Oh, god. I remember them. I remember them. I've seen them before. I've seen them –

CLAIRE: River!

SONG: I've seen them my whole life.

CLAIRE: Stop remembering and run!

[running footsteps, sound of hand-cannon discharge]

SONG: Okay. Okay, you have to go.

[unidentified audio]

[unidentified audio]

SONG: I can hold them off. I'm the one shooting them. You're just –

CLAIRE: No! I won't let you –

SONG: You know things. Maybe that's why you remember more. You've been remembering and you know things and I'm not the one they want. I can stay here, buy you some time.

CLAIRE: They'll kill you!

SONG: They want to stay hidden, right? So I make it loud and I make it messy. It's what I'm good at. Maybe it'll be too much of a risk for them. Maybe they'll back off. Either way –

[unidentified audio]

CLAIRE: Thank you. I'll . . . I'll remember this.

SONG: Oh, sweetie. How could you not?

[running footsteps continue, sound of multiple hand-cannon discharges]

[unidentified audio from multiple directions, volume wavering due to distance from microbead]

SONG: *[distant]* I remember you now.

[unidentified audio]

[unidentified audio]

[unidentified audio]

[Recording ends.]

[New recording begins: 25 December 5124, 11.59 p.m.]

CLAIRE: She got me off-world. There was a pilot waiting – some shuttle captain with a dreamy expression and a smear of lipstick he hadn't quite wiped off. I watched the moon get smaller and smaller and within a few hours I was somewhere else.

I can't say where. You should understand why. But I withdrew the last of my student loans from the college and now I'm just . . . out here, out in the universe, travelling to places that used to be just names on a map.

I'm out here now. Looking for . . .

Saturnyne is gone. A planet of ten billion lives. And nobody remembers. People have disappeared, hundreds of thousands of people on dozens of different planets and that's only the ones I've checked, and I only know they've gone because nobody mourns them and no one can remember when they were there.

But there are artefacts. A bracelet. A painting. A PhD student stubbornly staring at a section of the sky. A wedding ring. Even they are also fading now, as if erasing themselves over time. I have to listen to these tapes – my tapes – because if I don't it starts to escape me too.

I hope River remembers. And, if not, maybe someday I'll remind her, because that's what cartographers do.

They fill in the blanks.

I'm going to find out what happened. I'm going to find out why things are falling out of the universe, and what these silent creatures have to do with it. I'm going to copy these tapes when they start erasing themselves, and then when the copies start erasing I'll copy those as well. There are blank spaces – I keep finding blank spaces – but I've tried to explain them as best I can. Footnotes, I guess. Once an academic, always a . . .

I'm mailing them to you, Professor North, even though I'm pretty sure they killed you. But if they haven't I want you to know where I went. I don't want to be forgotten. I don't want to disappear.

My name is Donovan Claire, and my eyes are –

[unidentified audio]

SONTARANS

A SOLDIER'S EDUCATION

S ONTARAN SUBLIMINAL EDUCATION MATRIX INTRODUCTORY AUDIO FILE LOADED.

    . . . UNPACKING . . .

    . . . UNPACKING . . .

    . . . PLAYING NOW.

    Greetings, Hero of Sontar!

    You are hearing this because you have been born. Congratulations! Your first victory against the cold, uncaring universe. I am the voice of the Sontaran Subliminal Education Matrix, a database of a million military surveys compiled by the brave Sontarans who have gone before you. My purpose is to instruct you in Sontaran culture, military tactics and honour codes so that you, like the 7 million other soldiers in your batch-generation, may serve the Empire to the best of your ability.

You may have noticed that you are submerged in liquid. Do not struggle. This is merely the warm embrace of the Sontaran Cloning Pool. Ignore any discomfort. This is just the needles of the Sontaran Assessment System piercing your skin. Blood samples are required to make sure that you are not in any way defective.

While we check your vitals, consider this, newborn soldier.

All but 0.000000000000000000042 per cent of the universe is empty space. The natural state of the galaxy is freezing, hostile death – or stars, which are very hot and can also kill you. The chances of you being born in a location that would not prove immediately fatal are staggeringly low and, yet, here you are. You did not exist a moment ago, and now you do. The odds were against you, and yet you prevailed. You, Hero of Sontar, have single-handedly defeated the natural law of all of existence.

Take a moment, as we drain the Sontaran Cloning Pool and move to the next stage of the process, to assess what that triumph feels like.

Feel your noble Sontaran heart pounding. Listen to your strong Sontaran muscles twitch and stretch, yearning to crush all before you. Taste the adrenaline that, even now, is squirting through your veins, urging you onwards to the next victory and the next. Savour it! Victory is your birthright. Cherish the first time you feel it – it will not be the last!

And keep your hands by your sides. You are being loaded into a drop-pod, and losing an arm is classed as an immediate failure by the Sontaran Assessment System.

Over the next seven minutes of your infancy the Sontaran Subliminal Education Matrix will provide all the education you need in order to become a proper Sontaran. Data entries exist on a multitude of subjects: our technology, enemies of the Empire, famous victories. Prepare to be inspired by the glory of Sontar!

Choose a data entry to study now. And please ignore that loud exploding sound. It is just you and your drop-pod being fired into space.

DATA ENTRY 1 SELECTED: THE SONTARAN BODY (AND ITS USES).

An excellent choice! You will wield many weapons over the course of your service, but none so mighty as your own form. Generations of gene-splicing and DNA modification have resulted in you, Hero of Sontar.

Not for us the messy, squishy, chaotic nonsense that other races call 'breeding'. Not for us the randomness of evolution or these different and confusing 'genders'. No! We have approached the propagation of our race with the same strategic clarity we approach all warfare.

As previously stated, you are one of a batch of millions, one of a clone army birthed in a single moment, perfected for the waging of war. While other races indulgently enjoy a period of utter unreadiness called 'childhood', mewling and rolling around in their own filth, we are born and raised in minutes, educated in all relevant knowledge by the Sontaran Subliminal Education Matrix.

Every Sontaran body is crafted with extreme care. Traits such as strength and resilience have been selected and prioritised, while useless characteristics such as compassion and body hair have been reduced or removed entirely.

Every aspect of our bodies has been perfected, from respiratory to digestive. You will note, perhaps, an area of relative tenderness on the back of your neck. This is the probic vent (SEE RELATED DATA ENTRY 245), an opening through which your body can be nourished with simple energy. Other races are weak, needing a variety of vitamins and minerals for sustenance. Our diet is plasma and triumph!

As you can see, even unarmed you are already better equipped for battle than any other galactic species.

Unfortunately (and shamefully), many other races do not appreciate our streamlined design. Some have even learned that a sharp strike to the probic vent can render us unconscious – even slay us.

However, in its infinite wisdom, Sontaran High Command is aware of and has accounted for this potential vulnerability. Face forwards, Hero of Sontar! Face your enemy! Do not leave your probic vent exposed, and your invincibility is assured. This is the glory of the Sontaran Empire – even our weaknesses are strengths!

A note before we continue. It is possible that the first time you face a member of another species they may point out that the mighty Sontaran stature (a product of our high-gravity origin world) is less . . . towering than that of other races. It is also possible that they might mention our height in a mocking or derogatory way.

Sontaran military strategy does not advise engaging in conversation with enemy races, if at all possible. There is no honour in *verbal* sparring. However, if immediately murdering them is not a viable option, simply remind them of three indisputable facts.

1) We are not short. We are compact. This makes us a more difficult target to hit.

2) A more compact structure means fewer resources are spent on armour, thus freeing additional assets to be spent on ammunition.

3) All races are the same size when laid out with a blow.

Then you may immediately execute them. This is called 'irony'.

RELATED DATA ENTRIES:

- 325: NURSES – NECESSARY OR COWARDLY?
- 390: HOW MANY FINGERS DO YOU POSSESS? A CAREER IN SPECIAL FORCES COULD BE FOR YOU!

DATA ENTRY 2 SELECTED: SONTARAN ARMOUR.

Ah, another excellent choice. This is only the second minute of your existence and already you are displaying a keen sense of tactical nuance. Be aware that when presented with the same options 4,300,008 of your batch made inferior choices. You are moving up the ranks!

You may also be interested to know that your drop-pod is now hurtling into the atmosphere of an enemy world. This is a perfect opportunity to educate you in our innovations in military technology.

There is nothing dishonourable about wearing armour. The Sontaran physique is robust, and our enemies are pathetic – but they can be cunning, and anything that prolongs combat effectiveness is crucial to our cause.

But worry not! You have already been encased in the Sontaran Empire's finest Mark VII Battle Armour: sturdy, form-fitting and proof against all but the most determined blade or bolt. This armour offers extra protection for your probic vent and can be modified for the inclusion of a perception-camouflage matrix and other advanced technologies.

Please hold your head still as we lower the Mark VII Tactical Helmet. This will guard the noble dome of your valuable skull and enhance your senses with an intuitive, ever-updating heads-up display connected to our forces in orbit. No Sontaran sees alone, hears alone or fights alone with a Mark VII!

Now, as the Mark VII Tactical Helmet connects to the systems of the Seventh Sontaran Battlefleet, you should see our ships in orbit, and details of the planet below. Do you see the green icons entering the atmosphere? That's you! The 5,960,000 who have survived this far, to be exact, which, considering the sheer volume of anti-aircraft fire being levelled at you from the surface, is actually well within acceptable fatalities for this stage of your development.

Another note: like any good Sontaran soldier eager to serve, you may be wondering whether the Mark VII Battle Armour – or, indeed, your sturdily constructed drop-pod – has been reinforced to survive the barrages directed at you from the planet's defences.

Fortunately, the enemy's weapons are so advanced that not even our properly shielded command ships are safe. Revel in the heady rush of knowing that you, like our most celebrated generals, may die at any moment – and, remember, dying *above* a battle is still dying *in* battle!

RELATED DATA ENTRIES:

- 247: PROBIC VENT CARE – WHY A MIRROR IS YOUR BEST FRIEND.
- 357: HELMET POLISH PROCEDURES – GET A SONTARAN SHINE.

DATA ENTRY 3 SELECTED: SONTARAN WEAPONRY.

Ah, eager to spill some blood, I see! Very good. A healthy thirst for violence is a key component of the Sontaran mindset, and we enhance this with some of the most advanced weaponry in the galaxy.

Such is our tactical strength that even our enemies can become weapons when combined with Sontaran principles and might. Example: the ATMOS Stratagem, just one of our many successful campaigns against the weaselly pink race known as humanity. Masterminded by our revered General Staal the Undefeated (SEE RELATED DATA ENTRY 2096), this plot exploited the meagre intellect of a human child known as Luke Rattigan.

General Staal allowed Rattigan to devise a hybrid human–Sontaran device to take control of humanity's primitive automobiles and drown the human home world, Earth, in a gas similar in composition to the liquid of your Sontaran Cloning Pool. Earth would have become a cradle world for whole generations of Sontaran soldiers.

Despite overwhelming resistance from a massive army, interference from an incredibly irritating time-traveller (SEE RELATED DATA ENTRIES 13–105) and despicable treachery from his human pet, Staal the Undefeated prevailed in his ultimate goal: to die honourably in battle. Truly an example to us all.

However, such complex strategies are for Sontaran High Command, our revered generals. You are a simple soldier, and a simple weapon will suffice. As the old Sontaran saying goes: 'Kill things with a rheon carbine!'

Rheon carbines are the habitual sidearm of Sontaran forces. Elegant, slim and versatile, the carbine is not just a metal rod that can disintegrate enemies; it is a badge of Sontaran ambition. A simple press of its controls will fire a charged stream of rheon particles that will immediately disintegrate most foes.

Should you advance enough to be allowed access to the hallowed grounds of the Sontaran Military Academy, it will also serve as a recording device and graduation wand. Should you rise to the literal heights of starship command, it can even be upgraded as a navigation sceptre. Impress us, Hero of Sontar, and that simple rheon carbine will not be only a weapon, but a symbol of your mighty rank. One that can also disintegrate enemies!

The rheon carbine is just one of the many weapons developed by our scientific divisions who seek to make up for not having the stomach for *true* combat by arming their more courageous brethren. Such weapons include the fragmentation grenade, the Skyhammer cannon, and devices capable of unimaginable destruction, such as the Warsong, an engine that can rewrite the surface of entire planets. The might of our military machine is unquestioned, Hero of Sontar!

A third note: like any good Sontaran itching for a fight, you might be wondering why we have not provided your drop-pod with weapons. The enemy is even now launching megatons' worth of munitions into the atmosphere in an attempt to stall your approach – it is only natural for you to want to respond!

Patience, young soldier. Weapons must be forged and tempered before they can be of use. You are an untested blade. Prove yourself with the trusty rheon carbine hanging from your belt, and the glorious weapons of the Empire will soon be yours to command.

Not long now!

RELATED DATA ENTRIES:

- 312: TANK-MOUNTED RHEON CANNONS – WHEN SUBTLETY IS A TACTICAL ERROR.
- 315: FRAGMENTATION GRENADES – WHEN TANK-MOUNTED RHEON CANNONS ARE TOO SUBTLE.

DATA ENTRY 4–159 SELECTED: FOES OF THE EMPIRE.

Now we come to it, Hero of Sontar. The universe is a hostile place, and we are not alone in it. Existence is full of

life-forms too foolish to realise Sontaran superiority – and this
is good! Even if they were to accept their betters, even if aliens
from the Medusa Cascade to GalSec Seven threw down their
weapons and offered their unconditional surrender, the
Sontaran Empire would not accept it. We *could* not accept it.

A design must have purpose, and we were designed
for war.

Should we be grateful, then, to our enemies for existing?
An interesting question, Hero – although be reminded that
philosophy, like recreation, is a waste of time. It is true that
many of our cleverest innovations were created as a response to
the threat of an enemy. This is a tradition dating back from
those revered, half-lost days of our clan culture, where Sontaran
would fight Sontaran to determine who was the strongest.

However, that fateful day when we first encountered an
alien race changed our culture forever. Our hated foes, the
Rutan Host, descended from the sky, and as a race we were
faced with a choice: waste precious Sontaran blood by
fighting each other, or evolve. Even then our military instincts
were keen, and those early Sontarans immediately allied with
each other, declaring war on everything not Sontaran.

On that day, the Empire was born.

There is your answer, Hero. It is not our enemies to
whom we should be grateful, but our own ingenuity! In the

centuries since, we have risen to every challenge and stared down every threat. The Sontaran Subliminal Education Matrix shall detail some of these threats for you now, so that you may also be ready to meet them, with carbine and blade.

One more note, as we are detecting that your heartrate is elevated and your skin is producing sweat at a higher rate than is normal. (Delighted to witness your excitement at the coming battle, soldier!) You may be wondering why we have not informed you which of our many hundreds of enemies are firing at you right now. That is an excellent question, and we have a very good answer for it – all in good time, soldier!

Three minutes to landfall!

DATA ENTRY 5 SELECTED: THE RUTAN HOST.

Hero, if we had a thousand years to educate you, it would not be enough for the Sontaran Subliminal Education Matrix to plumb the depths of our hatred for these vicious, gaseous fiends. The Rutan Host are our oldest foe, our most despised nemesis. The Sontaran Empire has warred with them from one side of the galaxy to the next, fought them to a standstill on a thousand worlds, and almost claimed victory a hundred times before having it slip from our grasp.

In many ways, the Rutans are our opposites. Where we are sturdy and solid, they are wafting, fragile things. Where we are monolithic and unshakeable in our identity and pride, they are literally spineless, quick to hide in the forms of others, without names or personalities of their own. They can also electrocute things with their minds, while Sontarans cannot – and would not, even if we could! Such dishonourable tricks are beneath us.

The Rutans' sole redeeming feature is that they are as dedicated to slaying us as we are to defeating them. It is perhaps telling that the only virtue they possess is mimicking *our* dedication and heart.

DATA ENTRY 11 SELECTED: DALEKS.

There is nothing wrong with good, clean bloodlust. There is certainly nothing wrong with wanting to go out and bend all opposition to your iron rule. On such things all Sontaran culture is based. However, we simply wish to kill our enemies, bury their women and children, and raze their cities to the ground. This is not a product of hatred. This is simply what honour and our own superiority demands.

There is something sick at the heart of the Daleks. Hate has squeezed the honour out of them. Hate has infected them, infested them. The rancour we feel for our ancestral enemies in the Rutan Host is but a shadow of what these ancient and terrible creatures feel for every living thing that is not a Dalek. This sickness ruins their plans as often as it motivates them, and it is the official opinion of Sontaran High

Command that it is this sickness that is the Daleks' greatest weakness, even as it makes them a particularly dangerous foe.

They are the right height, though. We must allow them that.

DATA ENTRY 8 SELECTED: CYBERMEN.

It shows a commendable amount of self-awareness to be able to admit inferiority and the need for upgrades, but if the Cybermen possessed true Sontaran efficiency they would be like us and do it before birth.

DATA ENTRY 12 SELECTED: TIME LORDS.

The Sontaran Empire has stretched for thousands of years and, thanks to our military might, will stretch for thousands more. And yet, against some races in the galaxy we are naught but children. Children with guns.

The Time Lords are an ancient race, kept alive only by secrets and the incredible technology they wield – technology that gives them power over time itself. It is perhaps no wonder they are so arrogant when they have spent aeons playing with the very fabric of reality.

It is true that there was a time when Sontarans pursued this knowledge as well, but such efforts have since been deemed dishonourable. We face our enemies. We do not sneak behind enemy lines, and that includes into their past or future. When we attack, we do so in full sight.

(This is also why every Sontaran drop-pod is painted a bright and reflective silver so that it can be clearly seen against the sky. Camouflage is cowardice, soldier!)

That is the true horror of the Time Lords. Face a Sontaran, and all you have to contend with is a moment of pain, subsequent death and the pride that you were destroyed by the finest military machine in the universe. But crossing the monstrous intellects of Gallifrey has far wider consequences, not just for you but for every you that has existed or may exist.

Only the Time Lords truly understand the damage they cause, whereas we are rats in their maze, our lives manipulated without our knowing, at the mercy of fickle gods.

Perhaps the Sontaran you were yesterday is not the Sontaran you are today.

Perhaps Sontarans have even stood and fought on Gallifrey itself, only to have the memory of those victories stolen away.

Perhaps there is a universe-spanning war going on just out of sight, an apocalyptic crusade fought in the space between one second and the next.

Luckily for the Empire, Gallifrey's might is matched only by their disinterest. Distant and alone, they have no interest in the affairs of the galaxy, and are content to play with time and prattle their arrogant philosophies.

All of them but one, that is.

DATA ENTRIES 13–105 SELECTED: THE DOCTOR.

Hero of Sontar, though I am naught but an automated set of recordings based on the military teachings of our greatest minds, I have been programmed with the same judgement protocols and scorn settings as any good and honourable Sontaran. If more proof was needed that the principles of the Sontaran Empire are good and right, consider that even I, a mere machine, feel them as strongly as if I possessed a Sontaran heart.

Though the Rutan Host remain our greatest nemesis, there is one foe, a single alien, who has foxed and foiled and flummoxed our Empire more than all the other meddling breeds of the universe put together.

Where we have honour, this foe is honourless. Where we have single-minded purity, they are polluted by compassion. Where we have a healthy contempt for those who are not of the Empire, this foe allies themself constantly with lesser races. Most confusingly, this Time Lord consorts with *humans*, even recklessly allowing their human pets access to a timeship and other advanced technologies.

Our records of this foe are even sketchier than is usual when dealing with a Time Lord of Gallifrey. Although they do not meet the normally impeccable standards of Sontaran records, Sontaran High Command has deemed it necessary to share them anyway, as we seem to encounter this ludicrously dressed menace nearly as often as the Rutan Host.

DATA ENTRY 14 SELECTED: FIRST ENCOUNTER WITH THE DOCTOR – 'THE TIME WARRIOR'.

In a clash with the hated Rutans, Commander Linx of the Fifth Sontaran Army Space Fleet was forced to land on Earth. With the practicality typical of our race, he immediately claimed the fertile planet for the glory of the Empire, even taming a group of local barbarians and commanding them to help repair his ship.

However, Linx's innocent kidnapping of humans from Earth's future (SEE RELATED DATA ENTRY 2235: THE OSMIC PROJECTOR) was curtailed when he and his human pets were confronted by the Doctor. This version of the Doctor – titled by Linx in his report as 'the Time Warrior' for his surprising martial arts ability – was a deceptively wrinkled, dandelion-haired scoundrel who was so lacking in honour that he shared our probic-vent vulnerability with mere humans. This treachery availed him not, however, as Linx easily defeated the Time Warrior before going on to achieve his true goal of dying honourably in battle.

DATA ENTRY 15 SELECTED: THE SCARF-WEARER.

It was Field Major Styre who next encountered the renegade Time Lord, learning that Gallifreyan duplicitousness is actually also biological, with this new version of the Doctor wearing a different face and different mannerisms, and even seeming to be younger than the first. Note that at this time we were unaware of the Time Lord capacity for regeneration.

Field Major Styre was compiling knowledge of humans and testing them for their usefulness – a process all components of the Sontaran war machine must undergo. As you no doubt understand, Hero of Sontar!

(Ninety seconds! Also, due to that last glancing hit from some laser-fire, you will be landing very close to enemy lines. Most efficient!)

Further details of this conflict have been redacted, but know that after his actions the Doctor was classified a Class 2 Nemesis of the Sontaran Empire. (RELATED DATA ENTRY 246: PROBIC ENERGISER MAINTENANCE – WATCH WHAT YOU EAT!)

This encounter, however, did provide us with useful knowledge of Gallifreyan biology, such as the revelation that the Doctor is colour-blind, based on the garish garment he was wearing round his neck.

DATA ENTRY 659 SELECTED: HUMAN CUSTOMS.

Earth is a fertile world, so it made complete sense when Commandant Stroll of the Sontaran Special Insertion Forces suggested lightweight green cloaks for an attempted scouting mission. Human population centres had also adopted a red-and-white scheme as part of the festival dubbed 'Christmas', and so it was deduced by Stroll that incorporating these colours with the green would facilitate a successful infiltration.

Intelligence gleaned from the mission was . . . spotty. The team successfully infiltrated a human shopping temple, where children had queued to prostrate themselves before the 'Father of Christmas'. (Human breeding is a mystery.) Suddenly Stroll and the other commandos were beset by humans wishing to take photographs 'with the elves'. One human consumer tried to buy Stroll so she could 'put him in her garden'. A riot ensued, and tactical retreat was advised.

Commandant Stroll was never seen again.

DATA ENTRY 17 SELECTED: OTHER SIGHTINGS OF THE DOCTOR.

General Staal's reports from the ATMOS Stratagem, though unfinished due to his death (and rightly so, as only a cowardly intellectual would sit and take notes when battle could be joined), describe the Doctor as different again: pin-striped and spindly, with a ridiculous crest of hair, as if trying to engage in some futile human mating ritual.

These are but a fraction of the times our noble Empire has crossed paths with this devious alien. There are even archival military reports that suggest we have faced multiple versions of the Doctor at once, presumably because not even his own people would wish to ally with him. Unconfirmed reports have also reached us from the hotly contested Regalis Sector that the Doctor has reappeared with a new form, topped with a wild blonde mane and a higher-pitched voice, which is no doubt some form of ruse meant to confuse us.

DATA ENTRY 19 SELECTED: THE DOCTOR'S PETS.

Normally, humans are beneath notice, but those allied to the Doctor have undergone considerable training, not unlike our own Sontaran attack rhinoxes, and these youngsters must be guarded against with a care not normally required. These particular humans, mostly small men with high voices, accompany the Doctor everywhere, fouling good Sontaran work with their clumsy, five-fingered interference. One in particular, a Sarah Jane Smith, was also instrumental in complicating both Commander Linx's and Field Major Styre's great works in exploiting humans' potential as a servant race.

DATA ENTRY 105 SELECTED: THE DOCTOR – CONCLUSIONS.

The treachery of Time Lords is nowhere more apparent than when dealing with the Doctor. Even this Time Lord's name is a curse: a 'doctor', someone who unnaturally extends the life of those who should have died in combat. It is the lowest of professions, reserved for only the weakest and most dishonourable of Sontarans. I hope that, in the coming engagement –

(Sixty seconds! It appears that you will be landing *behind* enemy lines. Perfect opportunity for a pincer attack!)

– if you should perish, you do so cleanly and without feeble recourse to medicine, bandages or any kind of ease from pain. Pain is life, Hero of Sontar, and anyone who tries to get in the way of that is stealing your honour.

And speaking of honour, soldier, you are reaching the end of your time with the Sontaran Subliminal Education Matrix. In the remaining fifty-five seconds of your education please choose two more data entries and ready your rheon carbine. Your graduation is at hand.

DATA ENTRY 179 SELECTED: BAKED POTATOES.

This phrase is a curse originating on Earth and often levelled at Sontaran soldiers when humans realise that they

are outgunned, out-thought and out-matched on the field of
war. No further explanation or research is required.

(Fifty seconds! Hold on to the stabilisers provided.
Engage counter-jets to facilitate the best chance of survival.)

DATA ENTRY 1500 SELECTED: SONTARAN
ART.

Art is pointless.

(Forty seconds! Brace for impact.)

SONTARAN SUBLIMINAL EDUCATION
MATRIX GRADUATION SPEECH LOADED.

. . . UNPACKING . . .

. . . UNPACKING . . .

. . . PLAYING NOW.

Here at last, Hero of Sontar! Just seven minutes from
clone-birth to full deployment on the battlefield: a new
Sontaran record, and a new victory for us all! I am delighted
to inform you that over half of your batch-generation, despite
fierce bombardment from the planet's surface, are about to
land on their first battlefield and face their first foe. As to this
foe's identity –

(Ten seconds!)

– we ask you this, soldier. Does it matter? Do you need to
know, when you have millions of your brothers around you,
when a new clone-generation is already being prepared above

you, younger brothers all ready to learn from your glorious example?

(Eight seconds!)

In these last moments before you land and unleash the full might of your Sontaran bloodlust, remember the feeling of that first victory. Remember how you took on the entire universe and prevailed against all odds.

And remember you did not do it alone. You exist by the might of the Empire's science, and it is your duty to repay that in conquest and triumph. When you march, it is not as a single soldier but as a component of the Empire, a link in a chain unbroken since the first Sontaran, millennia ago. When you march, the Empire marches with you. Where you tread, the weight of a billion Sontaran boots fall. This is your birthright –

SONTARAN SUBLIMINAL EDUCATION MATRIX NAME SELECTION ENGAGED.

. . . LOADING . . .

. . . NAME CHOSEN.

– Strax of the Seventh Sontaran Battlefleet. This is what you were made for, and we are already proud. Go forth and conquer!

SONTAR-HA!

SILURIANS

THE RED-EYED LEAGUE

It was in December, as humans would have it. For Va'stra, hunter of criminals and daughter of Pangea, now known in this older, lonelier world as Madame Vastra of 13 Paternoster Row, it was not so simple.

It did not seem right, in the moments when she let herself think of it, to take humanity's calendar. It was inaccurate, first of all; utterly self-centred, in the way these human things were. It was not that she blamed them for being ignorant of her people – the Silurians had not wanted newcomer races to know of them and so they had not – but humanity had made calendars into trophies, beginning anew every time one of their infant empires drew breath.

'The year of Our Lord 1884.' Such an adolescent boast. As if one could lay claim to a year instead of powerlessly watching it pass.

Warmbloods. The year grew colder, and took her patience with it as it went.

It was four years into Vastra's new life in Queen Victoria's London, and she was buying a book. Piccadilly had become a confection, all snow and raspberry-red bunting, and she wound through crowds with her veil pinned low. A mixture of scents assailed her: cinnamon, cheap ink, the earthy warmth of nightsoil and flesh.

Those who time-travelled – that modest, odd fraternity – kept their own calendars. It was a defence against that nauseating loss of perspective that came from seeing the world from a height reserved only to a few. Vastra did not possess a TARDIS, but there were many ways to time-travel. She had closed her eyes in one world and opened them in another, and it had become necessity to find significance in dates of her own choosing.

Vastra did not care for Christmas, but she did care for Jenny, and they were to mark two years together at the end of 1884.

Hatchards of Piccadilly was a low-ceilinged warren, full of dark nooks and overflowing shelves. Booksellers scurried beneath caramel lights, so quiet you could have believed them Dickensian spirits, had their scent not been thick on Vastra's tongue.

'My dear madame, a pleasure continual!'

Master Wills was the shape and shade of a chest of drawers, with a disposition so bright Vastra could have stretched out beneath it like a sunbeam. She'd solved a theft for him months ago, a minor affair, but Wills was generous in his gratitude – so generous, in fact, that they'd needed to extend the library at Paternoster Row. Twice.

'Master Wills. Things are looking busy.'

'*Christmas.*' He said the word with a predatory relish that would not have shamed a Silurian. 'How those seasonal cards have caught on! Who would have thought?'

'Not I,' Vastra said mildly. So far the fat little cherubs glaring happily from each stiff paper card had done little except make her wonder what Strax was preparing for dinner. 'And have there been any deliveries?'

'Ah,' Wills said, cheeks flushing with the effort of containing his grin. '*Your* delivery? Christmas present for a lucky gentleman, I assume?'

Vastra smiled behind her veil. 'Halfway right, Master Wills.'

The bookseller looked stricken. 'But how lucky he is, madame! The snow has slowed matters, but I promise you it will be here soon and when it arrives –'

Vastra didn't disbelieve him. There were *some* human arts she admired, and bookbinding was one of them. She could almost smell –

'The cover is hand-massaged leather, the gold lettering pin-engraved, each page an example of the finest artistry.'

She suddenly caught a whiff – sharp, acrid – muscling aside the soft notes of paper and wood. It barely seemed to fit in this world at all.

'Out of my way, feeble intellectual!'

Sontarans did not enter rooms; they invaded them. Shoppers made way with a chorus of yelps before the bullet skull and egg-curve bulk of Vastra's manservant. He marched up to his mistress, pinning Master Wills with a belligerent glare.

'You, sir. Are you the proprietor of this . . . this temple of weakness?'

Wills didn't even blink. Not for the first time, Vastra admired the lion's heart beneath that portly chest. 'Do I detect a military man? Well. I have just the –'

Strax leaned closer. 'You should be *ashamed* of yourself.'

Vastra eyed her manservant witheringly. 'I do hope whatever Lady Horrinthal had to say is worth this interruption.'

Strax blinked. 'How did you –'

'You have the paw prints of a King Charles spaniel on your left leg, your right cuff is stained with azalea pollen from fighting your way through her jungle of a garden, and you have that look you get when she flirts with you.'

'What look?'

'Scrambled,' Vastra said archly. 'Now, what is it? She's already paid us for getting back her stolen gems. What does –'

And then it came to her: honeysuckle and strawberry, and the richest blood beneath.

'Hello, ma'am.'

Jenny Flint was five foot two of dimple, grin and barely contained violence. She wore the attire of a maid, yet owned every room she'd ever entered five seconds after entering it. Pursuers of wrongdoers were not supposed to have hearts, but it had taken Jenny no time to lay claim to Vastra's as well.

'Strax, what are you –' Jenny paused. 'Madame Vastra. Buying a book?'

Silurians did not blush as humans understood it, but there were similar responses that Vastra had decided to keep to herself. She shot a look at Master Wills, who, professional that he was, busied himself elsewhere.

'Surely it does not take two of you to deliver the Lady's message?' Vastra said.

Jenny's smile disappeared. 'What message? I came here about this.'

She held up a copy of *The Woman's Signal*, a periodical of which Vastra was passing fond, and showed Vastra the symbol scrawled on its front. For a moment, the image meant nothing – just slashes of ink dipping into one another as if searching for meaning in themselves – and then it resolved, like a familiar face in a crowd.

There are many ways to travel through time.

'It's Silurian.'

There was no snow on Number 13. It was the only house on Paternoster Row to feature that recent and ingenious Russian invention known as the 'radiator' – and, furthermore, the only one to have married it with a Sontaran power generator, which heated the water to a point where everything within four feet of the house's walls felt as muggy and deliciously warm as the Cretaceous period.

Sometimes Vastra thought herself selfish for inflicting such heat on the other inhabitants of Number 13 . . . but her warmblood wife had a whole world, and all Vastra had was her.

'You're sure, ma'am?'

There were pages – dozens of pages – by Vastra's locker on which she had traced out words in the Old Tongue because she was afraid of forgetting what it looked like. She had only stopped because she had realised she could no longer remember whether she was forming the letters correctly or not.

Vastra had woken wrong, perhaps, or had left something behind her in sleep. Memories had blurred, over the course of aeons, and it was hard to reassemble a world that time had unmade.

'I am sure,' she said, for she was. No other language mined such meaning from simple curves, webbing across paper like frost on a windowpane. It was just hard, millions of years on, in a house of sharp human lines, to recall what the letters meant.

'The true mystery are these scratchings below. Look at them. Angular where this symbol is –'

'Foolish reptile!' Strax barked, in the delighted manner of a child figuring out a puzzle. 'It is a map. And this circle here a disused human chapel in Spitalfields.' He peered closer. 'I assessed it as a hideout in case Number Thirteen became compromised, but there are too many possible entrances and an unstable floor just crying out for sabotage.'

The contrast between the map and the symbol was painful. Human cities were like human words: sharp and jagged and mostly without grace.

'Thank you, Strax,' Vastra said. 'I will investigate.'

'Alone?' Jenny asked.

Clumsy and blocky as it was, human language could have more than one meaning too.

'Yes,' Vastra said. 'This is . . . meant for me. And, Strax, you said something about Lady Horrinthal?'

'Yes,' Strax said. 'Dreadful man. Looks like a cushion. And he's let his jewels be stolen again. I propose we find the group responsible, execute them with massive prejudice, and then execute Lady Horrinthal for wasting our time.'

Vastra could not drag her eyes from the image in front of her. She had forgotten the *elegance* of Silurian – the manner in which it drew your gaze, the way it spoke to you rather than being simply read.

'Yes,' Vastra murmured distantly. 'You do that.'

She looked up. Strax appeared delighted, which was never a good sign. Jenny had no expression on her face at all.

'It means something,' Vastra said. 'The symbol.'

'I shall bring a large gun,' Strax said solemnly. 'Two large guns. And I've had some success with detonation rats . . .'

'Yes,' Vastra said. 'It's an invitation.' *And a plea.*

The Church of Latter Day Emergence had been abandoned by all but the snow. Falling white had softened its lines, mounding on its half-collapsed roof and spiked railings as if trying to erase it from existence.

Wearing the black mask and lightweight armour of her profession, Vastra eased her way in through the rusted gate, leaving barely a mark on the pristine white of the path. The door of the chapel opened easily under her claw.

To four of her senses, the inside was as deserted as the outside. Hard wooden seats clustered under the eyes of the humans' disapproving saviour. Snow had trespassed through the hole in the ceiling. The place had that particular silence only found in houses of worship, though the distant noises of the city still murmured at her back.

But each deep sniff told her the church was not abandoned. The air had been disturbed. It should have hung dead and still and heavy with dust, but many bodies had churned it – or a single body in much distress. The floor, too, was marked with a hundred circling prints. It reminded Vastra of the way she would pace when sleep would not come, when irrational terror told her closing her eyes would cause her to wake thousands of years in the future. Alone.

She slipped a hand round the hilt of her sword.

'Will you slay me?'

The voice came from everywhere and nowhere. It slid under the seats and dripped from the rafters, but most of all it penetrated Vastra's breast and curled about her heart, for she knew that language, if not the voice that spoke it.

It was a language she had not heard since waking, a language she had not heard in 443 million years.

'Have I slept so long only to die?'

Vastra had been born strong and lean and sharp of sense, and so, in the manner of a civilised society, had been trained to be a solver of crimes and a detector of truths. There were Silurians born for study, and those born for war, and then there were those marked for a higher path.

'Priestess,' Vastra said haltingly. She had not spoken Silurian in a very long time. 'I am kin.'

A pair of red eyes appeared in the gloom.

'Blessed be.'

It was late when she returned.

Jenny and Strax abandoned their map of Lady Horrinthal's estate as soon as they heard Vastra's sword slip into the umbrella stand.

'Repulsive thieves!' the Sontaran barked by way of greeting. 'They must have –'

'The note, ma'am,' Jenny interrupted, laying a shawl round Vastra's shoulders in the manner she always did after her wife had to brave the cold. 'Who sent it?'

*

'I am Kisimos.'

She was smaller than Vastra, for priestesses were bred for wit before war, but when she spoke it shook snow from the windowsills, for they were also bred to have voices that could reach into earth and sky. She wore the scaled and spiked ceremonial mask that had been assigned to her at birth, its eye lenses red as coals, and even to look upon them made Vastra remember the warmth of the jungle when the earth was young.

'She is Silurian. A priestess of our kind.'

'Right,' Jenny said. 'Why is she here?'

'There was a machine. A drill. I felt it scrape along my stasis pod and . . . I woke. There was pain.'

Vastra had nodded. 'My waking was similar. Workers extending a tunnel. Humans, with axes.'

The priestess's eyes had glittered behind her mask. 'Is that what the apes call themselves? I was the only one of my clutch to survive. The "humans" had broken open the pods, like monkeys with unguarded eggs.'

She had stared down at her claws then, and been silent for a long time. Around them, the church settled further into decay.

'I killed them. I killed those operating the machine, and those who came after, but when their numbers seemed inexhaustible I took a translation bead, my robes, and I fled.'

Red eyes, boring into Vastra's.

'Did you kill those who woke you?'

'Yes.' It was not something she allowed herself to dwell on. She had been different then. Half awake, blind with rage, her memories incomplete. 'Most of them. Until I met another stranger to this world. He showed me how the world had changed, and I realised that the apes did not know their own deeds, and do not deserve the sword.'

Kisimos had taken Vastra's claws then and, surprised, Vastra had not pulled away.

'One of the humans saw my skin. I heard him tell his fellows that he had heard rumours of a similar creature. It took a long time to find you.'

'I . . .' Vastra said. 'I am glad you did.'

'You wear the uniform of a hunter of wrongdoers. Is this an omen, to meet a keeper of our laws? Tell me. Have I committed a crime? In this new world?'

Jenny was staring at her.

'And you talked? What about?'

*

'No,' Vastra had said. 'You did not know what you were doing. You were afraid. You did what you had to do.'

Kisimos had nodded solemnly. 'What is your name, finder of truth?'

'Vastra.'

The priestess laughed then, high and clear and cold as winter. 'You have not spoken the tongue in a long time, Va'stra. Is it good to hear it pure-spoken again?'

'Many things,' Vastra said eventually. 'She knows little of this world. And –' *It was good to speak my own tongue again.* She cleared her throat. 'What did you learn at Lady Horrinthal's?'

'They came in over the roofs. Graceful like. Not a snowflake out of place.' Jenny frowned. 'And then they tore the bedroom to pieces looking for the gems. You'd think a gang that professional would have carefully searched the place. And . . .'

A hesitation then. A rise in pulse.

'What is it?' Vastra asked.

'And what does a hunter of criminals do now, in this ape-ruled world?'

The next morning brought an answer to that question, and tragedy besides.

'I am sorry for your loss,' Vastra said gently, as she and Master Sook gazed down at the smouldering shell of the Widow Inn. A smudge of soot marked the old man's cheek, and his hands shook in a manner that had nothing to do with the early-morning chill.

'Just before dawn, Madame,' he said. 'Only for my aching knee that keeps me up at nights we might have slept right through it.'

The Case of the Widow's Wail had occupied no less than a month of Vastra's time – a record, according to Strax's embarrassingly detailed notes. The name had been his too – one of the first cases they had tackled as a team. After the knave attempting to blackmail Sook had been revealed as the famed dictator known as The Tiger of San Pedro (or, rather, the alien parasite controlling his nervous system), the Widow had remained one of the Paternoster Gang's favourite venues, and Sook and Carmille their firm friends.

It shook Vastra to see all three so drastically reduced.

'Who would do this?' Carmille whispered. He had never been strong, but the loss of the Widow had demolished him thoroughly, turning him frail and ashen as a moth's wing. He'd been repeating himself since she arrived. 'Who would do this?'

'I don't know,' Vastra said, trying not to wrinkle her nose against the stench of the burnt hops with which they brewed their ale. When Silurians had ruled the young earth, foresters had carefully curated seasonal wildfires so that certain plants could flourish. From flames came growth. Human dwellings, however, were rank with chemicals, and the smoke tasted acrid on her tongue.

A bud of pain had lodged itself behind her eyes, and she found herself battling the strangest sense of resentment, as if it was the fault of these two Masters that she was here.

And where else would you be, Va'stra?

Jenny was eyeing the one remaining wall with a spyglass. Strax had suggested orbital bombardment – though whether as the cause of the fire or the solution was unclear. Vastra tried to focus, but the bud had bloomed into a headache and her thoughts slipped and slithered like Silurian script until she found herself back in an old church, hearing the stories of her youth.

'Ma'am,' Jenny chided gently. 'Are you listening?'

Vastra had not been, as a matter of fact, which made her feel at once guilty and angry about it. What was wrong with Jenny? Vastra had come when she called, despite having to leave Kisimos alone in a world of which she knew nothing. What more did Jenny want?

Carmille was craning his neck now, peering despondently at the inn as if trying to see through to a timeline where the

Widow still stood. She could see his pulse fluttering the papery skin of his throat, and her headache began to pound in time.

'Vastra!'

She blinked.

Jenny's cheeks were flushed. 'I'm sorry, ma'am. You seemed . . . distracted.'

Carmille hadn't taken his eyes from the destroyed inn, but Sook was looking confusedly between them both. Vastra gave him an awkward nod, then took Jenny by the arm, piloting her away from the inn-keepers.

'Jenny. You know that, barbaric as these times are, we must at least appear to comply with their customs. A maid does not speak to her mistress so!'

'I don't know that, actually,' Jenny retorted. 'Since when am I supposed to know that? You never normally –' She took a deep breath. 'I was just saying, *ma'am*, that the pattern of the fire is odd. It was started by one of the inn's oil lamps.'

'An accident?'

'Not unless they swung it round a few times before they dropped it. There are looping patterns of deeper charring, as if the arsonist doused as much of the floor of the inn as they could with lamp oil then dropped a candle in it.'

Vastra scowled. 'The inn had no tenants last night, Jenny, and I hardly think the proprietors would have set fire to –'

'*Listen*, ma'am. Of course they didn't set fire to it themselves. This is arson, plain and simple. But what arsonist shows up empty-handed, hoping to find something to use?'

The headache was pounding harder now, as if trying to find a way out of Vastra's skull, her veil lank and sweaty on her brow.

'A crime of opportunity, then.'

'I found scratches on that last standing wall, ma'am. Whoever it was went in a second-floor window. They must have had ropes. A harness. It doesn't make any sense.'

It was as if the smoke had spread out through Vastra's skull. Her head ached, with the stink of ash and the scrape of cloth against her scales and the red pulses all around her.

'Oh, nothing you mammals do makes sense!' Vastra snapped.

There are many ways to time-travel, and in that moment Jenny looked the way she had the first time she had seen Vastra: that dizzying shock of realising that the world was bigger and stranger than she had ever believed. And then, as time passed, that shock had dissolved to warmth – a warmth Vastra had not felt since her people had slept. It was that warmth that kept Vastra going, into an age not her own.

But now that warmth had disappeared, and Vastra was suddenly glimpsing a timeline that had gratefully passed them by.

'Jenny,' Vastra said. 'I . . .'

And maybe she could not be blamed for not having the words to say. It was her second language, after all.

'I'm going to check on Strax,' Jenny whispered, and fled.

'What are they to you?'

Kisimos had lit a fire in the centre of the church. The sight of it had worried Vastra – what if it drew the curious or the concerned? – but it *was* unforgivably cold, and so they had kept it, stuffing rags in draughty gaps to trap as much of the heat as they could.

Shadows danced like worshippers come to hear old tales of the young earth.

'What do you mean?' Vastra had asked. This had been the way of it, these last few nights. Face unreadable behind her mask, the priestess's queries roamed: one moment Vastra would be interrogated on where humans got their clothes, the next it would be on the network of London streets or the Christmas decorations Kisimos had observed in the residences nearby.

But Kisimos seemed to have forgotten she'd asked the question, turning the periodicals Vastra had brought over and over in her hands. The translation bead extended only as far as the spoken word, but Vastra had a mind to teach the priestess letters too – though the thought of instructing a priestess seemed almost blasphemous.

'They're everywhere, these humans,' Kisimos said. 'I've ranged further and further each day.'

She'd taken to sitting cross-legged on the altar, a shadow draped in shadows, shapeless on the other side of the fire.

'You shouldn't do that,' Vastra warned. 'You'll frighten –'

'I shouldn't do what? Explore? Walk around in this new world? Like you do?'

'No, it's just –'

'I sought to find an edge to the settlement. This settlement.'

'London,' Vastra said.

'Yes.' The priestess shivered. 'And I could not find one. I struck out – robed against the sight of apes, do not worry.'

Vastra smiled. Kisimos did not.

'And I ran and I climbed and I searched for an end to this sprawling stain on the earth, on *our* earth . . . and I could not find it.' There was horror in her tone. 'It could not be found.'

'They are a multitude,' Vastra said eventually. 'They have had a long time to spread.'

'Have you seen the river?' Kisimos said abruptly. 'Have you seen what they've done to it? The dirt? The pollution?'

'I have,' Vastra said. 'It shocked me too.'

'And does it no longer?'

'I . . .'

The priestess should have been naïve. She should have looked to Vastra for guidance in this new world, but instead it was Vastra who felt like a hatchling on her first day of tutoring, the priestess doing as priestesses did: educating, criticising, demanding more than Vastra could give.

'They are a young race,' was all that came to her lips.

'It is no excuse,' the shadow on the altar said. Theirs was not a forgiving god. 'You tolerate more than is proper. Especially for a keeper of laws.'

That stung, and Vastra could not help but respond. 'With respect, the old rules of the young earth no longer apply. The humans have inherited this planet, and they must learn to respect it as we did.'

'And what do we lose, while they learn?'

It was something they were taught. Vastra was sure of it. Deep in the caves, closest to the eternal fire at the world's core, that was where the priestesses were taught to reach deep into the hearts of their congregations, to make the universe feel as if it could turn on a single word.

'Do you love them?'

Silurians do not blush, but the priestess noted the darkening of Vastra's scales.

'You live among them. Dress like them. Hide your sword as if ashamed of the order that forged it. And you solve their petty crimes while they commit far greater sins.'

The stink of burnt hops and chemicals was still raw in Vastra's nose.

'You must love them greatly to forget who you are.'

'I remember who I am,' Vastra lied, as she had become accustomed to lying on the long nights when sleep would not come and she looked out on a city not her own. 'I remember our people. I remember that they chose to sleep. I remember –'

'We sang. Do you remember that?' The priestess was full of sudden mirth, and the fire seemed to leap at the sound as if it remembered too. 'The great jungles stretched from pole to pole, and every tree was ours. We hunted. We were hunted. And both these things were right because the world was ours and we were the world's. And we sang.'

'Of stars,' Vastra said hollowly.

'And moons,' Kisimos murmured, voice rolling like a tide. 'Of the empire that our people had built. And now the world is so loud, and so silent, and none of the old songs will ever be sung.'

'They are not sung because we are sleeping,' Vastra said, but her protest was frail.

'No,' the priestess said. 'They are not sung because we are forgotten. Because you have forgotten us.'

Vastra growled. She had not growled in a long time, and it was at once a noise of pain and a sound that felt wholly right. Humans saw animals and thought they were different; Silurians saw animals and knew they were the same.

'Good,' the priestess hissed, and the words were nearly a growl themselves. 'Do you remember, finder of truths? Do you remember what we would do if we found a kin-mate violating the earth? If kin forgot our laws and acted of their own accord? If kin turned on kin, or stole from kin, or hurt kin?'

'I remember,' Vastra said softly.

'Say it.'

'What?'

'Say it. What would you do?'

'I would hunt them.'

'Yes.'

'I would slay them.'

'Yessss.'

'And all would be reminded of who we are.'

'I am glad that I found you,' the priestess said, rising suddenly to her feet. She stalked towards Vastra, flicking back her hood so that the firelight burnished her scales like a temple idol, graven and gold. 'I am glad you are finding the truth once again.'

Vastra did not immediately return to Paternoster Row. She knew she should, but the thought of the human dwelling, with its narrow corridors and artificial heat, was suddenly repellent. Instead, she wandered London's streets – Spitalfields to Finsbury Square to Holborn – and everywhere she looked there was truth.

Her world was going. Her world was gone. Moving backwards in time was beyond her, and as the years marched on cities would swarm like ants, eating space and shrinking green. They would make concrete of it all, these infant apes, and if a day ever came when her people returned they would find their beds paved over and turned to tombs.

Only the smell of azalea buds informed her that she had wandered as far as Lady Horrinthal's gates, and it was simplicity itself to shimmy up the side of the building opposite, her claws making short work of the brick. She stared at the boarded-up roof window, an easy leap across, and thought of the Widow and the harsh smell of hops.

She had helped them. She had used the skills her people had given her to hunt down precious gems for a greedy old woman, and foiled a tyrant just to save an inn. Even the memory of her work for Wills seemed to mock her. She would have hunted him for prey an aeon ago. Not ran for him. Not *liked* him.

These humans had built their petty little lives in the graveyard of her people, and she had helped them cement their hold on a world that was never theirs.

But it is theirs. And that was the only truth to find. The world had travelled through time and her people had not. There was a new calendar now, and she had no place in it, and soon she and her people would be only a memory, and then even that would melt like snow.

Number 13 Paternoster Row was silent but for the chug of the heating. Vastra eased the door open and, despite herself, something softened in her chest when she stepped inside. Plants clasped each other in the corners. Art from a dozen cultures hung on the walls.

This is real, she told herself. *I built this.*

'You came back.'

Jenny was standing at the top of the stairs. She was dressed for war, with her swords at her waist.

Vastra smiled. A blade should be an extension of your body, and it had taken them a long time to find two as sharp, as wickedly curved.

'Who do you intend to fight with –'

Jenny stared at her, and it was a moment before Vastra realised she had spoken in Silurian.

'Sorry,' she said in English. 'Who do you intend on fighting with those?'

Jenny's face was stone. 'Master Wills is dead.'

'What?' Sudden shame filled Vastra at her previous scorn. He was a rosy-cheeked hamster of a man, yes, but one with the heart of a lion. She had even thought about telling him who she really was. The joy he would have felt, knowing that there were other species out there in the void, whole new volumes he could have read.

'Jenny, I'm so sorry. What –'

'He was coming here,' the maid said. 'With a copy of *The Art of War* by Sun Tzu for Strax. And then four masked assailants attacked him. They had knives, the doctor said. His wounds were . . . It was messy, ma'am.' Her hands were white on the hilts of her swords. 'A burglary we solved. An alien we defeated. And now a friend, taken from us. Three attacks. And do you know what they have in common?'

Vastra's eyes narrowed. 'You're not suggesting . . .'

'Us,' Jenny finished. 'We're the only thing that connects these three cases. I wonder what that means?'

'It's a coincidence, surely,' Vastra snapped. 'Kisimos would never . . . She barely knows this world. It frightens her and . . . and I can see why!'

Jenny padded down the stairs and took her coat from its hook.

'You don't understand, Jenny,' Vastra said, half angry, half pleading. 'She is of my people. I can talk to her. You don't understand how lonely I've been.'

'Because you haven't said anything,' Jenny retorted. 'You turn cold, and you turn silent, and your response is to tell me that talking to someone else is easier? Someone who shows up out of nowhere, at exactly the same time our old cases are being unravelled before our eyes?'

'Stop it,' Vastra said. 'Just stop. She is a priestess of –'

'Of what? Of your world? It isn't –' Jenny took her hands from her swords. 'You are ignoring evidence because a piece of the past has returned, and I want to understand that, but I won't let it get in the way of the truth.' She sighed. 'Do you think this age is easy for me? I'm your *maid*, Vastra. Do not tell me that there is no hardship here for me.'

'Not like mine,' Vastra said. The words were out before she could stop them and she knew from Jenny's face that they could not be taken back.

'Well, let me make it easy for you,' she said, and brushed past Vastra to open the door. 'You have her now. You have a part of your past back. You don't have to be –' She blinked furiously. 'You don't have to be stuck with us any more.'

'Jenny, wait –'

But she was gone, into the street beyond, and Vastra stood in the doorway between one world and the next, and knew that when one disappeared it would be gone forever.

The fire had gone out in the Church of Latter Day Emergence when Vastra arrived, a bag clinking over her shoulder. Packing it had taken less time than deciding to pack it. So few things were needed, really, to end one life and begin another.

Kisimos was waiting for her, standing over the smouldering embers like a trailing wisp of smoke.

'I am glad you have found your truth, Va'stra. Now the work can begin.'

'What would you have me do?' Vastra asked, savouring the feel of the Old Tongue – *her* tongue – on her lips. She had missed it. She would speak it more from this day on.

'I have prayed for guidance,' Kisimos said. 'And nothing has happened that could not be reversed. We could wake our kin. We could take back our world. It never stopped being ours. That is the truth.'

Vastra nodded slowly and laid down her bag. None of what the priestess said was a surprise.

'I just have one question.'

Kisimos cocked her head.

'Why kill Master Wills?'

Silence, but for the fall of snow.

'Was it because I helped him?' Vastra asked, her voice neutral, her sword coming free with a rasp of steel. At her feet, her bag was twitching, but the priestess only had eyes for her. 'Is that why you burned down the Widow? Stole Lady Horrinthal's jewels? Are you trying to undo my cases one by one?'

The priestess stepped backwards into the darkness. If she ran, Vastra would catch her, for that was what she had been bred to do.

'I didn't –'

'This fire nearly hid the scent of burning,' Vastra said, indicating the embers with a sweep of her sword. 'But I smelled the hops on you. Was it murder you planned, before you found the lamps? Should I be grateful that you only stooped to arson?'

'Va'stra –'

'I should have recognised the claw marks on the wall. At Lady Horrinthal's, too. No climbing gear required.' She raised a claw. 'Not for us.'

'Va'stra, I –'

'No lies, Kisimos. Not to me. I am a finder of truths, and the truth is that you murdered an innocent man just to remind me of it.'

'I'm not lying,' the priestess said. 'I didn't kill your little pet.'

Five sets of red eyes appeared in the darkness behind her.

'My servants did.'

No one knew by what means the temple assassins were chosen. There were stories of hatchlings born with dead eyes and a lust for blood, of infants who strangled their siblings in the cot. They hissed as they unfolded themselves, all sinew and claw, tongues panting poisonous spittle through the grilles of their masks. There was nothing of recognition in their gaze when they looked at her, and Vastra understood that they were not chosen for something they possessed, but for something they lacked.

A mind and soul were essential to find truth, but only the soulless joined the Raptorae.

'I did not want to have to do this alone, Va'stra.' The priestess scratched behind one of the assassin's crests until it crooned and kicked its feet. The others were constant and jittered in their motion, heads darting back and forth every time they heard the skitter of rats in the walls. 'But the miners who woke me, the miners I tortured – they had all sorts of stories about your exploits, and I knew that only by taking them away could I remind you of who you really are. And what you are not.'

Kisimos lifted her mask away. Behind it, her eyes were soft and yellow. Like Vastra's. They could have been sisters, a long time ago.

'You are not one of them. You can parade around in their ridiculous clothes and parrot their ridiculous tongue but it won't make them love you. Only mock you. Fear you.'

A sudden crack, like the breaking of bone, and one of the slinking Raptorae was flung backwards in a tangle of limbs. The other four recoiled, shrieking like cats, and even Kisimos shrank back, composure wavering.

Somewhere above, Vastra could hear the *click-clatter* of Jenny reloading.

'You're right,' Va'stra said. 'I'm not one of them.'

She snapped her fingers, and somehow the snap echoed, multiplied, chased itself around the church. The whole floor rocked with a lurch of broken stone, and Vastra leaped cleanly backwards as the floorboards gave way.

Kisimos and her assassins tumbled into the sudden gap, so it was unlikely they heard the words that Vastra said next, or would have understood them if they could.

'But I'm not one of you either.'

After that, it was all over, bar the apologies.

Strax was livid that Vastra had commandeered his detonation rats without asking. It had been scant comfort that the new knockout-gas recipe he had concocted had incapacitated the rogue Silurians so thoroughly.

'What will you do with them?' Jenny asked, wrapping a shawl round Vastra's shoulders.

'Put them back to sleep,' Vastra said. 'I don't want the world she wants, but I will not kill kin to make it so. I've contacted the Doctor for help repairing the stasis pods and, provided he arrives sometime this century, Strax's supplies of gas should hold out.'

Jenny nodded, squeezing Vastra's shoulders through the cloth. There was something tender in the movement.

'I'm sorry for my actions,' Vastra said. 'I was lonely, and nostalgic, and foolish, and I ask that you forgive me.'

Jenny smiled. 'You get like this, ma'am. People do, in the winter. Especially people with cold blood. Just . . . talk to me about it. Don't hide it, or pretend it's not there. Because I see more than you think.'

Vastra laid her head against Jenny's arm. 'I will. And I have something for you.' Sadness touched her voice. 'From Master Wills. It finally arrived. Merry Christmas.'

She drew a package from under the table and unwrapped it. The book was indeed beautiful, bound in soft leather with engraved golden lettering. Every page was gorgeous, and every page was blank.

'Ma'am, it's beautiful, but . . . what is it?'

'A dictionary, eventually,' Vastra said, smiling. 'I would very much like to teach you Silurian.'

OOD

THE HEIST

Now

First, the alarum-globes.

They drift through the atmosphere like jellyfish, a shoal of silver spheres, each one laced with awareness nodes and detection fronds. Deceptively aimless, they gently collide, then drift apart, weapon systems flushing red. They are small and they are delicate, and any one of them is packed with enough firepower to bring down a battlecruiser.

Thirty-two million of them clog the atmosphere, and the trait-pods fall towards them like plummeting sycamore seeds.

The pods look like sycamore seeds too: folded clasps of cartilage, sleek husks as long as a human is tall. They don't look like much. They certainly don't look sturdy enough to survive planetfall. But that is why they were grown. That is their design. Their Krillitane tenders call them trait-pods because, like the Krillitane themselves, they evolve to suit and overcome their surroundings. Each pod bristles with sensors, with awareness – a readiness to learn, adapt and change.

If they are even a hair too slow, the heist ends here.

Then

Three thieves met in an unnamed bar on an unnamed world, and Agrakos the Krillitane laid it out over pale Jovian wine.

'We're going to rob the Maldovarium.'

'Waste of time,' Vertebrae said, resting his feet on a battered stool. 'Place is untouchable.'

The Silurian wasn't wrong. The bar they sat in was just a grubby little dive, the kind of run-down bolthole you found on every world: a refuge for those who lived on the wrong side of the law, who stole or sold or made people disappear, who didn't look up from their drinks on anything less than a three-stabbings night.

But scattered across the universe were those singular establishments, those bars of legend. The Kiasmos, carved into the shell of a living star-whale, or the Cheem bar Lux, where all the drinks were wavelengths of light. There was the

Sun Deck on Midnight, the meta-cocktails of the Ruke, the Harbour Bar in Bray . . .

And not one of them compared to the Maldovarium.

Half-bar, half-bazaar, mostly illegal and always full, the Maldovarium clung like a secret to the side of a deserted, barren moon. You could get anything in the Maldo – a glass of sunfire whiskey infused with the light of a star, diamond daiquiris at a hundred thousand credits a glass . . . or micro-explosives, stealth-ships or passage to the darkest rim of space.

They'd all been there. Buying rare gear, trading information, hunting targets. Everyone passed through the Maldovarium. That was the saying. And, every time you did, Dorian Maldovar took a cut.

'I'm not denying,' the Silurian continued, baring long and back-hooked teeth, 'that it would be a score. Score of a lifetime, maybe. But there's a million credits' worth of alarum-globes in the atmosphere, and that's just the stuff we know about. The place,' he repeated, 'is untouchable.'

Vertebrae the Silurian, a reptile safe-cracker with a brutal streak. Agrakos the Krillitane, who they said had once been a spy, and Kiz Head-Taker, the assassin, anonymous behind armour of dull and featureless black.

'And what if,' Agrakos countered, with an oily smile, 'it wasn't?'

Now

Each alarum-globe is equipped with different sensors to cover all possible threats. The first scans for organic body heat, but before it detects the descending infiltrators the trait-pods' rudimentary brains are already devising a response, hardening each pod's shell from cartilage to bone. The bioships glaze white like lakes in winter, thickening their skins to hide the passengers inside.

Sensing nothing, the first alarum-globe moves on.

Density scanners. Motion detectors. Pheromone sniffers. Alarum-globes flock and cluster, curious as bees, but muscles flex and glands spurt and the specially designed bioships evolve and adapt and warp and change to stay one evolutionary step ahead.

Finally, sixty metres above the ground, a single message is sent from one pod to another.

'Head-Taker,' Agrakos whispers. 'You're up.'

Then

Krillitane were shapeshifters, but Agrakos had arrived in his true form to show open-handedness, or honesty, or trust. Unfortunately, since Krillitane derived their shapeshifting abilities by eating their enemies and harvesting whatever genetic traits they deemed useful, and since the word on the street was that the Krillitane Empire was about to declare war on just about everyone they viewed to be either hostile or delicious, *and* since Agrakos's true form looked like a skinless bat with a crocodile's snout, the desired effect was lost.

That it was this particular Krillitane didn't make things much better.

Agrakos was ex-Krillitane military, and there were rumours he still worked contracts for them, which, by the elastic and ever-evolving standards of the criminal community, was very close to a mortal sin. Not even they would dirty their hands with government work.

Without stretching his head, Agrakos could count four thugs of various species with hands on their guns, a drunk Sontaran muttering to himself and trying to remember where he left his grenades, and a band of Bessan raiders sharpening their knives. There were plenty of patrons with reason enough to take on the predatory, conniving Krillitane.

The only reason they hadn't was Kiz Head-Taker.

Now

The belly of the trait-pod opens outwards like a wound, like a mouth, and Kiz Head-Taker steps out into freefall.

This is my last job, he tells himself, for the thirtieth time.

This is not a fact he has shared with his comrades. Kiz Head-Taker does not have comrades. There are only three things Kiz Head-Taker has amassed over his thirty-three-year career: a reputation, a high price, and a blade of folded Gallifreyan zinc – the only thing he has ever actually stolen. *Until tonight.* He is not a thief. He is a murderer, and after tonight he will not even be that.

Twenty-five metres up, Kiz draws his sword.

It is a thing of genuine beauty: perfectly balanced, incredibly sharp, so thin the edge is invisible straight-on. The archivist he stole it from had no idea what it was, and Kiz sometimes thinks about how she could have easily paid off her gambling debts by selling it, and then Kiz would never have been hired at all.

Seams open along the limbs of Kiz's armour, and antigrav units rev up, turning Kiz's plummet into the graceful swoop of a hunting bird. Below him sprawls the Maldovarium – a great silver tulip of a dome – and the guards, just as Agrakos had said, looming on the roof's edge like polished silver gargoyles. They register on his armour's systems as gleaming stars, the neural link binding them together like a drawing of a constellation in a children's book.

Kiz hangs in the air, choosing his moment. This must be perfectly timed. It is why he was hired – that, and the

prize inside the Maldovarium, the prize that only he and
Agrakos know exists. When he has that, he will stop being the
Head-Taker. For the first time in thirty-three years, he will be
just Kiz.

Not for the first time, he wonders whether he remembers
how.

There. The guards are neural-linked, but the connection
is imperfect. There is a lag, as everything the first guard sees
and hears is bounced to the second, and then the third, and
then the fourth. If one of them sees him descending like a
spider, then they all will, and they will open fire, and the
alarum-globes will descend.

But if he is fast enough to race that pulsed connection, to
strike down the first guard just as the link transmits, and then
the second, and then the third . . .

Kiz dives, and prepares to earn his nickname one last
time.

Then

'It's not just the alarum-globes,' Vertebrae said, picking a
morsel from a fang, eyes locked on the Bessan raiders as if
daring them to go for their knives. Vertebrae had a reputation
too. 'He has those toy soldiers. Eight Cybermen. Neural-
linked. If one of them spots an intruder they all see it.'

'Twelve, actually,' Agrakos said. 'You gotta admire him. If the Cyber-Legions ever found out . . .' He lazily waved a hand at the black-clad assassin at his side. 'You know Head-Taker?'

Kiz no longer winced at the nickname. Nicknames were useful. Good for business. Kiz had been Head-Taker for thirty-three years. It was a persona now, a role.

Recently, it had begun to feel like a cage.

'By reputation,' Vertebrae said. There was an edge to his voice. Sometimes people heard nicknames as a challenge, or the chance to earn one of their own. 'And reputation or not, if one Cyberman goes down, the alarm goes up.' Kiz could feel the calculated insult in Vertebrae's voice. 'What's the plan for that?'

Thirty-three years. Kiz has killed Cybermen before. He had killed Judoon, and Axons, and even Krillitane – a fact of which he was sure Agrakos was aware. Not that it mattered. Krillitane ate their own kind as readily as everyone else's.

And it wasn't Kiz who met Vertebrae's stare with the smooth, flat curve of his helm. It wasn't Kiz who kept his hand purposefully away from his sword hilt, as if a six-foot-tall reptile with dagger talons and a repeater crossbow was nothing more than a curiosity.

Head-Taker's voice was cold. 'Me.'

*

Now

He takes their heads.

Maybe it's because it's been a long flight, and his muscles need warming up. Maybe it's because he doesn't trust Vertebrae and he doesn't trust Agrakos and he wants to remind them who he is. Maybe it's because the guards are Cybermen, and to Kiz they're not people, though in his faceless, shineless plate he looks just as inhuman as they do.

Maybe it's because he is saying goodbye to this life and he wants to feel that rush one last time.

He takes their heads. He drifts from the sky like a mobile patch of night, movements sped by careful antigrav bursts, and that blade flashes soundlessly in the moon's dry air. Only one of them manages to get a weapon up, and Kiz delicately takes its hands before decapitating it as well. The rest don't even register. Few kills do any more. Kiz feels strange about that.

You have to remember. You have to remember to feel things, if this is going to work.

He's sheathing his sword when the first trait-pod lands, its narrow snout now massively swollen. *An airbag.* The Krillitane think of everything. The pod settles on its side, and Agrakos tears his way free, shredding the pod like paper. Vertebrae is next, shivering and slathered in juices, glaring down at the bioship that has delivered him here as if personally offended.

They all stare at the dissected Cybermen at Kiz's feet.

'Head-Taker,' the Silurian breathes, and picks up one of the heads, slipping it like a trophy into his pack. 'Nice.'

Kiz ignores him.

Beyond, the massive central dome rises, a pocked steel bulge like a bruised fruit. Usually, the whole Maldovarium is lit up like Christmas, red and green neon blaring prices at the sky. Normally, Dorian's unctuous voice blares across every radio channel, offering everything a sentient being might need or want.

Now, though, it is shuttered and dark. Now, a single word repeats over every radio channel but theirs.

'CLOSED. CLOSED. CLOSED.'

'There's an access hatch to the Maldo's inner systems just there,' Agrakos says, pointing. 'Vertebrae?'

'On it,' the reptile growls, and shoots Kiz a combative grin. 'We all got reputations here.'

The alarum-globes keep to high orbit, so they are now out of range but neither they nor the guards are the Maldovarium's only defence. This is where Vertebrae shines, pulling away the access hatch to reveal a thick cluster of wires that he takes apart like a game bird. Sections are sliced, spliced, rerouted, defused. He produces his own connectors, weaving them through the bar's systems like a surgeon grafting veins. Somewhere inside the Maldo, screens freeze, or loop, or shut down entirely, and with a satisfied hiss the Silurian flicks a switch and fifty metres away an airlock swings open with a grinding of gears.

A second later, a head pops out.

'Took you long enough,' says Dorian Maldovar.

Then

'So what do we get out of this?' Vertebrae said, eyes still on the assassin sitting across from him. Vertebrae Rax, of the aquatic Silurian genus, a lithe humanoid with dark scales, heavy-lidded eyes and a sharp and snapping beak. Known for safe-cracking. Better known for not particularly caring about anything else getting cracked along the way. His body count is nothing like Head-Taker's, but if you're counting necessary kills versus unnecessary . . .

'What do you want?' Agrakos said coolly, one predator regarding another. 'Money? My intel says there's at least thirty million credits in Dorian Maldovar's vault. But that's not what you're really after, is it? I've heard you've been asking around for a vortex manipulator. Unregistered time travel doesn't come cheap, my friend. When you looking to go?'

The Silurian shrugged. 'Earth. Back when it was our
Earth. Before all this co-existence with the humans got
started. Back to when the Sea Devils ruled. That's what they
used to call us, you know. The terrors of the deep.'

Kiz and Agrakos exchanged glances.

'What?' the reptile hissed. 'They *did*.' He scowled.
'Whatever. Fine. A third of the take, and the vortex
manipulator, and I'm in. Though I don't think Dorian
Maldovar is going to let us just stroll into his bar and take
what we want.'

'Dorian's off-world,' the Krillitane said. 'That's what my
intel says. Maybe it's a holiday or something. I don't know.
But he left in a hurry, and that means the whole place is up
for grabs.' He leaned forward. 'Look. I know what I'm asking.
On a job this big, it's the variables that get you killed. But
that's why I'm doing this. I have the whole place mapped –
every security system, every weapon and trap. It's perfect.
Like a key in a lock. All we gotta do is show up and be us.'

'You're putting a lot of stock in this intel,' Vertebrae
muttered, knocking back the last of his wine. 'You sure it's
good?'

'The best,' Agrakos replied. 'Trust me.'

'Ah, but that's the thing,' the Silurian continued. 'I don't.
I'd be a fool to. And not just because you're Krillitane and

you spend ninety per cent of your time sizing up how much of a meal I am. But, if this is accurate, you've got the biggest scoop on the biggest score in three galaxies. What are you getting out of it?'

'What?' Agrakos said. 'Ten million credits isn't enough?'

Kiz felt the Silurian's gaze flick to him. Wondering why he wasn't asking these questions, no doubt. Any sane thief would. They both knew the rumours about Agrakos, and the rumours that the Krillitane were ready to kick off a war.

There was no such thing as family in this business. Some had their family within the business – bonds forged in combat or crime, relations by blood spilled rather than shared. But Krillitanes were all one family, tied together by mutual hunger, a single bloodline from the Brood Mother down. Working for Agrakos was one thing; working for the Empire was a war crime.

'And why the assassin?' Vertebrae continued, beady red eyes gleaming. 'You thinking of taking me out after I break whatever safe is in there? Hey, I'm asking you, Head-Taker. What does an assassin want with the Maldovarium? Running low on cash? Have to slum it with thieves?'

Reputation.

All Kiz did was angle his head, and the words dried in the Silurian's throat.

Family.

'I lost something,' he said. 'And I want it back.'

Now

'Autons give me the creeps,' Vertebrae murmurs.

Entering the Maldovarium as a patron is a complicated affair. There's the Dorian Gate, a boulevard vast and plush as the man himself, lined with opportunistic merchants too broke to afford renting a stall inside. Giant holo-statues of Dorian gleam on either side of the red carpet, laughing and gesturing and knowingly nudging the air, urging you to spend or drink or gamble just that little bit more.

You can afford it. You know you can.

Treat yourself. You're at the Maldo.

The thieves, however, enter through Service Hatch 11B, a dank tunnel of rusted steel that smells of smoke and neglect. In the cramped passageway, the Auton duplicate stands out like a gem in a landfill – blue-skinned, bald-pated, clad in bright red robes, with that luxurious lightness of foot exhibited by large and pompous men.

'Don't you like it?' he preens, swishing his sleeves to beckon them down the corridor after him. 'It's very roomy. Oh, and don't let that door close!'

Vertebrae pauses halfway through the service hatch.

'All the doors here use one-off codes. Once it closes, they recalculate. You'll need to prop each one open with –'

Kiz pulls the Cyberman head out of Vertebrae's pack and wedges it into the frame. It glares at them impotently.

'Handles,' the Auton riffs. 'Welcome to the team.'

'Sassy for a copy,' Agrakos murmurs, and bids them follow him into the first of the serviceways that climb the great swell of the Maldo's dome like the veins on a leaf, splitting and branching and doubling back on themselves, away from the discerning eye of paying patrons.

'That's what you paid for,' the Auton says, fastidiously holding his robes clear of a spill of oil.

'This is your intel,' Vertebrae says, eyes narrowing. 'You had an inside man.'

Agrakos shrugs.

'But I thought Autons were just mindless golems, driven by the Nestene Consciousness. No offence.'

'None taken.'

'So what's one doing here?'

'Dorian likes keeping trophies,' the duplicate says. 'I've been here since the Pandorica opened.' He grins at their confused expressions. 'Don't ask. So, when Agrakos –'

'Negotiated a one-time deal with the Nestene Consciousness,' the Krillitane interrupts smoothly. 'Dorian *thinks* it's been wiped, but I came in one day when the place was open and uploaded a reactivation code, a new personality template.'

'Sarcastic, amoral rogue,' the copy says, saluting. 'With qualms about personal risk and a fourteen per cent chance of betrayal, so I'd keep an eye out for that.'

'And,' the Krillitane interrupts once again, 'he's been sitting in the corner, recording every single movement and key press Dorian's made in the last year. I have it all. We are covered, gentlemen.'

They walk for nearly an hour, stopping and starting as the Auton disarms defences and the Silurian unlocks doors, making their way in slow revolutions up through each level of the dome. Kiz imagines the shabby luxury of the Maldo on the other side of the walls – all gaudy neon and clashing gilt – and how eerie it must all be now that it's deserted.

'Okay,' the duplicate says, as Vertebrae splices open the thickest door yet. 'Now we ditch the serviceways and enter Plaza Three, just two levels beneath where Dorian keeps his vault. There are inner defences that will only respond to me – Dorian, that is – so I can cover that. Then it's Vertebrae's turn.'

'Yeah,' Vertebrae says, and Kiz hears the unmistakable click of a safety. 'About that.'

Then

'How did you find out?'

Vertebrae had gone to the bar, or possibly to stab someone in the cloakroom – Kiz wasn't sure. Either way, this was the first moment he and Agrakos had been alone face-to-face since the Krillitane had contacted him three weeks before.

The snub-nosed pistol gleamed in the assassin's fist.

'I'm not going to ask you again. How did you find out?'

The Krillitane didn't appear at all perturbed. 'You're going to shoot me in front of all these witnesses?' he said, indicating the crowded bar.

Kiz snorted. 'They'd probably chip in together and pay my fee. You're not liked, Krillitane. Now spill. How do you know I have a –'

'When you've made such an effort to hide it? When you've carefully erased any evidence of an existence before "Head-Taker"? I have to say, I don't know why you bothered. It's all so very pedestrian. Why did she abandon you? Could she not handle the career? The highs, the lows, the body count? Or did you not tell her and then she found out? Or –'

Kiz clicked off the safety.

'That's it,' the shapeshifter purred. 'You left her, to keep her safe. Rode off into the sunset because you knew what kind of man you were, without ever knowing that she was –'

'I will put a hole in you,' Kiz growled. 'You touch a hair on their heads –'

'Relax, assassin,' Agrakos said lightly. 'She's done an excellent job of covering her tracks. Learned that from you, did she? We have no idea where your old flame is, and to be honest we don't care about your family. We care about ours. You don't know where she is either, do you? But the data-banks in the Maldo do.'

Vertebrae was returning. Kiz made the gun disappear.

Agrakos smiled indulgently, like a parent who'd got their kids to play nice. 'Looks like we both get what we want.'

Now

'Is it very important?'

That same calm tone. *How often,* Kiz wonders, *does Agrakos get guns pointed at him?*

'I've never got this far into a job without knowing why everyone's involved.'

Vertebrae herds them into the wide expanse of Plaza 3, a cavernous, velvet hemisphere studded with dozens of gambling tables and a circular central bar. There are still glasses on the tables, food congealed on plates. Dorian did leave in a hurry, after all.

The Silurian's crossbow is firmly levelled at Agrakos, and there is a slim little piece in his other hand, pointed squarely at Kiz's head. 'That goes for the assassin too. Is he here to take us out when I get you in?'

'I don't want to alarm anyone,' the Auton said, hands raised. 'But there are quite a lot of defences *inside* the Maldo, and they tend to get antsy when guns are drawn. I can voice-disable them if –'

'Shut up,' Vertebrae says, and Kiz realises that the Silurian has chosen his ambush spot well. Maybe they could all take the reptile. Maybe he'd only cut one of them down before the other took him out. But Kiz can hear whirring noises in the walls – the subtle unveiling of gun ports, the charging of laser cells. If one of them shoots, they all die.

'Your call,' Vertebrae says casually, as the charging weapons in the walls begin to ping with target locks.

'For the next eight seconds,' the Auton adds helpfully.

'You're bluffing,' the Krillitane snaps. 'You'll die too.'

'At least I'll see it coming,' Vertebrae says.

Another second, the rising whine of loading cannons and –

'Fine,' Agrakos snaps, and the Auton strides out into the centre of the floor.

'Deactivate security,' he calls.

Kiz hears the security wind down.

The Krillitane sighs. 'Dorian takes a cut of everything that comes through the Maldovarium. Sometimes it's credits. Other times it's information – travel manifests, censuses and the like. That's what Kiz is after. And, a couple of years ago, a broke biologist specialising in dangerous and extinct animals lost a poker game here and put up his life's work. A bio-library. DNA samples.'

Suddenly it all makes sense.

'And you want to eat them,' Vertebrae says flatly.

Even the Auton looks faintly nauseous, a flush darkening his borrowed face.

'I *knew* it,' Kiz breathes. 'You're still a spy for the Krillitane. You're looking for new traits to give you an edge in the war. This isn't a heist. This is *politics*.'

'You can split my share,' Agrakos says abruptly. 'That's fifteen million each if you get me into his vault.'

'Oh,' Vertebrae says. 'Okay.'

'What?' Kiz snaps. 'Seriously?'

'Um, yeah,' the Silurian responds, holstering his weapon. 'Let them at it. I'm heading to the past anyway.'

'Then why do you need the credits?'

'Because,' the reptile says, as if it's obvious, 'fifteen mill is a much better send-off than ten. And who knows what kind of supplies I might need in prehistory?' He turns back to the Krillitane. 'I'm in. What about you, plastic man?'

'I don't have free will,' the Auton says, 'so it's much of a muchness to me. The Nestene's already negotiated my co-operation in return for a peace treaty with the Krillitane.'

'Can't eat plastic,' Agrakos says with a smirk. 'So . . .'

Kiz just stares at them. With bio-gains like that, the Krillitane Empire will become a hundred times stronger than before. A thousand times. New and terrifying forms of Krillitane will be unleashed upon the universe, and it will all be because of them.

'I'm not doing this,' he says.

'Suit yourself,' Agrakos says. He gestures, and the others begin to make their way through the deserted plaza. It is the first time anyone has turned their back on Kiz in a long and storied career. 'It's a family thing. I guess you wouldn't understand.'

The words follow Kiz back into the serviceways, stalking through corridors dank with rust and run-off, stepping gingerly through the propped-open portals Vertebrae laboriously unlocked.

This is the second time you've walked away. The second time you've given up on a chance not to be Head-Taker.

He shuts out the voice. It has been years. She definitely doesn't want to see him. She's probably forgotten he exists. And, even if he was to help, even if he was to sell his soul one last time for a cheque and a job well done, he'd still be unleashing misery untold on the galaxy and everyone in it.

You never cared about that before.

He turns the corner to Service Hatch 11B, and those instincts hard earned over a long and brutal career don't even have a chance to kick in. It isn't that the heavy metal hatch has closed, or that the light in its centre has changed from a welcoming green to a harsh and unforgiving red. It's that someone has removed the Cyberman head formerly propping the door open and placed it directly and purposefully in the centre of the floor. They've even cleaned it, wiping away the dust it sustained in its death and restoring its former polish.

Somehow, the motionless face looks amused.

They're locked in.

Someone has locked them in.

Level 1 is reserved for the super-rich and Dorian's personal guests. Its is a long shaft, rising to the very tip of the Maldo's pointed dome. In stark comparison to the showiness below, it is uncluttered and pristine, a simple platform of steel hanging from the roof like the basket of a hot-air balloon, littered with mold-form couches and discreet screens on which all manner of entertainment can be summoned.

Above, security droids cling to the ceiling like bats, clicking and whirring in digital slumber.

Entering across a low bridge, the thieves see that the lower half of the shaft has been flooded. The churning black water is almost unbearably fresh and salty after the dead air of the tunnels and the sickly-sweet scent of Levels 2 and 3.

The Maldovarium resides on a barren world. In the universe of interstellar commerce, where long-haul voyages and months between resupplies are common, water is litre-for-litre more expensive than fuel. It takes a gesture from Agrakos to hurry them from the bridge to the platform, so stricken are they by this display of wealth.

'Where's the vault?' Vertebrae whispers, his voice dry with awe.

'All around us,' Agrakos says. 'And nowhere.'

The Silurian scowls. 'I can still shoot you, you know.'

'No sense of dramatics.' The Krillitane sighs. 'Fine. It's a pocket dimension. High-level time-and-space folding technology. No idea where Dorian got it, but it's telepathically linked to him – keyed to his thoughts, not his voice or appearance. No codes to enter, no wall panel to hack. He just asks, places his hand in the portal, and there it is.'

'Then why are we here?'

'Because,' Agrakos continues, 'Dorian isn't going to place his greatest treasures somewhere without having two ways to get to them. He's worked in a failsafe. A captive-thought form – like leaving a key with a neighbour. If we find the hidden activation panel, it will think like Dorian, and we'll just have to ask it to give us whatever we want.'

'Not going to pretend I understood half of that,' Vertebrae says, 'but if you say so. Where's the panel?'

Agrakos's gaze drops to the roiling water below.

'Ah,' Vertebrae says. 'I suppose we can't just drain it?'

'The real Dorian can,' the Auton said. 'My thought patterns aren't a match.'

'And you couldn't just grow gills and do this yourself?'

Agrakos folds his arms. 'Fifteen million. I thought you liked water, *Sea Devil*.'

The reptile withdraws a scanner from his pack, and takes a deep and deep and *deeper* breath, his three mighty lungs swelling in his chest. He gives both the Krillitane and the Auton a warning look.

'Don't start looting without me.'

And he flings himself off the platform with a crack of his powerful tail.

Planning. Foresight. Closing down variables. It is the only reason Kiz has survived. The only reason any of the thieves have survived. Those on the inside of the law imagine those outside of it as living chaotic and brutal lives, but only half of this is true. To survive in lawless space every risk must be analysed, every corner checked, because there is no law to catch you if you fall.

Kiz is distracted when he enters the Level 3 bazaar. It nearly costs him his life.

Someone has reactivated the security systems. Gun ports are already open. Plasma coils are charged. Kiz darts into Plaza 3 on plumes of antigrav, intent on warning the others, and an entire bazaar's worth of weaponry opens up on him. The air catches fire with dozens of laser bolts. Airborne security droids dismount their charging stands and swoop in, chattering bullets from bulbous pods.

Only a lifetime of extreme reflexes saves him – that, and the knowledge that someone somewhere along the line has either betrayed or thoroughly failed him and, either way, they are going to pay.

He tries to contact the other thieves, but there's some sort of jammer or blocker in place and all he can hear is that toneless voice.

'CLOSED. CLOSED. CLOSED. CLOSED.'

There are, by Kiz's experienced count, thirty-five different weapons currently unloading on him, chipping away at the hulking chance machine he has taken shelter behind, warping the metal, shaking the frame.

One last job. One last fight. *It's a family thing.*

He takes a deep breath and draws his sword. It's a long way up to Level 1. He hopes its edge does not fail him now.

Vertebrae dives. The first few seconds are disorientating. There are hidden jets in the shaft, churning and agitating the water until it feels like an ocean in a storm and, contrary to what he told Agrakos, he has never swum in a real sea. Earth is a mega-city now, and swimming in actual water is reserved for the sickeningly rich.

But this is what he was born for. Growing up in the high slums, his father raised him on stories of the Sea Devils' noble, vicious history. The ultimate predators of the deep. Whole oceans were their kingdom. They rose up to feast on weak, pink humans and descended to the darkest depths to fight the monsters who roamed there – great soulless thickets of blubbery flesh with arms as long as trees and eyes the size of dinner plates.

His ancestors were not afraid. He is not afraid now.

His powerful legs kick, the webs between his toes splaying wide like flippers to propel him forward. His pupils have dilated, dragging in every photon of light. His inner-ear membranes have descended, protecting him from the whirling, roaring, swirling sea of sound.

There. A light. *The panel.*

He kicks towards it.

'I think I'm going to kill Dorian.'

Twenty-five minutes have passed since the Silurian dived, and every second has been a one-sided conversation. Agrakos is perched on top of a couch, wings folded round himself, staring off into space, while the duplicate paces in front of him with the genial awkwardness of an employee hoping for a promotion.

'Would that be all right? I've been here for six months listening to him, and I think I'd really quite like to kill him. It's up to you, obviously – you're holding my contract – but honestly, if you could just leave me propped up in here, then the second he comes back I'll just grab him by the throat –'

The unsealing of Dorian's vault is announced by the man himself, his voice ringing out from empty air. 'Greetings, me! I hope your exploits are proving as fruitful as ever . . . and that you've fired that waitress on Level Two, Section B. She's stealing cutlery. You know she is.'

'He's like this all the time,' the Auton mutters. 'Which brings me back to killing him . . .'

'Well, you know how this works. You ask, I deliver. Or is it the other way round? How delightfully confusing.'

'Enough,' Agrakos snaps. 'Ask it for my DNA collection.'

The Auton clears his throat. 'Search for DNA sample collection.'

'Searching! Ah, yes, here it is. Filed under categories "DNA", "DNA Samples", "Esoterica" and "Owner Was Bad At Gambling".'

There is a small table in the centre of the platform and, as the search completes, the air above it trembles. A swirling vortex appears – a knot of whirling, sparking light – and from it slides a small steel case. The Krillitane wipes his mouth and crosses the distance with a single wingbeat, claws reaching out –

That's when the security droids open up.

Clicking and clattering to each other, the spider-like droids fill the air with laser-fire, skittering across the roof to get better angles, some engaging thrusters and actually taking to the air. Agrakos snatches the samples and flings himself behind a mold-form couch that immediately begins to melt, and the Auton looks faintly perturbed as a barrage of light cuts him in half.

'This is because I bad-mouthed him, isn't it?' he yells as he begins crawling towards cover, and then the security droids chitter and giggle as a third figure enters the fray, dipping and weaving through the storm, firing expertly placed single shots.

'Something's wrong!' Kiz roars, spinning in mid-air to avoid a haze of laser-fire.

'No? Really?' Agrakos snarls. He's snaking underneath couches now, lithe body pressed low to the floor. 'What gave it away?'

'This is *your* fault, Krillitane!' Kiz pirouettes, antigravs flaring bright, and puts a round through the targeting sensor of a droid at ten metres. 'You and your plan. "All variables covered," you said. Well, you missed something. There's someone else here. They sealed the airlock. They reactivated the security. They *cleaned up.*'

Agrakos's voice is low and dangerous. 'Duplicate. You said all the staff had been dismissed.'

'They have been!' The Auton is attempting to hide what remains of his borrowed bulk underneath a table, flinching whenever a shot comes too close.

'See?' Agrakos retorts, scampering from one piece of cover to another, samples held tight under his arm. 'It's –'

'Except for the Ood, obviously.'

The Krillitane's voice falls dangerously quiet. 'What?'

'The Ood. Dorian has an Ood.'

They both stare at him. Kiz deflects a las-bolt without turning around.

'Did I not mention that?'

Vertebrae feels like he has been swimming for hours. The shaft must be longer than his instruments are telling him, because every time he thinks he's close to the light it pulls away. His first two lungs are almost out of breath. He should open his third, but after that . . .

Even Sea Devils can drown.

Still, it's just a fraction out of reach, and it is only when Vertebrae forces his last remaining strength into a kicking, frantic lunge that it steadies and grows from a speck to an acorn, from an acorn to a fist.

It's almost close enough to touch.

Motion.

Motion in the water around him. He can feel it, and old reptile instinct tells him that it isn't the churning jets, but another body. There is something else in the water with him.

Twisting in the water, claws at the ready, his eyes strain to pierce the black. Is it a guard? Some kind of vicious alien pet? He reaches one last time for the light. It's all that stands between him and kicking for the surface.

The glow brightens, and Vertebrae sees what is in the water with him.

He sees its pale body, its sleek, domed head. He sees it cut through the water around him like it was born there, its boneless undulations cast in corpse-light by the glowing orb in its hand. Vertebrae opens his mouth in shock, and suddenly there are tentacles round his neck, rubbery coils squeezing out the last of his precious air. The eyes above them are giant, and soulless, and hungry.

Just like the stories, the Sea Devil thinks as the darkness closes in. Just like the demons that live in the deep.

'I didn't think it mattered!' the Auton wails, trying ineffectually to pile cushions over himself and hide.

Kiz is a blur of motion, antigravs straining red as he takes on an entire roomful of security droids by himself, deflecting blast after blast on his stolen Gallifreyan blade. It is a superlative display of swordsmanship, and he absolutely cannot keep it up for much longer.

'Agrakos,' he snarls. 'There's an Ood? You said you knew everything about the Maldo!'

'I thought I did!' Agrakos snaps back.

Kiz can't see the Krillitane. If he could, he might risk getting shot simply to take him down as well.

'Duplicate!' Agrakos says. 'You were supposed to give me every detail, every staff member –'

'It's an Ood,' the Auton squeals, as laser-fire stipples the decking around him. 'They're barely sentient! It didn't occur to – Why are you looking at me like that?'

The rate of fire is increasing. Security droids are converging. The Maldovarium is waking up. Every screen in Level 1 is cracked and flaking glass, and the mold-form couches are eroding under the weight of fire like a time-lapse of a storm-tossed beach. Soon, there will be nothing to find cover behind at all.

'Agrakos! Where are –'

There is a blur by the entrance to Level 1. Only the enhanced systems in Kiz's armour and a lifetime spent looking for movement in the corner of his eye let him see it. There is a shape, though the light bounces from it oddly, like rain from the back of a water bird. Then it turns and grins at him, mouth wet and red in empty air.

'I've always wanted to see Head-Taker at work,' Agrakos says. 'And you haven't disappointed. But I've got a family to get back to, and a war to win.'

Kiz snarls. He cannot help it. This was why the Krillitane had been wearing his own form, why he hadn't simply prepared a form that could have dived into the water. He'd been saving himself for the moment he left them all behind. Droids skitter and swoop obliviously above him, entirely focused on the assassin in black.

'Hope you find what you're looking for.'

He turns, and is gone, closing the door behind him. It locks with a click as quietly menacing as the pin leaving a grenade.

'Agrakos!' Kiz roars, pirouetting between laser blasts, splitting light on the edge of his blade. A stray shot catches his shoulder guard and spins him off balance enough for another two to find their mark. His armour flexes under the strain. He cannot take much more.

'Listen, I am *really* sorry about all this.' The Auton is babbling now, trying to rearrange his robes over the space where his legs used to be. 'That's the problem with this model. You have to be really specific, bit like the vault –'

The vault.

That swirling vortex is still there, rippling occasionally as laser bolts pass through it, and Kiz doesn't even think. His antigravs flare and, as more droids activate and bolts finally find the Auton and the air seethes and cooks with weapon discharge, he dives.

It's what he came for, after all.

Agrakos is halfway to the airlock when he hears the noise.

The serviceways are deserted. Every security droid is massing on Kiz's position. He's actually very impressive. Agrakos had calculated that he'd only last half that time, and that was with the Silurian helping him.

It's not a successful heist unless you get away, and for the Krillitane to get away clean there had to be someone left behind. It is possible he could have pulled this off with a strike-force of his own people, but Dorian Maldovar has connections to a Time Lord who has a particular contempt for the Krillitane, and it is far better that they think this is the work of an assassin and a reptile with an unhealthy regard for the past.

It is the future that concerns Agrakos now, and that is when he hears the singing.

Distant singing. A high, sweet note. Agrakos's ears are a predator's ears – he evolved them specially for this occasion – and as soon as the sound reaches him they snap back against his skull. *The Ood.* That stupid Auton – but no matter. The

Ood have been assessed by the Empire and have no useful features whatsoever. One Ood – even an Ood who somehow locked them in and reactivated the security systems – is no threat at all.

For a second, he looks down at the case under his arm.

Seventy samples of strange and dangerous species, weaponised nature, predators red in tooth and claw. He could . . .

No. The Brood Mother would have his hide.

The reflective scales blurring his form hide him from all but the most careful scrutiny. He goes low, slithering across the floor, using the walls and the ceiling as he hunts his prey. He should have just used Krillitane for this, and damn the Doctor if he came to hunt them down. Relying on other people is a mistake when you can simply *be* those other people yourself. The Krillitane are the only race that need to exist, when they can showcase the best features of every race themselves.

Another noise just ahead, and temptation once again streaks across Agrakos's mind. He hadn't really intended for any of the others to survive, but he can't ignore the fact that, while reactivating the security systems is one thing, the Ood also managed to delay or disappear Vertebrae, one of the nastiest killers he has ever had the fortune to meet.

Wouldn't the Brood Mother want me to bring back the samples safely? Isn't sixty-nine samples better than none?

'Greetings, me! And what do we have here?'

Kiz floats in darkness.

'A live specimen? How decadent! Activating soporific field.'

It's hard to think. To move. He came here to . . . he came here because . . .

'Attempting categorisation. Facial recognition scan, DNA test, accessing armour systems . . .'

Lights play over his face. A prick sends pain sluggishly moving around his arm. Text scrolls across his faceplate as the vault reads his armour and, through it, him.

'Ah. Head-Taker.'

'That's not who I am,' Kiz tries to say, but the words won't come.

A face materialises in front of him, and for a moment he believes it's some sort of judgement, some arcane science of the vault, but it's from his records, playing on the systems of his armour.

'First kill: Valten Sastos, Draconian. Second kill: Mabras de Pointe, human.'

'That's not who I –'

'Third kill –'

'Stop showing me –'

'Fifth kill –'

'PLEASE!'

On the tenth name, Kiz begins to scream.

Agrakos sets down the case with shaking hands. Popping the lid, he selects a solution containing the DNA of a Camoleoas goreraptor. The Krillitane has seen vid-docos about them. Claws like swords. Senses that verge on the preternatural. It is challenge season soon, and the Brood Mother is getting old. Maybe she will object to Agrakos taking this one sample, and maybe it is time for a king to take the throne.

He slugs the sample down.

Inside the Krillitane, specially designed organs go to work. They analyse the new DNA, dismantle it for the traits that will prove most useful. Agrakos closes his eyes, feeling the familiar pain rack his form. The camouflage scales turn the dead white of shedding skin. He can suddenly see himself again.

Good. I want to watch this.

His snout shudders, and he waits for the pop of new teeth . . . but something is wrong. His snout droops like a trunk, and suddenly his sharp nose is dead, his skin paling further, his skull growing, his pupils spasming from thin slits to black circles.

Agony as his snout splits. Flesh runs and whitens like wax. There is something forcing its way out of his mouth. He can taste himself. He tastes unfamiliar.

Agrakos opens his mouth to scream, and a hundred tentacles spill out.

Thirty-three years later, the list stops.

'Soporific field disengaged.'

Kiz is lying on his back. Above him, clinging to the ceiling of Level 1, are hundreds upon hundreds of security droids. He tenses, but they are dormant, grumbling uneasily to themselves, their weapon pods shuttered and dark.

'What . . .' His voice is hushed. 'What happened?'

The vault's voice is quiet.

'Compilation search complete. Passenger manifests, intergalactic censuses, surveillance footage and government records indexed. Individuals formerly associated with the assassin known as Head-Taker are resident on the planet Kratos, in the capital of Pater, at Number Fifteen Saint Maso Boulevard.'

The vortex shivers and expands, and Kiz sits up to see a woman sitting on a balcony, staring out over an unfamiliar city of spires and towers. There is a young man beside her. They are talking, laughing silently on the rippling screen. They look happy.

Kiz hears footsteps behind him, but does not turn round.

'They *are* happy, aren't they?'

The Ood is silent.

Kiz looks around at the shattered remnants of the droids he has destroyed, the Auton's blank, staring eyes. Vertebrae and the Krillitane are nowhere to be found, though he cannot imagine they got far.

She is laughing at something her son is saying. She's older, but it doesn't weigh on her at all. Instead, each year seems to have added to her beauty, until she is so much more than she was before.

'They don't need me. They don't need me coming into their life. They've already built one for themselves.'

Again, the Ood is silent.

Variables. That's what kills you, in the end. It's variables that ruin your life.

'Do I die now?' he says, and is strangely unaffected by the thought. 'Is that what happens?'

There is no reply. Kiz reaches up, unhooking his helm, and stands there for the longest time, but there is only silence. Finally, he turns round. The Ood is gone. The door is open.

He looks at the black helm in his hands, and gently places it on the floor.

ZYGONS

THE KING IN GLASS

'Y'ou have to promise not to be mad.'
Rory blinked.

His wife had her arms folded, the soft light painting her blue and copper-gold, and behind and below and above and around was the soft hum of an impossible room in an impossible machine. Oh, he knew it *was* possible, all right, because it was happening, but if he allowed himself to think about it the whole thing just gave him a headache.

'I said,' Amy Pond continued, 'you have to promise not to be mad.' Now *she* sounded annoyed, which was more familiar ground.

'I'm not mad,' Rory said cautiously. 'I'm never mad. I'm fairly sure that was in our vows . . . What am I not mad about?'

He took a tentative look around the control room. It wasn't fair to say that he felt crowded in the TARDIS. The ship was roomier than most planets, with ample nooks and crannies for him and his wife to be, well, married in. Unfortunately, considering the rate that the TARDIS exploded, crashed, phased out of existence or got possessed, it was generally safer to stay as close to the control room as possible – which did *not* lend itself to private chats.

Luckily, the Doctor seemed to have vanished. Not *vanished* vanished, presumably – though that did occasionally happen – but, at the minute, the control room was empty. All except for Rory and the woman he'd loved since before he even knew what the word really meant.

Now she was smiling. Somehow that worried Rory more than her annoyance.

'You know I love my boys,' Amy said. 'And I love to see you getting on.'

'We do get on! What about Venice? Venice was nice. And we had to team up when you –' He swallowed. 'At Stonehenge. When I hurt you. We had to work together then.'

It wasn't just the dimensions of the TARDIS that made Rory's head ache. He had died, been resurrected as an Auton, then stood guard over a wounded Amy for 2,000 years, only to have that entire timeline folded out of existence. Only the memories remained, warped as if seen through plastic. And it didn't seem right to try to forget them.

Amy's voice softened. 'One: you didn't do it on purpose. Two: you made up for it two thousand times over.' She frowned. 'Also, didn't you punch the Doctor in the face at Stonehenge?'

Rory flushed. 'I . . . don't remember. And we worked together just yesterday!'

'Yesterday' had been the thirty-second century and the midnight-black sands of Gauss Electra. The Doctor had hoped to dispel what he'd called Amy and Rory's 'unnatural British pastiness', which Rory thought was a bit rich for someone who spent most of their time inside a box. However, their sunbathing had been cut short when a freak lightning storm had reminded the sand it was in fact the disintegrated remains of the Gaussian Omni-Witch, and she'd started to reassemble herself.

'Well, anyway,' Amy continued, 'I never got my sunbathing in, and me and the Doctor thought it would be nice if you two –'

'It works!' The Doctor bounded past Rory so close he flinched.

How *did* he do that? Rory knew the Doctor had made a 900-year-long career out of being the loudest and most arm-wavingly *present* person in the room. He was tall and he was spindly and he moved as if various parts of him were trying to signal for help. So how was it that he was always able to sneak up on them?

It's the TARDIS, Rory thought. *They're colluding.*

Amy, for once, looked just as perturbed as Rory to see the Doctor. 'Doctor, I –'

'Took a while, Pond, but I got there. No small feat, hooking the long-range communicators to the voice interface's holographic projectors.'

'Doctor –'

'Had to clear out a lot of old junk to do it, too – old error messages, notes I'd left to myself, dramatic monologues when I thought I was about to die. I do record an awful lot of those.'

'Doctor –'

'For a while, it was stuck on Donna Noble. You would have loved her. Fellow ginger. But! We are finally ready. I haven't pulled a holographic fast one in *years*. Rory will never know you're still back on Gauss Electra. He'll think you're still on the –'

'Doctor!'

Slowly, very slowly, the Doctor turned to stare at Rory, who gave him a small, solemn wave.

'Hi, Rory,' the Time Lord said. 'I didn't . . . see you there.'

Behind him, Amy flickered like an interrupted TV signal.

'What am I going to be mad about?' Rory asked.

Numina Vitri was celebrating. Every screen in the TARDIS displayed the parades thronging its capital city, everyone cheering so loud Rory could nearly hear them from orbit. Spotlights spun through the sky, their beams splitting like prisms on sharp-edged skyscrapers until the whole sky was teeming with rainbows.

On the screens, dancers with limbs artificially extended into long, shimmering spears somersaulted and pirouetted through the crowds. Seismic engines embedded in the planet's crust had set the roots of each tower to trembling so that a single wavering note filled the air, like a wet finger rubbed around a glass of wine.

'It's amazing,' Rory said.

The Doctor grinned. 'You humans don't know how good you have it. A whole planet packed with every sort of resource you could want – ores, gems, treacle – whereas the Vitri have to make do with what they have.'

'What do you mean?'

'Numina Vitri is a barren world. Nothing much there but sand and the planet's molten core, which is why –'

There was something about the gleam of the towers, the way the light struck the city . . .

'It's glass,' Rory finished. 'The whole city is made of glass.'

'Why not?' the Doctor said, fingers moving over the control console like a pianist delivering a crescendo. 'Conductive, versatile, one hundred per cent recyclable. There are worse materials to build a life on – or from.'

Rory nodded. He found it best to, when the Doctor said cryptic things while pressing buttons that may or may not fling them out of the universe. He used to have to close his eyes every time the TARDIS took off.

'Rory?' The Doctor was flicking through stations on one of the viewscreens. 'Could you go open the door, please?'

'The door? Have we landed?'

The Time Lord didn't look round. 'Sure!'

Rory was at the door and turning the latch before his brain managed to kick in, and by then it was far too late. That was the danger of travelling with the Doctor for too long. Rory was a lot less susceptible to it than Amy was – which was obviously because she had travelled with him longer, and not for any other reason – but, when you went through enough life-and-death experiences with someone who at least nominally seemed to know what they were doing, you got into the habit of jumping to.

They had not landed. They had the opposite of landed. They had, in fact, parked in orbit and tilted at an angle, which, combined with the thundering gale trying to tear off his ears, made Rory feel like someone who had rather stupidly stuck their head out of a cellar door in the middle of a hurricane.

And then he saw their destination and abruptly forgot to be terrified.

They'd had to park in orbit, because it was the only way to take in the entire tower at once. It was so tall it started on the ground and ended as a silver line against the blackness of space. Clouds had formed around its mid-section, as if the titanic structure had bruised the atmosphere on its way up, and its sides were smooth all the way to the summit, where they split and sharpened into long barbs.

Like a crown.

'"Take him to a party," she says,' the Doctor growled delightedly. 'Well, there's no party like a coronation.'

Amy's instructions had been simple. All of space and time to choose from, and they hadn't got anywhere *near* a good party. Surely, while Amy stayed behind on Gauss Electra and got the sun her Scottish skin desperately needed, her two boys could find a proper knees-up – and pick her up a commemorative plate (or the local equivalent).

It wasn't a terrible plan. It was actually a very good plan. And Rory hadn't even been mad when he'd found out. He just . . .

'I have a healthy level of concern. That's all.'

The Doctor had donned a tuxedo and was trying to examine his bow tie in the glass panel of the door.

'Concern for what?'

'This,' Rory said. 'I think it's a great idea. Go away on a bit of a –' the phrase 'boys' night' came into his head and then immediately left again, embarrassed – 'night out. And I like parties. But parties are about timing and venue, and that's not something you and the TARDIS tend to get . . . right all the time. No offence.'

The Doctor raised an eyebrow. 'None taken.'

I was talking to the TARDIS, Rory thought.

'Rory, you just have to get into the spirit. Once we get into the coronation, it'll be improbably sized canapés and glasses of bubbly. You just have to –'

They stepped out of the TARDIS and directly into the sound of twenty cocking guns.

'Relax,' the Doctor said out of the corner of his mouth.

You never got used to it.

Not having guns pointed at you – though yes, that too, actually – but seeing an alien. Any alien, and at this point

Rory had met quite a few. Rory had dedicated his whole life to studying the human body, and it was disconcerting to know that he could spend a million more and not even scratch the surface of what was out there in the stars.

The inhabitants of Numina Vitri were tall and slender as reeds. Long-limbed and plated in armour of smoky crystal, there was a jerkiness to their every movement that made Rory think of sparrows or old stop-motion films. They were constantly moving, bobbing from hoofed foot to hoofed foot, their bright, long-lashed eyes darting everywhere as if eternally curious or wary.

The gleaming glass rifles they held didn't move at all.

'Hello, I'm the Doctor. We're here for the . . . party?'

The TARDIS had materialised in a long corridor of shimmering glass. Its sides were slightly curved, narrowing gently like a champagne flute round a massive circular door, in front of which were massed the aforementioned guards with their aforementioned guns.

The guards parted to allow a new Vitri to step forward, its thin chest and spindly shoulders draped in a mantle marked with spirals of gold. When it spoke – whispery, breathy – it did so with the particular horror of an organiser who had taken great pains to make sure everything was *just right*, and was now dealing with gate-crashers.

That was the other unnerving thing about meeting aliens. Some things were a constant the universe over.

'Are you . . . Are you trying to skip the queue?'

The Doctor gave the assembled weapons a sickly grin. 'Of course not. We wouldn't do something like that. Would we, Rory?'

Rory vigorously shook his head.

'You materialised at the top of it,' the Vitri hissed, and Rory could have sworn the air in front of those bulbous rifles began to shimmer with anticipated heat.

'Ah,' said the Doctor. 'Well. Time Lord. Bad at queuing. Could I possibly show you our invite?'

Ten guns tracked his hand slipping into his pocket.

'We could just go to the back of the queue,' Rory offered, having flashbacks of his sole sojourn to Leadworth's only club, The Vortex, which he had been barred from for simply standing next to someone who had tried to skip the queue. In fairness, that someone had been Amy, and he wouldn't have gone in without her, but bouncers – they were all the same.

'Rory,' the Doctor said. 'The coronation of the King in Crystal is pretty much all the Numina Vitri's Christmases come at once. Maybe with some New Years thrown in. Remember the parades packing the streets?'

'Yes.'

'That was the queue.'

'Oh.'

The Vitri in charge took the psychic paper from the Doctor and scanned it, unaware that the paper was scanning him right back and displaying whatever credentials the Doctor and Rory needed to get in. He seemed to stare at it for an awfully long time. The Doctor's grin began to waver at the edges.

Finally, he nodded, waving a long hand at the guards, who stepped aside with a clatter of glass.

'Of course, you may come in.'

It was hard to tell, with the way the Vitri bobbed and shook, but did it seem . . . worried?

'I am High Vizier Camadaras, and I formally welcome you to Numina Vitri and the Palace of the King in Crystal.'

A sudden chorus of angry mutterings sounded from behind the TARDIS, but Rory tried to ignore them in favour of the sudden elation he felt at passing a bouncer. They had arrived. They had got in! Maybe things were going to work out as planned. Yes, a lot of guns had been aimed at them, but that was all sorted out now. And, who knew? Maybe that was going to be their quota of life-threatening experiences for the day.

I am going to have a ludicrously coloured drink, Rory thought, with growing triumph, as the High Vizier led them down a long, low corridor of fogged, unreflective glass.

'How did you know to come here?' the Vitri asked quietly.

And whatever the local equivalent of a cocktail sausage is.

'Oh, I've always meant to,' the Doctor said. 'I love a coronation. It's spending all that time in England. I've also developed an unhealthy fixation on scones.'

And then I'm going to see about commemorative plates.

'What are you talking about?' Camadaras snapped, which was a fairly standard reaction to the Doctor's small talk. 'Your credentials – we didn't call investigators! We haven't even told anyone about the murder!'

'Wait,' Rory said. 'The what?'

The throne room of the King in Crystal was spectacular. A domed ceiling of shining glass seemed to stretch away into infinity, held up by crystal pillars wider than Rory was tall. Smoky glass statues of guards lined the walls in silent repose, and every surface was polished to mirror brightness so that, when Rory and the Doctor entered with Camadaras, a thousand reflections seemed to walk with them.

But, as awe-inspiring as the throne room was, it paled in comparison to the suit of armour in its centre. It was a construction on a scale with the palace itself: a looming fortress of glass plates and jagged edges, everything shorn to sharp perfection. The mask gleamed like an axe-blade, dazzling diamond, sweeping upwards in a forest of glittering points.

'The Mantle,' the Vizier murmured, 'of the soon-to-be King.'

It was majestic. That was the only word for it, and it made the body lying beneath it all the sadder.

Rory went for the body immediately. It was what he'd been trained to do. The Doctor whipped out his sonic screwdriver, panning it around the room and checking the results. He hadn't even glanced at the body, but Rory knew him well enough to know that, although it might *look* like he was examining statues and taking readings and measuring the relative distance between light shafts and the angle of the planet's axis, what he was really doing was searching for any possible reason why somebody might have lost their life there.

She was a woman. Human, not much older than Rory – though her scars and the hard set of her jaw, even in death, made her appear a lot older. Reflective cloth wrapped her limbs, making her almost invisible against the crystal floor, and a bag made of the same material lay torn open at her side.

She was slumped in front of the throne as if trying to kneel.

Rory had seen death in Leadworth. Most people didn't actually die while on adventures; they died in homes or in bedrooms. Most of all, they died in hospitals, and that should have made Rory used to it but it didn't. *Why did you die here?* he asked the woman silently, but his quick and respectful examination provided no answers.

'When does he take the job?' the Doctor asked, peering into the elbow of one of the statue-guards.

'Pardon?'

'The Mantle of the King in Crystal,' the Doctor said, pointing at the huge figure on the throne. 'That's what the party is for, isn't it? An empty suit of armour waiting for its king? Though armour's an overly simple word . . .'

'The donning of the Mantle is a sacred ritual,' the Vizier said stonily.

'Sacred ritual?' the Doctor said. 'It's a death sentence.'

'What?' Rory said, looking up from the corpse of the woman. 'How?'

'The King will sit in vigil before the Mantle for a night before donning the armour. Then it seals shut after him. Life support, augmented strength, rejuvena systems – the Vitri want their money's worth from a monarch, so it keeps the lucky king or queen alive for centuries, makes them strong, makes them mighty. Everything a ruler should be.'

Now it was the Doctor's voice that was cold. 'Behind a pane of glass.'

'It is tradition,' Camadaras growled. 'We are not humans, changing our rulers every season or so. A single monarch ruling for a millennium is more noble. More efficient.'

'Efficient?' Rory said. It sounded horrible. 'What do you mean, efficient?'

'He means the Mantle is a crown and a burial chamber all in one.'

Suddenly Camadaras knelt, falling to the polished-glass floor as if an unseen puppeteer had cut his strings. The Crown Prince – for there was no one else this could be, with robe and mask of shining gold – swept by his Vizier as if he didn't exist at all.

'Presenting,' Camadaras called out in a sing-song lilt, 'the Protector of the Peace, He Who Shatters and Reforges, Master of the Shining Guard, the Crown Prince Maanaster of Numina Vitri.' His voice lowered. 'Sire, you are not supposed to be here before the vigil begins. Laying eyes on the Mantle –'

'Is something I've been doing since I was old enough to know my own name,' Crown Prince Maanaster murmured, and there was wry weariness in his voice. He was young, Rory thought – much smaller than the other Vitri, and his voice was high and thin. 'I doubt another glimpse will take the shine off.'

The amusement drained from his voice. 'Besides, one of my subjects has died. I would like to know why.'

'She's an alien,' the Vizier said flatly. 'A thief, come to steal the Mantle. I was just about to deploy the Shining Guard, place the whole city under martial law.'

'Were you?' the Prince said mildly. 'That's odd. I think I'm in charge of them. It's in my name and everything.'

The corner of the Doctor's lip twitched.

'Sire, I know tradition demands two weeks of celebration and prayer, but if aliens are trying to steal the Mantle you must hold your vigil as soon as possible. The idea that the coronation might not go ahead cannot be countenanced!'

'That's easy for you to say,' the Crown Prince said. 'You get to go home afterwards.'

Rory was starting to like Maanaster, which made those empty glass eyes glaring from the throne all the harder to meet.

'And who are these people?'

The Vizier cleared his throat. 'Investigators, appointed by the Shadow Proclamation. Z Division, I think it said? Unexplainable Intergalactic Crime?' His voice hardened. 'Though I must say, sire, we are a sovereign race, and this uninvited intrusion feels like –'

'Unexplainable and intergalactic? Sounds like us. I'm the Doctor,' the Time Lord said with a bright smile. 'This is Rory. And I've solved the crime, actually.' His smile disappeared very suddenly. 'This woman wasn't a thief. She thought she was, but she can't have been. She didn't even lay hands on the Mantle.'

'She wasn't?' the Prince said. 'How do you know?'

The Doctor didn't reply, instead reaching into his jacket pocket and pulling free a tiny sphere that looked a little bit like a grape carved out of smoke.

Camadaras frowned. 'Is that . . . a canapé?'

The Doctor shrugged, then flung the grape at the Mantle's face.

The Vizier let out a shocked snarl, but he needn't have worried. As soon as the grape came within a metre of the diamond mask, the nearest statues raised hands in a synchronised and dazzling salute. Rory flinched as light pealed from their open palms, turning the canapé to a drizzle of ash.

'That's how I know,' the Doctor said. 'Breaking in to the throne room was one thing – though the doors did have matter lines, aceline locks. She must have had tools to bypass them but where are they?' He stared down at the not-thief's ripped-open, empty bag, then shook his head. 'But even if she got in, and she did get in, only those destined for the Mantle can approach it, am I right?'

'Visual sensors in the statues,' the Prince said. 'Yes.'

'Then she can't have approached, or we wouldn't be looking at her right now. And –'

Rory got there a second after the Doctor did.

'And how was she going to steal the Mantle? It's huge.'

Prince Maanaster's voice was quiet. 'It's packed with antigrav units, augmuscles . . . Apparently when you wear the Mantle, it feels like a second skin.'

'So, what?' the Doctor said. 'She was going to wear the most famous suit of armour in the solar system into packed streets during the biggest celebration this planet has had in a thousand years?'

Camadaras was shaking his head. 'Sire, it is clear foreign agents wish to sabotage the ceremony. We must complete it as soon as possible, before whoever's responsible –'

'Oh, that one's easy,' the Doctor said. 'It's you.'

'What?' Rory and Maanaster said together.

'How *dare* you, you alien heathen!' Camadaras drew himself up to his full height, long fingers clenched into fists.

The Prince cocked his head. 'This is a serious accusation,' he conceded. 'Do you have evidence?'

'Evidence?' the Doctor repeated. 'Well, it's the Vizier. It's always the Vizier. Or the Chief Advisor. Or the Grand Chancellor. It's *always* the Vizier. I've seen it a million times. Has nobody read their Pratchett?'

They all stared at him.

'Thank you for your analysis,' the Crown Prince said, his voice carefully devoid of amusement. 'But I feel we may need stronger evidence.'

He turned to Camadaras. 'Deploy the Shining Guard. Have our scientists analyse the body to discern the planet of origin. I want travel manifest and pict-capture records for the last month, and a list of entities that could sell something this rare, or benefit from its disappearance.'

The Vizier blinked.

'Now, Camadaras.'

'And the vigil, sire? I do not believe we can –'

'It will happen tonight,' the Crown Prince said. Rory could see them all reflected, tiny and insignificant, in the Mantle's depths. 'I know what I have to do.'

'Cool,' the Doctor said. 'Can we come?'

'Is it just me,' the Doctor said later, for the tenth time, 'or is it really suspicious that the Vizier said yes?'

It was nearing dawn, but the revels outside showed no signs of slowing down. Fireworks burst and flared above the throne room's great dome, flooding every reflection with red and gold. It sounded like an awful lot of people having a really good time.

Rory, in contrast, had spent the last eleven hours learning that there really was no way to make yourself comfortable on a polished-glass floor. And throne rooms generally only had one chair, and it was probably immensely rude to try to sit down on it. Besides, doing so would have disturbed Prince Maanaster, who had knelt down in front of the Mantle as soon as the doors closed, and hadn't moved since.

'The Vizier is a good servant,' Prince Maanaster said now, without looking up. 'He wants things to go as they should.'

The thief had only deactivated the security systems, not disabled them entirely, so it hadn't taken long for Camadaras to 'get everything in order', which to Rory sounded like a polite way of saying 'lock them in'. At least, with the ceremony imminent, the inner systems had been disabled, which meant that Rory didn't have to worry about straying too close to the Mantle and getting incinerated.

But that wasn't what was bothering him.

Who were you?

The body of the thief had been removed, but Rory's eyes kept ghosting back to the spot where she had lain. Some things never changed, no matter how far from home you got, and all he could think about was who was going to call her family. Did people do that, in space? Did she have anyone to call?

'And what do you want?' the Doctor asked.

'To serve my people,' the Crown Prince replied simply.

''S a good answer,' the Time Lord said, staring at the silent rows of statues. 'Have you practised it often?'

Maanaster was silent for a long time.

'Yes,' he said finally. 'Is that wrong?'

He seemed very young in that moment, and very old.

'I know I'm missing something,' the Doctor said eventually, and it wasn't clear whether he was talking about the murder or what the Crown Prince had just said. He turned on a heel, prowling towards the regiment of statues crowding the back of the hall with that expression on his face – the one that said he had worked out every facet of the puzzle but one, and was just waiting for inspiration to arrive.

'If you boys could talk . . .'

He disappeared into the crystal regiment, muttering to himself and leaving Rory and the Prince alone.

'So . . .' Rory said. 'This is a big honour, right?'

Maanaster nodded. 'The children of noble families compete to become a crown prince – games of intellect, statecraft, diplomacy – and the victor must know this world inside out, its every flaw and gleam. Royalty is not something given here. It is earned.'

Rory eased himself down on to the floor. 'It sounds . . . intense.'

'I care,' the Prince said simply. 'The Vitri are old, and powerful, and many of us – like Camadaras – want to stay aloof from the galaxy. I think we can do good instead.' His gaze travelled back to the glaring eyes of the diamond mask. 'I just wish I could do it as me.'

'What do you mean?'

'I've studied for this all my life,' the Prince replied. 'And the one thing no book or tutor has been able to tell me is –' he waved a hand at the hulking monstrosity glaring down at them – 'what I can do in there that I can't do as myself.'

The Last Centurion. Rory had no idea where the name had come from, but there had been days . . . years . . . centuries where it had been easier to think of himself as a symbol rather than a person whose heart had been placed in a box and left in the ground.

'I think,' Rory said carefully, 'that, to protect people, sometimes you need to be bigger than you are.'

'But what if that makes you . . . different?' the Prince asked. 'It doesn't hurt. From what I've read. But they talk about being more distant. About being separated from the world. Things look different from up there.'

'I can imagine,' Rory said, staring at where the Doctor had stood.

'I just don't want to forget that I care,' Maanaster admitted. 'I don't want to become . . .'

'A thing?' Rory offered, and the Prince nodded.

'I spent two thousand years being a thing once,' Rory said. It was such a strange sentence to say, with so much bound into it. In a way, it was a little like how he felt about Amy – an emotion so large and complex and terrifying that he could only express it in three simple words. 'Do you know what kept me going?'

'What?'

'Not wanting to be. Hold on to that.'

'Your Highness!'

Rory and Maanaster looked up. The Doctor was backing out from between the standing statues, wearing the other expression he frequently deployed: the tight grin of someone who had just stepped on a patch of ground in a minefield and heard a quiet click.

'What is it?'

'I am going to talk very quickly for a minute,' the Doctor said, easing himself from one backwards step to the next.

'You always talk quickly,' Rory said.

'Well, in this case, it's because something is going to try to kill us.'

From somewhere in the maze of crystal statues came a low and burbling growl.

Rory and the Crown Prince abruptly got to their feet. It was that kind of noise – the kind that reached into your spine via your ears and pulled you up like a marionette.

'She had no tools,' the Doctor said. 'No thieves' tools to bypass outer security. But she wasn't a thief, was she? She just thought she was. Someone lied to her, wound her up to watch her go. They *used* her.'

'Doctor,' Rory said, trying to watch everywhere at once while being very aware he had no idea what he was looking for. He'd heard more hungry growls in the last year than in all the rest of his life put together.

'She was a delivery system.'

Another growl, and this one had amusement laced through it like arsenic, red and raw and delighted.

'Because, if you think something has been stolen . . .'

The Crown Prince's voice was trembling. 'Doctor?'

'You don't ask what might have been left behind.'

One of the statues began to move.

It moved the way a scab clotted – jerkily, from the edges in. Shoulders shivered. Fingers twitched. Feet *tap-tap-tapped* against the floor. Then, with a convulsive shudder that was utterly lacking in Vitri grace, it took a step forward. Then another. Then a third, its head lolling on its crystal neck.

'Didn't suit you, did it?' the Doctor said softly. 'Taking an inorganic shape. You pretended to be tools and used a compression field to shrink yourself down. But, between that and the statues, your molecules are having commitment issues, aren't they? Does it hurt?'

'Agony,' the thing hissed, its body crooked as a stepped-on tent. Rory jumped as another statue suddenly twitched into movement, its jaw lolling open to admit the sudden growth of long needle teeth. 'But worth . . . the pain.'

'Not for her, it wasn't,' the Doctor snapped. 'You hired her. Told her there was what? Treasure? Technology? Even provided her the tools to do it. She just carried you in. And you killed her for it.'

'Doctor?' Rory said. 'What are these things?'

'Zygons,' the Doctor said.

'Not for long,' came a voice behind Rory, and he and Maanaster whirled to see a statue near the door slump like melting plastic, and its glimmering surface open in cratering sores. 'Soon one of us shall rule.'

'You mean to replace me,' the Crown Prince breathed.

The Zygon's laugh was like chugging oil. 'Will become you. You become the King. An empire becomes ours.'

The others began laughing too, even as the effort disconnected one's jaw and left it hanging from a string of flesh.

'The wars we'll start. Shards of glass grinding into the meat of the universe. All this beauty made a wreck.'

Habit drew Rory's hand to his waist, but his sword was back in the TARDIS. *They need to start letting me wear my sword all the time.* The Zygon blocking the door raised a half-formed hand to swipe at them, and Rory yanked Maanaster back.

The young Vitri was now shaking so hard he was practically vibrating, but Rory knew without asking that it wasn't fear for himself. It was fear for what a Zygon could do wearing the mantle of a king.

'Doctor?' Rory called. 'Ideas?'

'I really thought it was the Vizier,' the Doctor said. He sounded extremely disappointed. 'But Zygons? This is so typical of you. You'd rather *be* other races than learn from them. Experts with glass, the Vitri.'

He withdrew his screwdriver – just a little wand of steel and plastic that seemed utterly pathetic against the drooling half-glass creatures advancing towards them.

'Do you know what the difference is between Vitri glass and a bunch of Zygons forcing their molecules to do their best impression?'

The Zygons paused. Saliva hung in ropes from their jaws. The Doctor held up the sonic like an exclamation point and set it purring.

'Vitri glass is sonic-proof.'

The purr turned into a shriek, and the glass Zygons broke.

Cracks opened like screaming mouths, and the Zygon facing Rory fell on shattering limbs, its molecules too rigid, its disguise too good. It roared as it tried to force its body under control, the raw red suckers of its true form abruptly bursting from its back.

'Great,' Rory yelled through the din, turning to Maanaster. 'Now we just need to –'

But the Prince was gone.

Beyond, one of the other Zygons was on its knees, caught halfway between crystal and flesh. As Rory watched, reflective skin turned scabby and scarlet, and its struggles began to still.

He didn't see the third Zygon at all.

'Doctor? It's wearing off!'

'I know! I'm trying to think!'

'We will not be stopped.' The third Zygon rose amid the stark silhouettes of the glass statues – a burnt wedge of flesh, ringed by blisters, crowned by welts. Its eyes were the hot yellow of pus . . . and then they weren't. They were Vitri. They were Maanaster's.

'I will crack this world under my stride,' the Zygon-Prince hissed over the faltering sound of the Doctor's screwdriver. 'I will break cities down and sharpen the shards to knives.'

It was horrible to see. Its fellows had retaken their true forms, circling Rory and the Doctor until human and Time Lord were back to back, but the true awfulness was seeing something wearing Crown Prince Maanaster's skin stalking towards them with all the belligerence of a conqueror and nothing but darkness behind the eyes.

Its voice was full of childish glee. 'Mine. This world will be mine. And I will *ruin* it.'

'No.'

And a new day dawned. Caught and magnified by the glass cunning of the Numina Vitri, light came down fierce and molten as a lightning blast, haloing the throne in dazzling gold.

The Zygons stared.

Rory did too.

It was empty.

'Long live the King,' the Doctor whispered, as the Zygons turned to look up, and up, and up, and the King in Crystal drew his glittering sword.

There's always a point in a party where thoughts turn to the next day. People remember themselves, or home, or work, and gently start to slip off into the real world. Nobody had seemed to tell the Vitri this, however, and the party showed no sign of stopping. It was nearing nightfall when the Doctor found Rory leaning against a pillar, suspiciously eyeing a canapé in case it was poisonous – or a Zygon.

'That should be edible,' the Doctor informed him. He paused. 'Are you all right?'

The throne room had been opened to the public, and now the light of a thousand torches turned the impassive figure of the King in Crystal into a glittering, shifting mosaic. If Rory didn't know better, he could have imagined that there was no one inside that armour at all.

'He did it for us,' Rory said. *To protect people, sometimes you need to be bigger than you are.* 'To save us.'

'He did what he thought he had to do to keep people safe,' the Doctor said. 'It isn't a bad start to being a king.'

That great spiked head had turned, as if it had heard them speak.

'RORY WILLIAMS. THE DOCTOR. APPROACH YOUR KING.'

A hush fell upon the chamber.

'THANK YOU FOR YOUR SERVICE TO THE THRONE OF NUMINA VITRI.'

The Doctor bowed gracefully and, after a moment, Rory did the same.

'PLEASE ACCEPT THESE TOKENS OF OUR GRATITUDE.'

Servants came forth, proffering dazzling mirrors the size of Rory's torso. It wasn't quite a commemorative plate, he thought, but Amy would like it all the same.

'Good luck with . . . um . . . everything,' Rory said. *Oh, god. What do you say when* . . . Try as he might, he couldn't help but look for some sign of Maanaster in there, but the mask just showed him back his own face, pale and small.

'With your blessing, Your Highness,' the Doctor said. 'We might take our leave.'

The huge head nodded, and the revellers began once more to move.

'RORY.'

Rory turned back.

'TWO THOUSAND YEARS?'

'Yes,' he said. 'Two thousand years.'

The mask gleamed.

'I AM LESS AFRAID NOW, HAVING MET YOU.'

Rory nodded solemnly. 'I'm glad.'

They made their exit, navigating the huge crowds still making their way up through the tower to look upon their King. *All their Christmases come at once.* That was what the Doctor had said. Having met Maanaster, Rory could believe it.

The largest delay seemed to be beside the TARDIS, where a bedraggled and vaguely familiar Vitri was having an argument with two guards.

'What are you talking about?' he was saying. 'I am the Grand Vizier Camadaras! A Zygon jumped me, took my form. There's an impostor in the court, I swear.'

The Doctor turned to Rory with an expression of utmost delight. 'Fourth Zygon?'

'Fourth Zygon,' Rory said, and sighed. 'You want to go looking for it, don't you?'

The Doctor grinned, and adjusted his bow tie.

'I did promise you a party,' he said.

'Fine,' Rory answered. Amy could wait a *little* longer. 'But I'm bringing my sword.'

DALEKS

THE THIRD WISE MAN

It was in the first year of the Time War, though we did not call it that at the time. We were not to know what it would become.

Indeed, it was only much later that we realised it would be a war at all. For too long, we believed it a simple series of skirmishes, similar to the clashes along the raw border of the time field separating us from the wretched and primitive races of the universe. It was in those patrols that I gained my captaincy, piloting one of our few Battle TARDISes against the aliens foolish enough to seek our technology, or those who simply blundered into the constellation of Kasterborous and the Seven Systems – our home.

We Time Lords are jealous of our secrets. We must be. We do not seek to preserve our way of life simply for ourselves. We do it because only we are advanced enough to wield the power that we do. Anything else would be catastrophe. I am convinced of it, even now, as the younger races' awe of us has been lost and our enemies hammer at our doors.

In a way, that is what this entire war has been about.

The Daleks came for us in that first year, and we did not see it as war. We saw it as pest control. They amassed in their millions, and rather than face them as equals on the battlefield we simply detonated the nearest star and consumed their entire fleet in fire. Such was our power. Such was our arrogance.

War is poison. We wished to demonstrate this to the Daleks, to sicken them with might, dissuade them from challenging us. There are battlefields on Gallifrey from before the Stellar Age where the fighting was so fierce that the ground ran with blood and the soil was sown with arrowheads like seeds. There are places war has poisoned so completely that nothing will ever grow again.

Shock and awe. Those were our watchwords in that first year, when we were buoyed and comforted by knowing that *we* were the most superior, that *we* were better defended and that, at the end of it all, we simply had more *time* to respond than any other race.

We did not understand our enemy. For all our knowledge, we knew nothing.

The Daleks were indefatigable. They were remorseless. Everything we did, every attempt to scare or reason with or deter them was met with the pathological, twitching hatred with which they draw every breath. We learned this after Spiral Furl, when Harlan Castellos turned the death of his TARDIS into an electromagnetic extinction event and Daleks fell from the sky like hail. We learned it after the first volleys of the Anything Gun crumpled space–time like fire consuming parchment. We learned it as battle overturned the universe like a child raking dirt, and the lesser races squirmed and died like worms exposed in our wake.

You cannot intimidate a Dalek. You cannot frighten them.

I will speak now of the Nightmare Child.

It was supposed to be a small battle. There had been silence along many fronts for weeks now, and there was hope blooming on Gallifrey that perhaps the new generation of Battle TARDISes had proven our superiority. There were those on the High Council who still believed that the attacks were simply Daleks being Daleks, and not steps on the way to all-out war. 'One more battle,' they counselled. One more crushing defeat, and the little monsters would flee.

I was in the Scaveline system, investigating some
intercepted Dalek communications. My own TARDIS led a
strike-force – even then, the military language felt strange to
me – of a hundred recently grown battleships. Scaveline's
star was a white dwarf, struggling against its own weight to
stay in the heavens. I remember wondering, as we emerged in
the system, whether any of the planets had ever been
inhabited.

Curiosity was not a trait that the Time Lords ever
encouraged. What need had we for it? Everything in the
cosmos was there, waiting – every time, every moment – and
we could observe it all as completely as we desired.

'All ships are in-system,' my lieutenant, Orlock, murmured
at my side. 'Awaiting orders.'

We were not a warrior people. We had never had to be.
Belligerence had gone the way of curiosity, because all of time
and space was ours. Our tiny contingent of warships (of which
I commanded a significant portion) were stretched thin across
space, and many were still adolescent and untested.

No TARDIS takes to war with relish. I knew it pained
some of those under my command. TARDISes were not
ships, were not dumb beasts of burden or mere transports
across the heavens; they were our allies and our compatriots,
and we did them a disservice.

I mourn them still.

We inched through the Scaveline system, scanners at maximum. General practice during manoeuvres in uncivilised space was to take the form of ships designed by lesser races – a way to hide our own advancement, or a tactic to create confusion in our enemies. A competent commander can make much use of a moment's hesitation. For a Time Lord, a moment is an eternity.

However, such tactics fared abysmally against these new, frenzied Daleks. The simplicity that had once been a flaw in the Daleks became in war a hideous strength: they simply opened fire on every ship, no matter its origin.

My own Type 94 had therefore taken the form of interstellar debris: a slowly spinning chunk of rock made pale and shimmering with ice. Its interior was designed after the manner of an old observatory – a spherical space with seats on gimbals so that my crew could swing from console to console, and myself on a central leather chair. The entire arrangement looked rather like the model of a solar system, with the console our gleaming, silver sun.

'Scouts,' I murmured, knowing my TARDIS would relay my words to every other ship in the fleet. 'Range forward, pattern nocturne.'

Pattern nocturne: caution. The less-armoured Type 90s and 91s peeled off and dematerialised. Some ranged out into the system, rendered invisible by their chameleon circuits, and others darted into the timestream to scan the approaching seconds for peril. It may seem strange, the idea that our foes were not immediately detectable, but a star system is a gigantic place, even to craft such as ours. There are many ways to hide. Much of space warfare is not attacking or defending, but simply finding your enemy before they find you.

'Sir, this is Scout Circle Eight. No sign in the system's western quadrant.'

'Sir, Scout Circle Three reporting. No Dalek presence five minutes from your now.'

Strange. There was a psychotic honesty about the Daleks. They never encrypted their communications, never used stealth, never fled from battle even against terrible odds. There was a desperate, crazed need to them – either something inherited from their mad creator, or a behavioural side effect of being just a few tatters of flesh smeared over the trigger of a gun.

That was why I took the risk I did, my fingers dancing over the communications relay that connected me to my fleet.

'Pattern daylight. Show yourselves so that we may draw them out and end this. Scout Circles Three and Eight, loop back round and cover our retreat.'

'Yes, sir. How far?'

'A day. But be sure to stay hidden.'

'Understood. Should we establish a position in the future as well?'

'Negative,' I responded. *Not until I know what happened here. Not until I can be sure they're not waiting for us.*

Scaveline continued its turgid spin. I stretched in my chair, one eye on the scouts' reports. The fleet hovered awkwardly on the system's edge. I could not help but check and recheck the space–time co-ordinates, though the idea of a TARDIS getting lost was ludicrous. As the long silence stretched, I began to stupidly hope that the High Council had been right. Maybe this war *was* no war. Maybe for once in their pitiful, cyborg lives the Daleks had admitted that they were not the superior beings in the galaxy.

'Sir, we have something. Transmitting co-ordinates now.'

We are not the only race to have discovered time travel. Our battle to keep it so failed; a fact which is now even more painfully clear. But Time Lords were the first, and understanding time will always be as easy to us as breathing.

My screens showed me two star systems – the mundane, physical movement of planets, and the swirling overlay of the timestream beneath. Physical and chronological movement, like a flower blooming in four dimensions at once.

I could see the slow roll of asteroids from one moment to another, and the bacteria-like scurry of life still clinging to a couple of distant worlds.

The other TARDISes were like stars, each one a flare of time energy skating towards us like stones across the top of a lake. They looked omnipotent, perfect, navigating the fabric of our universe so deftly that it was impossible to imagine anything laying them low.

We followed the shining scouts as they led us into the shadow of a broken planet on the system's far edge. Something had dug into the world's crust, scoring a hole the size of a continent – huge by planetary standards, big enough to hide a fleet of Daleks in, but minuscule on a stellar scale. *That* was where they were hiding.

Clever. They were getting cleverer all the time.

'There, sir,' Orlock said.

For all our vaunted foresight, I had not anticipated this.

I do not relish the death of my enemies, and it chilled me at the time to hear some lower crew members whoop across our shared communications. It is unbecoming – and seductive – when dealing with such a terrible enemy to take pleasure in destroying them. My reaction upon seeing the debris was more akin to my TARDIS's. They do not hate the Daleks. I believe, if such a thing is possible, that they weep for the marriage of flesh and metal the Daleks have created, and the potential of such a symbiosis.

No such symbiosis was possible now.

Something had come upon these Daleks like a storm, tearing through them so completely that not a single fragment of their casings was left. Something had eviscerated them, cracked them open like crustaceans, the soft creatures within mercilessly flung to the void. Each rubbery cycloptic tangle floated alone, stiff with interstellar frost.

And floating serenely within that nebula of shredded Dalek was a small blue box.

Picture again that battlefield on Gallifrey. The pocked earth. The ruined soil. Picture something that may have been handsome, may have been habitable, made monstrous by war. Know that those buried arrowheads will never be pulled free, that it will take a thousand years for anything to grow, and that some trace and fossil of the pain will linger forever.

'Ho, travellers,' the Renegade said. It was the first time I had seen that face.

Warrior. Doctor. President. Failure. This old man had more names than he had faces, and it did not redeem him any in the eyes of Gallifrey that the Daleks hated him more than all of us put together.

He stood, grainy on my central screen – or maybe that was simply exhaustion deepening the trenches on his war-ravaged face. His TARDIS was a dim cave, starred by flickering gold.

'They can't be true,' Orlock said behind me, quietly enough that my relay node would not transmit his words. I had patched in the other strike-force captains, but the ability to respond was mine and mine alone.

Orlock hovered behind me like a nursemaid, straining in his chair.

I raised an eyebrow at him.

'The stories, I mean. They can't be true.'

'Which ones?' I asked quietly.

'All of them,' Orlock said. 'I mean . . . look at it. It's a Type Forty. I'm surprised it's even airborne.'

'Is insulting the ship floating in a sea of dead Daleks considered a clever strategy?' the Renegade growled in a voice like a whetstone sharpening a blade. 'No wonder the war is going so well.'

Orlock flushed, and I leaned forward.

'Then this is your handiwork,' I said. 'You killed all these Daleks.'

I would have believed it. Old and creased and bent double with spite he may have been, in a barely running Type

40 that looked like an outhouse, but I would still have believed he had killed them all.

I had heard the stories too.

'No,' the Renegade said. 'Not these Daleks. This wasn't me.'

I didn't bother asking him why he was there, if that was true. Asking the Renegade anything was an exercise in futility; I had learned that from the High Council. He would arrive in his battered TARDIS to shore up beleaguered defences or pull off a devastating attack run or, most inexplicably, lead a defence of a world outside Time Lord space.

I had heard that, in the first months of the war, he had avoided conflict, only helping those non-combatants who had no means of escape. But something more than his face had changed in the last few months. Suddenly, like a sad, inverse echo of what was to come, defensive had become offensive, and a man who had once named himself Doctor had gone on the attack. Though the High Council sought to quell it, talk resounded around war rooms all across Gallifreyan space of missing Daleks, daring raids and the old Type 40 at the heart of it all.

There were darker rumours, too. Rumours that only approached the devastation I saw here. But if he wasn't responsible . . .

'I have to ask.' I was careful to ensure a neutral tone, aware that every other captain in the fleet was watching me. I had no desire to show support for someone who flouted our laws at this, a time of need. Loyalty to Gallifrey was all. 'If you did not do this, why are you here?'

There was soot on his jacket, darkening the greying tangle of his beard. I wondered if he had been in battle recently or had simply stopped noticing.

'Just stopping by,' he said.

I gave him a calm smile. 'With respect . . .' I said, navigating the pause where a *sir* might have been, 'it is a big universe. Are there civilians in this system you were helping to evacuate? Could we offer assistance?'

It was a jab. A calculated one. His mission to save civilians was well known.

His eyes narrowed. 'Nice try, commander. But no. I was brought here by a distress signal.'

Orlock spoke up. 'But there hasn't been any Time Lord activity in this system for –'

I shot Orlock a warning glance, as the Renegade smoothed his scarf down in irritation.

'Fourteen Level Three civilisations, eight Level Ones with potential to grow, and over eighteen billion different life-forms that have evolved specifically to live in a star system being abandoned by its sun. The creatures here have never known light – did you know that?' His face crinkled. 'Of course you didn't. Of course you don't. Time Lords aren't the only ones who can send distress signals.'

This time Orlock remembered his discipline, and looked to me to answer.

'So it was one of these races, these early creatures, that summoned you?'

The Renegade's lips split in a grim smile. 'You offered to help, yes?'

Lights blinked across my console, a hundred captains offering their silent condemnation of this man, this renegade who flouted everything we held dear at a time when it was being so casually despoiled.

I met the Renegade's gaze. 'Yes, I did.'

'Then follow me.'

There are deadly places in the universe. I do not mean the huge tracts of space from which life is absent, for those are many, even before the Time War left vast stretches of the universe inimical to existence. But there are areas where the cosmos has turned on itself, where the ancient forces of gravity and physics and heat have conspired against each other to create a reflection of a mythical hell.

The Gates of Elysium is such a place.

I struggle to describe it even now. The colours, migraine-bright and shifting, as photons struggle like flies in amber. The antimatter cascade unfolding from black space like a waterfall, a purling tongue of unspace that murders the very atoms for a hundred light years in every direction. Something had gouged reality here, by accident or a design as far above the Time Lords as we were above the rest of the universe, and now raw unmaking bled from the sore like pus.

There are no words. Not even in Old High Gallifreyan, a language built on a celestial scale. It looked . . . it looked like madness. Let us leave it at that.

And above it hung a space station.

'That's impossible,' Orlock said as we materialised, our sensors already shuddering at the unnatural sight. 'Antimatter *undoes* matter. That station should be destroyed. It can't just hang there!'

'Oh, right,' the Renegade said, across our relays. 'Well, that's that then. Good to know.'

Our chameleon circuits disguised us as shimmering patches of black space or curls of icy dust, but his Type 40 just floated there, defiant against a setting of utter cosmic chaos. I wasn't sure if its chameleon circuit was broken or whether it and its pilot were just stubborn.

'That's a Dalek station,' one of the scouts murmured unbidden over the comms. I had ordered them forward, their cloaking fields engaged. She was right – there was no mistaking that blunt, brutal architecture, that barbarous and aggressive design. It hung in space like a poisonous barb, fat with venom and arrogance, suspended impossibly over an infected wound in space.

'Doc–'

'Don't call me that!' the Renegade snapped, and for a moment I saw a terrible rage in his eyes, the rage that told me the only reason he had not killed those Daleks at Scaveline was because they had already been dead. 'That's not who I am.'

'I understand,' I said, surveying the glittering syringe of a space station. 'But the signal you received – the distress signal. This is what it was warning you about? This is the threat you came here to face?'

The Renegade was staring at his own screens. I could see the glow of the punctured universe in his eyes.

'Not exactly,' he said. 'Look. Look at the outline of the station. It's Dalek-made, yes, but look at the design. There's something different about it. Something alien. And the outline here – it's blurring, as if in flux.'

'Some kind of shield?' Orlock offered, and the Renegade's scowl deepened. I began to believe that he did not care very much for my lieutenant.

'Against antimatter? It would unmake the shield, and then unmake the thing making the shield. It's *anti*matter. It antis matter. Do you need me to speak more slowly, or do you think you should just stop talking entirely?'

All of this was said in a monotone, without the Renegade so much as taking his eyes off the screen. I wasn't sure if he was even aware he'd spoken. I ignored my lieutenant's glare to focus on the station itself. Staring at the gates pained me in a way that I was not entirely sure was physical. We Time Lords believe ourselves custodians, guardians of the cosmos. It is hard to see the universe tearing itself apart.

'The signal,' I said. 'Where did it come from? You followed it here. Was it left by whatever killed the Daleks? Have they come here to finish the job?'

And should we be assisting? I didn't say it, but I knew the Renegade understood.

'I'm approaching the station.'

'In a Type Forty?' Orlock said, and the Renegade gave him a withering glance before shutting down his comms.

I turned to my crew, knowing as I did so that on ninety-nine other TARDISes across the fleet captains were waiting for my word. And, just then, my personal comms crackled. To this day, I have no idea how he found my command channel.

'What do they tell you,' he said, in a voice only I could hear, 'in the Academy? After they show you the Schism – that horrible maelstrom of infinite moments, everything that ever can and ever will exist – and then put the controls of a TARDIS in your hand?'

He knew. He knew that. Every cadet did.

'There is only today,' I said. 'Orlock. Take us in.'

We approached the wound in space. Communications flurried as I gathered half the TARDISes into a war formation – an arrowhead of ships with shields extended, ready to burst apart like shrapnel into a dozen different time periods – and spun the rest out in a loose cluster between one second and the next, that tiny sliver between future and present.

Weapons were readied: chronal torpedoes, chronic tripwires, ghost clusters and parallel beams and living weapons that thought for themselves, and it was almost enough to make you believe in Time Lord superiority again.

They should have attacked us. They should have swarmed like wasps from a kicked nest. We advanced, and my scanners began to pick out individual Daleks – a hundred thousand, more – looping round the station in glittering lines.

Some screens gave us the whole fleet – the massed, teeming horror of it, like a river, like a flood – and others magnified so that each and every mechanical monstrosity could be seen.

I had TARDIS captains in my ear.

'Sir, these are not the fleet we were targeting –'

'Reading weapons discharge. No targets –'

'They're just firing randomly, sir –'

Shots began to crackle over our shields, but the captains were right. It was sporadic, an afterthought. A hundred TARDISes flitting down upon them should have been the delight of their black little hearts. A chance to kill, to rage, to show that hard-wired, gene-bred allegiance to Emperor and hatred. Instead, they shook and scattered and emptied their weapons at the airless void.

'Renegade,' I snapped, and it dawned on me that I already knew the answer to my question before I had asked it. 'What is this? Whose distress call are you answering?'

'Traitor,' Orlock snarled, and I heard a hundred other exhortations across the comms, though none of the ships pulled away from their advance. Discipline – something this old fool clearly lacked. Something he had never possessed. Anger gripped me then, unbecoming of my command.

'Have you brought us here to *save* Daleks? How dare you. How *dare* you –'

'Not Daleks,' the Renegade said, those pained old eyes flashing up on my screen. 'Not them. See the ship beyond the station?'

I had not. The Gates, that roiling pit of clashing realities, had hidden it from my scanners. The sheer interference from the waterfall of antimatter could hide a multitude of sins. *Perhaps*, I thought, *that is why they chose here.*

There *was* a ship, although it slipped in and out of my sensor nets with every moment. A Dalek command saucer: huge and round and bedecked with bulges of arcane equipment I had never seen before. That was where the pure hatred of the Daleks became weakness – they were slow to innovate with anything except cruelty, because they believed their own civilisation too pure.

This ship was Dalek, but it was also something else.

The Renegade's voice was quiet. 'I came for him.'

'Doctor. I dared not believe it.'

Had my comms not been connected to the Renegade's, we would not have heard it. Oozing like oil from a ruined machine, the words were for him alone. Each syllable seemed a great effort, as though throat and lungs were drowning, and although I could not see the speaker I recognised the voice. We all did.

'Davros,' the Renegade whispered. 'What have you done?'

And the station came apart.

It was not mechanical. No gears or pulleys or hinges could move so smoothly. It was more like the bursting apart of a flock of birds, a huge and singular shape now suddenly millions of fractured pieces, all swirling and swooping as if directed, like a black blizzard with a single mind. There was something of the jellyfish in its undulating, and something of the shoal, but before our eyes or sensors could even begin to track it Daleks began to die.

Thousands of them.

The blizzard split them. It peeled them. It disassembled them on a molecular scale. They shrieked as they fired – the horrific, horrified shriek of a Dalek denied the chance to kill – and then perished like sand before a tide.

'Pull back,' I snarled. 'Pull back!'

But it was too late. The razor wind twisted in on itself and flurried around one of our forward scouts. The TARDIS's shields flung it back in an orb of blinding light, but that only drew more of the swarm, like ants detecting prey. The shields pulsed again, weaker this time, and then abruptly cut out beneath the heaving weight of a million glittering shards.

It was not the first time I had heard a TARDIS die, but that was the moment I learned that they could scream.

'Scatter!' I roared, and the TARDISes flung themselves back and away, as much with horror as from their training.

Still that battered old Type 40 advanced, weaving its way through the jerking, squirming horde of Daleks that sought to somehow defeat the annihilating cloud.

'Davros!' the Renegade yelled. 'What is this?'

That lone saucer, that single ship, just hung there, between the antimatter cascade and the voracious cloud. Daleks died. TARDISes died. And that voice came again, wet with madness and glee.

'*My triumph. My undoing. The Dalek Emperor promised me acceptance. He promised me a legion of my own. If I would . . . if I would . . .*'

Now we were in it too – dipping and soaring through a chaos of Daleks and this abomination. Our screens were a turmoil of weapons discharge and dying ships, our sensors struggling to make sense of the *thing*. There were recognisable glints of Dalek tech – their nano-conversion swarms, their dalekanium hulls – but it morphed and fluxed too fast for our scanners to read. It felt . . . alive.

'*It's a Dalek,*' Davros said dreamily. '*I made a new Dalek.*'

'*Focus*, you lunatic,' the Renegade said, desperation shivering through his voice. 'I came. I shouldn't have, but I did. I don't know if I came to help, or to watch you die, or to

kill you myself, but I *came*. Now tell me what's happening.'
Frustration bled from his voice, as poisonous as the antimatter
seething below. 'You've *always* done this, Davros. You built a
race that can only hate, you wired them so that anything un-
Dalek is impure, and then you've spent the last thousand
years desperately trying to get them to love you. You *idiot*. You
can try all you want, but they're not capable of revering
anything but themselves.'

'*Yes, Doctor,*' the clotted voice purred. '*The lot of the renegade.*'

'*Stop calling me that!*'

Daleks screamed their insectile, mechanical screams as
particles cracked lenses and poured down eye-stalks, splitting
them open like wasps in fruit.

'*But it's true, Doctor. You are my inspiration. The Emperor is
fascinated by you – the Time Lord who reviles the Time Lords, yet goes
to any length to save them. Loyal deeds without loyalty. You break all of
their rules, and that gives you power.*'

'Oh,' the Renegade said. 'Oh *no.*'

'*Oh yes. It pained me to do so, but I did it. There are Daleks who
can think independently, but always, always they are wired to revere
Dalek-kind, to acknowledge our perfection, and in doing so be unchanged.*'

A Type 93 TARDIS died in torment, gnawed to its
bones in a single instant. Its crew spun out into the void
before they were devoured as well.

'*So I built one that had no such strictures in place.*'

'Commander,' the Renegade said quietly. There was horror on his face. I had never seen horror on his face before. 'I want you to retune your communications to the Daleks' wavelength. Transmitting instructions now.'

'Why –'

'Just do it. Please.'

'*EXTERMINATE!*'

'*THIS IS DALEK CAAN. LORD DAVROS MUST RETREAT!*'

'*THE RENEGADE WILL BE DESTROYED. THE RENEGADE WILL BE DESTROYED!*'

And beneath their banal threats, their exhortations of violence, was a sound. A sound so low that it distorted the signal, like something gargantuan breaking the surface of the sea.

A scream. An abysmal, abyssal scream.

'*It is aware,*' Davros said, with terrible pride. '*It is wired with all the beautiful hatred of my children, but with no reverence towards its own form. It is entirely aware of the flaws of its race, so that it may evolve, and improve them.*'

'It's killing them,' the Renegade countered. 'That's what it's doing.'

'*I crafted it a body,*' Davros said. '*A perfect Dalek body, which it rejected with horror and scorn. Then it got into our systems, devouring* those of use and discarding those with none. We have been hunting it for weeks, and now I have driven it to ground.'

The lull in the war. Dalekanium in its body. The nano-swarms. Those Daleks in the Scaveline system had not been killed.

They'd been eaten.

'*It needs food*,' Davros whispered. '*It's a growing boy.*'

'And that's why you brought me here,' the Renegade said between clenched teeth. 'You can't control it. So you need me to stop it. Or . . . save it. It's your child. You made it. You want me to –'

'*Oh no, Doctor.*' Davros cackled. '*I just came here to make you watch.*'

And the saucer began to move. Slowly at first, then faster and faster, that arcane equipment unfolding wide. Crackling lines of energy began to dance round its edges, then out from it like a fest-day sparkler, then the legs of some electric spider ten miles across. Daleks whirled and died and lashed out at the cloud of nano-particles devouring them, and TARDISes died too as they fled.

And I hung there, my own crew shouting in my ears, demanding orders, weeping at the slain, and I suddenly realised that this is what it must be like to not be a Time Lord. This is what it must be like to be a lower race, like children, helpless and ignored before beings far beyond them. This is what it is like to be ground between the hatred of the great.

'Sir!' Orlock was shouting. 'Sir, what do we do?'

Davros's command ship was a blur now, and the abomination sent glittering tendrils out to escape, to feed, to multiply, but jags and strikes of lightning from the ship stung it back. He was herding it. He was pushing it back, the way a trainer would a lynx.

'Davros!' the Renegade cried. 'Don't do this!'

'I do it with pleasure, Doctor. Left alive, it will eat all my children – my true children. It will never stop. I tried to contain it, but it outpaces me at every turn. It is rather like fighting you, Doctor. It made me . . . nostalgic for your company.'

My strike-force, what remained of it, was making for deep space, abandoning this hellish system and the monstrosities at its core. Davros's ship was fending off the wretched creature, spinning a crackling wall of light thousands of kilometres across, but I could see it bending and breaking in places as this nightmare thing pushed through.

It would not be stopped. It would grow, and dissect, and feed on the whole universe before it was done.

Its hate relentless.

Its victory assured.

And not even that would bring it peace.

'Then why bring me here?' The Doctor was pleading now. Actually pleading, with the wretched being who had doomed the universe to a war unending and now signed its death-warrant outright. His TARDIS bobbed and weaved between the dancing lights, but could get no closer without being consumed.

'What is that old Earth legend?' The blurring, spinning ship lurched into motion, and I suddenly realised what Davros's plan was, why the station and this *thing* had been brought into existence at the Gates of Elysium, above a roiling vortex of the most destructive substance in creation, a substance that would unmake anything it touched. *'Two wise men and the birth of a child . . .'*

'That was always your problem, Davros,' the Renegade whispered. 'You're just not as smart as you think you are. It's *three* wise men. And you are a fool if you think I'm going to stand and watch you die.'

'I will not let it go free, Doctor. What kind of being would let their people die?'

'Drop your shields. I can bypass the cloud, materialise aboard –'

'No!'

He needed saving. I could see it, as plain as day. Davros's ship had ground to a halt, as the abomination – the *child* – pushed back, a hurricane of hunger with a waterfall of unmaking at its back.

As the Renegade howled at his mortal foe and the cackling scientist prepared to sacrifice his life for the children that would never care, I reached down to the controls and committed my own atrocity.

This would not stop. Renegades won wars when rules and law had died, and Davros was in his way a renegade too. The Daleks had come to him before, and would come to him again, hating him but never themselves, and sooner or later he would create something that would rival a Time Lord themself.

Again.

It's three wise men.

I activated my TARDIS's tractor beams, and held the Doctor in place.

'WHAT ARE YOU DOING?'

'*Goodbye, Doctor.*' He sounded calm now. Cool. Logical. A shade of the leader he had been. '*My nightmare is over. I fear yours is just beginning.*'

Screams from the Daleks. Roars from the cascade. The crackle and seethe of tearing space, and then Davros –

madman, inventor, genius – flew into the jaws of oblivion, taking his Nightmare Child with him.

'You had no right.'

'I had every right.' My voice was steady. Why wouldn't it be? I had seventy-five Battle TARDISes at my back, and he a decrepit old Type 40 that even now struggled against the void.

We hung in the black space above where the Gates of Elysium had once stood. The antimatter cascade, that thunderous outpouring of poisonous light, had closed, as if something had caught in its throat. I had visions of the creature within trying to claw its way out, and hoped that the constant unmaking field of the rift would hold it there forever.

'He could have . . . He was a *man*, commander.' The Renegade's face was pale on my screen. There could have been tears on his cheeks; in a face that lined and scarred, it was hard to tell. 'He was intelligent. He could have been . . .'

'What?' I countered calmly. I could feel my crew's eyes on me, and the surviving captains listening to my every word. 'Saved? Redeemed? Tell that to the billion billion other Daleks out there who tolerated him as a useful weapon when the time was right. And look at what that weapon nearly did.'

'He sacrificed himself,' the old man said. 'He gave his life rather than see his people destroyed.'

'After creating the means of their destruction,' I said. 'I made my choice. As we all must do in times of war.' My voice did not shake. I took great pains to make it so.

'I will not forget it,' the Renegade said coldly, and his TARDIS slipped away, a blue flash against time.

It would not be the last time we saw each other. There was the fall of Arcadia, and the Hellion Blaze, and that last day, that most awful day, when I stood, a General, as Gallifrey began to fall.

I never forgot the joy in Davros's voice as he saved his people.

What kind of being would let their people die?

As I say, it was the first year of the Time War. We were not to know what would come.

JUDOON

THE RHINO
OF TWENTY-THREE
STRAND STREET

'There's a rhino in Mrs McCarthy's garden.'

Patricia Kiernan didn't say it because she thought anyone was listening; people didn't listen to Patricia, as a rule.

There were two reasons for this. The first was that, while her father always announced the fact he was about to speak by snorting manfully and clearing his nasal passages like a dedicated player of the tuba, Patricia didn't start conversations because she'd never finished one. She'd begun talking at six months old and continued pretty much without interruption, a constant stream of observations, ideas and facts that washed around the Kiernan home like the background hum of a radiator – sometimes welcome but mostly ignored.

The second reason was that Patricia was ten.

'There's a rhino in Mrs McCarthy's garden,' she said again. The snow was coming down thick and fast outside, and her mam was darting between saucepans and her brother was begging Dad for a go of the record player and there was a rhino snuffling at Mrs McCarthy's holly wreath. Holly was poisonous – Patricia had read that. Mrs McCarthy had a bush in her back garden. Dad had been trying to convince Mrs McCarthy to get rid of it, but then she'd gone and died, which Dad said was exactly the kind of thing the woman would do just to win an argument.

It hadn't been holly that had killed Mrs McCarthy. She'd been old – very old, so wrinkled that her eyes disappeared fully when she smiled, which was pretty much constantly. She would have smiled at seeing the rhino, Patricia thought. Patricia had grown up in Mrs McCarthy's shabby living room as much as in her own house, and had once heard the old lady say that she loved surprises at Christmas, 'but the more Christmases you see the harder surprise is to find'.

The rhino, Patricia felt, would have qualified.

Rhinos lived on the African savannah, which was hot and flat and not quite a desert, and they lived in Sumatra and India and Java. They were megafauna, which meant they were not just animals but *large* animals, sometimes up to a ton in weight, and they were endangered because some people thought their horns were magic, which further darkened Patricia's already low opinion of magic.

(Patricia did not believe in magic, or wizards, or fate. She did believe everything happened for a reason, but she believed that reason was physics.)

There were only a few rhinos left, and they said that by the year 2000 there might be none. Patricia knew there were only a few places in the world where you could find rhinos, and nothing in any of the books she had read said that one of those places was a back garden in an Irish suburb a week before Christmas in 1966 – but, by the looks of it, this rhino didn't seem to mind.

'Dinner,' her mother said, and Patricia automatically clambered into position. The Kiernan house was so small that the chairs had to be pulled out from under the table in a specific order or nobody could get in from the living room, and Patricia, being the smallest, had to scramble round everyone else so that the system would work.

By the time she managed to get back to the window, the rhino was gone.

The nuns didn't teach zoology at Lakelands Convent School. It wasn't something girls needed. Girls needed language classes. They needed sewing lessons. They needed religion most of all, according to the Mother Superior, because sins were always waiting – legions of them, hidden like trapdoors in everyday life. There was a long list of sins, read out every morning at Mass. Some of them Patricia had to look up.

But the children who attended that grim, cabbagey-smelling school had developed an interest in zoology all the same, because it was essential when it came to dealing with nuns. The nuns wafted down the corridors, stark and white and terrifying as swans, all with different predilections (a word that meant habits).

There was Sister Jacinta's halitosis (a word that meant bad breath), Sister Miriam's inhuman aim with bits of chalk and Sister Victoria's tradition of telling the girls which of them she thought did and didn't have futures. When it came to surprise megafauna, however, there was only really one nun you could ask.

'Sister Agnes, what do you know about rhinos?'

Sister Agnes was stout and small, her face flushed as a new apple. There was a stretched shininess to her cheeks, as if they were unable to keep all that personality inside. 'I wager,' she said, with the lilting Cork accent that made every sentence a poem, 'less than you, Miss Kiernan. You've read all of our books on animals, I believe.'

Bragging was a sin.

'Yes, Sister Agnes.'

'And you still have questions?'

'Yes, Sister. Just a couple, Sister.'

'Well, the Lord admires an inquisitive mind,' Sister Agnes said, which to Patricia seemed to directly contradict quite a few of the Mother Superior's sermons, but maybe nuns were allowed to disagree.

She forged ahead. 'Rhinos live in the savannah, don't they?'

'I believe so,' Sister Agnes said. 'In Africa, anyway. I'm not sure of the exact address.'

This was a joke.

'And there haven't been any . . .'

'Any what?'

Escaped zoo rhinos. Rhino exchange programmes. Rhino sanctuaries in Ringsend. Lying was a sin, and so was keeping secrets, but until Patricia knew exactly what she was supposed to be saying, until she knew exactly what the situation was, telling anyone would also be lying.

Sister Victoria looked at the kids like she knew every bad word they'd ever said. The Mother Superior's stare could strip paint. But Sister Agnes looked as if she couldn't just see the thoughts inside children's heads but, uniquely for a nun, as if she understood them too.

'Patricia?'

'Nothing, Sister. Never mind.'

She took the long way home, skirting Sandymount Strand where Dublin fell away into the iron-grey sea, and the skeletal, fenced-off construction site where the Poolbeg towers were promised to rise, and everywhere she could she collected plants; colt's foot and yellow Alexander and wiry strands of beach reeds, until her bag was bulging with yellow and green. Rhinos ate almost constantly, and pickings were slim in Dublin in December, so she took everything she could. Maybe beach reeds were delicious to rhinos? She hadn't been able to find a definitive answer in any of her books. This was what Patricia's burgeoning scientific sensibilities thought of as the 'experimental' phase.

The last ingredient came from her kitchen, and for once Patricia was glad of being invisible – skinny and pale, just a slip of a thing with a crescent fringe and a gap in her smile. Technically she knew the satsumas in the kitchen were for their Christmas stockings, so she only took one and assumed the other would go to her brother, and then she was back out on the street.

It wasn't breaking in, Patricia told herself to quiet the nun in her head. She had her mother's key, orphaned from the fat set in the hall because Mam didn't quite know what to do with it and got a little weepy when Dad asked. Mrs

McCarthy didn't have any family. What happened to houses when nobody was there to claim them?

The house itself looked unworried about its precarious future – just another one-storey cottage huddling up against the others on the street. That didn't sit right with Patricia's ordered mind. She knew that physics meant that the world was always changing, even if we didn't see it, but the house looked exactly as it had when Mrs McCarthy was alive.

It felt disrespectful.

Patricia took a deep breath, opened the gate and stepped up to the door.

That was when everything changed.

Something swept over her, scudding and popping along her skin as if she'd just stepped through a soap bubble. It tickled like the precious cans of fizzy orange they were allowed on special occasions. Her ears went *gloing gloing*, the way they did when she was swimming, and all sound from the city outside seemed to stop.

It wasn't scary. That was her first thought. It didn't hurt and wasn't like anything she'd ever felt before, so she wasn't at all frightened by it. It was just . . . odd.

But then she looked up at the house, and *then* she was frightened, because something had come down through Mrs McCarthy's roof like a foot through a doll's house. It had torn a hole wider than she was tall, and impacted so hard that slates had popped free from the roof and cracks had spread down through the walls. The whole house looked *squeezed*, the brick puckering out a little the way cheese did in a sandwich that had been in her bag all day.

Slowly and carefully, Patricia backtracked through the bubble. Standing in the street, Mrs McCarthy's looked completely normal. No hole, no cracks. Standing in the street, she could hear cars and birds and Aunt Carol (who hated the Brits and put brown sauce in her tea).

She stepped into the bubble again – *Pop! Fizz!* – and spent a couple of minutes taking down notes in her copybook.

> There is a bubble round Mrs McCarthy's house.
> ~~It is hiding what is inside.~~ It is showing a different version of the house. Like TV.
> There's snow on the house when you're inside the bubble.
> No snow when you're outside it. Maybe the image is old?
> The image is hiding a hole in the roof.
> The sides of the hole are all glassy and burnt, like the thing that broke in was hot.

She took notes because that was what scientists did, and not because she was trying to work up the nerve to go through the door. That was the other thing scientists did: they discovered. A scientist would go into the house.

Mrs McCarthy's hallway was at once exactly and nothing like the way she remembered it. The pictures of Jesus and the Pope and Padre Pio were still all present, but they'd hopped off their frames. Huge cracks ran down the walls. The carpet was all churned and torn. It even smelled different – the warm apple smell that had always been there was squeezed out, along with the architecture, to make way for a muskier, earthier smell. It wasn't bad, exactly, just *big* – a smell she had to breathe around rather than through.

The rhino was in the sitting room.

It was definitely a rhino, now that she could see it up close. Nothing else had that huge slab of head, those strangely delicate, flicking ears, and nothing else had that horn – that magic horn, the horn that got them into trouble. She could tell it was a rhino, though its arms and legs seemed almost human-long, wrapped in some kind of silvery fabric, and she could tell that it was young (though its face was just as wrinkled as Mrs McCarthy's had been) and she could tell that it was sick, because it was on its side and its breath was coming in wheezing gasps.

'The holly,' she whispered, and then its liquid eyes rolled to her.

'No, no! Wait!' she yelped, but it had already panicked, staggering to its feet, its too-long forelimbs wrapped round its stomach. Only years of living in a small house with a large and inattentive father saved her from being crushed, because there was not a lot of room and quite a lot of rhino. It was shorter than her but far wider and, as she ducked the massive swerve of a shoulder, all she could think was that many, many more people killed rhinos than the other way round, and maybe this rhino also knew that and wasn't happy about it.

'Wait!' she said again, skidding on a pile of what had to be vomit and landing hard against the wall.

The rhino stomped into a turn, looking at her with first one eye, then the other.

'I brought food. I brought –'

A great, dragging snort then that would have reminded her of her father had she not been so afraid. It wasn't even up to her shoulder, but it was nearly as wide as her dad, and terribly, terribly strong. Most of Mrs McCarthy's furniture had been smashed to flinders and arranged in some kind of nest, and she could see splinters sticking to its silvery covering from where it had rearranged the house around itself.

With its great head lowered, it sniffed again. *Respect.* That was what professional zoologists said: you had to respect animals and they would respect you.

'Satsuma,' she whispered, and held it up.

The rhino lurched away, spooked at the sound of
her voice, and she winced as more pictures were ground
under its lumpen feet. There was something strange about
them, but it was hard to see with its massive head in
her face.

Rhinos always looked grumpy. It was how their faces
were made. They were like nuns in that respect. But when it
stopped again and stared at the satsuma, glowing in her palm
like a little chunk of sun in the cold December gloom, it
looked hungry as well.

'Of course,' she whispered. 'You've been sick. You're
probably starving. Would you like it?'

Her hand inched forward. Its head did too, and slowly,
very slowly, arms still wrapped around its stomach as if in
terrible pain, it turned to bite the satsuma from her palm. She
felt the fruit pop, and juice suddenly baptised her fingers,
sticky and sweet.

'There,' she said gently, as its throat worked. 'That's
good, isn't it?'

The rhino flinched back, its eyes fixed on hers – brown
as almonds, somehow bright and dark all at once . . .

Animals were smart. It was why Patricia had never asked
her parents for a pet, even though she wanted one so much it

was an ache in her chest. She wanted something she could love and look after, but she lived in a little house that was cramped already and she couldn't bear the thought of letting the pet down. The Mother Superior said that people had been put above animals and it was their job to serve us, but as far as Patricia could see the only difference was that people had voices and animals didn't, and so someone had to look after them.

And fair enough, the rhino was twice her width, but it was still afraid, and just like that it was Patricia's job to make sure it wasn't any more.

Slowly, she opened the bag at her feet and tipped out all of the plants she'd collected. She didn't want to rush things. The rhino had a lot to think about, and so did she.

'I'll come back tomorrow,' she said. The rhino was caught between warily watching her and staring with undisguised longing at the greenery on the ground. 'It was nice to meet you.'

'Miss Kiernan.'

All the other girls had left. The snow flurried against the windows and Sister Agnes had her arms folded, her eyebrows in what the staffroom had already begun to call 'the Patricia position'.

'Miss Kiernan, it's lunchtime.'

Without taking her eyes from her work, the little girl withdrew a flattened cheese sandwich from her bag and took a purposeful bite.

'Patricia, I appreciate your curiosity . . .' *Though others won't,* Sister Agnes thought, *and eventually quiet little Patricia is going to get noticed.*

Some of the other sisters thought it was a waste letting the girls have a library at all. Sister Victoria, who thought herself a poet despite lacking the empathy God gave a whelk, said that there was a cruelty in it, like putting a caged bird in a place where they could see the sky. But Sister Agnes didn't think like that, because it wasn't a teacher's job to decide what was good and what was bad. It was, technically, a nun's job, but that was why she had decided a long time ago that she'd rather be a bad nun and a good teacher instead.

'Patricia, what are you doing?'

'Research.'

Unfortunately, research had provided Patricia with more questions than answers. This initially did not bother her. That was what science was all about – learning the connections, figuring out how much you didn't know.

Certain facts had proved easy. She'd learned not to bring branches because, while black rhinos had beaky lips that allowed them to eat hard things, white rhinos had soft, square mouths, and apparently Ringsend rhinos did too. She wrote in her notebook:

Are you a white rhino?

She'd learned rhinos could live up to five days without water as long as they were getting greens, but she'd filled a bath up anyway and the rhino had cautiously drank. She'd even brought a bucket of mud, being careful not to ruin her uniform, because rhinos had thin skins and liked to armour themselves with muck.

But there were . . . inconsistencies between the Ringsend rhino and the rhinos in her books; inconsistencies that the books didn't seem to be able to explain. Its silvery clothes, for one – wrapping limbs long enough that its walk was more of a primate tramp than the waddle she'd seen in the rhinos at Dublin Zoo. It walked like a person, or nearly like a person, or more like a person than a rhino should.

And it had hands. That was the main difference. She hadn't noticed the first time she'd been there because it had been clutching its stomach, but now they dangled at the ends of its arms: thick, blunt and four-fingered, but definitely, actually hands.

'What are you?' Patricia whispered as she dumped out more grass. 'You're behind some kind of . . . hologram.' She'd picked up the word from a science-fiction show on television, which didn't feel very scientific, but it was better than nothing. She'd examined the bubble as much as she was able to without being the girl standing on the street staring at an empty house, and it seemed to just be a veil, like a painted backdrop hiding the reality underneath.

'Did you put that up? Are you . . .' She didn't want to say 'are you smart', because that seemed rude, but there were so many things here that made so little sense that she could only focus on one at a time.

Patricia had narrowed it down to three questions.

1. What are you?
2. How are you hiding the house?
3. Where are you from?

Unfortunately, the rhino wasn't talking. They had made some progress. It no longer retreated to a corner when she spoke; instead, it just sat there in the remains of Mrs McCarthy's chair, pushing reeds around the floor the way a kid might spaghetti. Once, she had patted it, and she'd thought it had nuzzled a little into her hand, but it might have just been hoping for more satsumas.

'Are you from Africa? The savannah? South Africa? Kenya?'

She was trying to be specific. Mostly because she was Patricia, but also because the nuns talked about Africa like it was a street, and they talked about 'the problems over there' like the whole continent was an aunt who kept coming over to borrow sugar. Only when she was safe behind the bubble did Patricia let herself think about the fact that she knew Africa had more than forty different countries and 2,000 languages and that if they did have problems it was probably the fault of the people who kept coming over and trying to tell them what to do.

A little part of Patricia understood that at some point she was probably going to get into trouble. Not because of the rhino – though yes, maybe – but just for being Patricia. She was small and she was well behaved, but sometimes she could feel the things she read filling her up and making her bigger, and eventually, like a rhino in a living room, something would get broken. It was a lonely feeling.

Maybe that was why she talked to the rhino so much.

Patricia wasn't surprised the rhino was a little standoffish. She had trouble understanding the people around her, and they were the same species. This creature – this shambling riddle with its almost-human form and huge, animal head – must have felt even lonelier than she did.

'Where are you from? Did you do this bubble thing? Do you know where you are now?'

One of those lumpish, thick hands reached down and picked up a reed, and then tipped over the pail of mud. Patricia yelped, jumping backwards as gritty water splashed over her uniform, staining the pristine white a dark and dirty grey. Her cheeks burned red; Mam had enough washing to do, and her dad would be so angry and –

The rhino just stared at the floor, the reed still clutched in its hand.

'Why did you do that?' she snapped. 'I'm already in trouble for getting caught stealing Mr Reilly's tulip bulbs, which I did *for you*, and now I . . . I . . .'

The reed scratched its way across the drying mud, as if the animal was ashamed, and Patricia trailed off, feeling abruptly bad. And then she realized. It wasn't ashamed. It was drawing.

Circle after circle after circle. Nine in all, some small and some big, and for a second Patricia thought it was writing in some sort of language, even though of *course* that was silly. It stared at her with its deep-set eyes, then ended the row of circles with a curved line so large it could have swallowed all the others, and that was when Patricia realised the truth was far more ridiculous.

Nine circles, then a huge one.

Deliberately, the rhino stabbed the third circle along.

Do you know where you are now?

It was answering her question.

The circles were the planets of the solar system. It was pointing at Earth.

It was time to tell a nun.

Rhinos were one thing. Rhinos with hands and clever, wounded eyes were another. But a rhino with hands and clever, wounded eyes who knew where it was in the solar system and was hiding behind what Patricia thought might be a hologram?

Sister Agnes would know what to do.

She'd thought about telling her parents, but she was afraid her dad would laugh at her the way he had when she'd asked him for a Young Scientist Kit!™. Mam had said she couldn't have one because they were saving to send her brother to technical school, but that didn't explain to Patricia at all why her wanting a science kit would be funny.

No. It had to be Sister Agnes.

Patricia pushed open the school's thick glass doors, for once not wrinkling her nose at the cabbage smell. It was after school, but most of the nuns lived at Lakelands as well as taught there, and sometimes there were meetings in the evening, presumably about sin.

Sister Agnes wasn't in her room. There was nobody in the staffroom either. Wandering the corridors, Patricia began to confront the fact that maybe her classmate Maebh hadn't been wrong about the nuns hanging upside down to sleep in the closets like bats. Finally, out of sheer desperation, she climbed the cold stone stairs to the Mother Superior's office, hoping she might meet Sister Agnes on the way.

Voices were drifting down the stairwell.

'I really don't see what the problem is.'

Sister Agnes. Patricia froze, her hand on the bannister.

'The problem, *Sister,* is that she will get herself into trouble. The smart ones always do.'

There was an arch and terrible fury to the Mother Superior's voice, an arctic, ever-present wrath at the world and all its failures, whether she was addressing 200 frightened girls or thanking the postman. It was why, despite every Sunday sermon, Patricia imagined hell as cold instead of hot.

'That's not –'

'It is, Agnes. You know it is. We've seen it time and time again. I already have her father on to me, saying that we're giving her notions with all these books. It's a disservice to her. Sister Victoria is right – songbirds shouldn't look at the sky. You'll leave her discontented with her lot, and you know where that leads.'

'Miss Kiernan is a very bright girl!'

Patricia went cold.

'That's the problem,' the Mother Superior said icily. 'All those books. Botany. Zoology. *Physics*. These are not the things with which a girl should be concerning herself. She's been going around taking flower cuttings. Did you know that? Making a nuisance of herself. She doesn't know her place, Agnes. And girls who don't know their place get themselves into trouble.'

'I just want her to be herself.'

'Why?'

A gasp. A tiny, shocked intake of breath.

'This is what happens, Agnes. We are not raising little girls to be bright. Bright girls get noticed. Bright girls get into trouble. Bright girls get taken away. There are institutions up and down the country full of bright girls, Agnes, and no one will appreciate bright little Patricia Kiernan. I can already see it. The way the other girls think of her –'

Patricia's cheeks were burning. There was a prickling in her eyes. Her heart was hammering so hard in her chest that she was afraid the nuns would hear it. She'd never really paid any attention to the other girls – they were confusing, and books were not. She'd never thought about whether they were paying attention to her.

The Mother Superior had laid her little life out so neatly, like a mouse for dissection, and Patricia just stood there listening, a tiny thing underfoot.

There was another list in her head. One she felt bad for keeping, but she did. All the jokes her dad made. The way her stomach felt when they talked about her brother going on to college – *college*, when he had only gone to school because otherwise the nuns would come looking for him – and about Patricia getting married. Not married *to* anyone, just married, like someone handing off a parcel.

And, underneath it all, the sudden fear. *Bright girls get taken away*. It happened. She knew it did, though the what and where was kept from her, and that just frightened her more. Mam and Aunt Carol talked about it sometimes, and sometimes they were angry about it and sometimes they were afraid too.

Sister Agnes's voice was subdued. 'I just wanted to give her a chance to not end up at the kitchen sink.'

'But that is where she's heading,' the Mother Superior said, and now her voice was gentle. 'The sooner she realises that, the better.'

Patricia had read thirty-three books where children ran away. She could recite the formula like a gospel. You went to bed dressed, and carried your shoes so nobody could hear you. You packed a torch, and sandwiches, and maybe a flask of tea, and just before you slipped out of the door you turned round and whispered 'Goodnight' to your family, because it was poignant.

Patricia did none of those things, because she shared a room with her brother and he would have noticed her being dressed in bed, and had she touched the food in the kitchen her mam would have said, 'Was your dinner not enough?' and she didn't stop at her doorway to turn round and be poignant because – and this made her blink tears from her eyes – her dad would consider poignancy notions (a word that meant airs and graces, and was very close to a mortal sin).

Instead, she just did what she assumed normal runaways did, which was hide awake and terrified behind her closed eyelids until 2 a.m., and then she got up to go to the bathroom and didn't come back. Her schoolbag was by the door, and she threw a coat on over her pyjamas and put a whole bag of satsumas into her pockets and then she ghosted out of the door.

Running away at Christmas should have been especially poignant, but in reality it was just cold. Thinking of that supposedly special day with Mass and lectures and getting an itchy dress instead of a science kit just made Patricia feel colder.

The night and the snow combined in a strange alchemy, turning the street she knew into something completely different: bigger, the spaces between the houses deeper, the streetlights only seeming to darken the darkness to a cold and vicious black.

The now-familiar fizz washed over her, and for a moment she thought that they could just stay there, living in a different-but-the-same world. But rhinos were hungry and she'd have to forage, and eventually someone would come to claim the house.

Too big. Too bright. Neither one of them fit the world any more.

'We're going to leave,' she said as soon as she entered the sitting room. The rhino eyed her suspiciously, until she withdrew a satsuma from her pocket, and then its look turned to suspicious hunger. 'Do you understand?'

Zoologists and respect, and it was the same in the books Patricia had read about girls befriending animals too. Usually by now there was supposed to be a bond between them, a kind of mutual respect, but so far all the rhino seemed to respect was the fact that she could produce satsumas. She'd brought it paper and pens in case it wanted to draw again, and even an encyclopaedia so it could learn about the world, but it hadn't so much as cracked the spine. She hadn't even got to fall asleep against its side or have a moment of shared danger or anything.

That was fine by her. Patricia was beginning to realise she preferred non-fiction.

'I've brought my dad's coat –' which was *not* revenge for his jokes, obviously – 'and I've made a list of hiding places. We can use one a night, until we get out of Dublin.'

The rhino sniffed, and turned away, folding its arms.

'We can't stay *here*,' she said. 'Neither of us. You have to listen.'

It just stared at the wall, and Patricia felt the anger building, buoyed up by all the knowledge inside her, the secret fact lurking underneath everything she had learned: that the world was unfair, and just physics, and all she had to do to fit into it was stop being herself. She could just say her prayers, and be good, and not get into trouble; so far looking after an ungrateful rhino had just got her scratched and muddy and looked down on, and wasn't she only going to end up at the kitchen sink anyway?

But that is where she's heading.

The Mother Superior's words wrapped round her like chains, like the bars of a cage, and she looked up to stop the tears from falling out. The hole in the roof was still there, the stars glittering beyond, and the rhino was staring up at them too – a trapped little thing looking at the sky.

The words sank through Patricia and, like a meteor entering the atmosphere, caught fire and came apart. Sometimes you didn't have to give respect to get it. Sometimes it had to be took.

'No,' she said, and the rhino's ears pricked up. 'We're not giving up. We're not staying here. The world is . . . the world is changing all the –'

There was a knock at the door.

A chill burned through Patricia's veins, driven hard by her analytical heart. It wasn't the thought of the Gardaí. It wasn't the thought of nuns. It was the sudden and scientific knowledge that for someone to have knocked on the door they had to be inside the bubble. And they had knocked anyway. Jauntily. As if they had all the time in the world.

That scared Patricia more than anything.

'Hello?'

The voice was female, but more importantly it was English. There were different English accents. Patricia knew that from the radio. This wasn't the glacial, precise English accent she had heard from politicians – every syllable smooth and sharp like a dentist's tools – but it was English all the same. English meant police. It meant government. It meant trouble, and suddenly what *else* the Mother Superior had said sent terror down Patricia's spine.

Bright girls get taken away.

She had to assume the same went for rhinos.

Moving faster than she had ever seen, the rhino reached out and grabbed her round the waist, lifting her as if she weighed nothing at all. Patricia let out a squeak as it dropped its head and *charged*.

Glass, and noise, and confusion, and by the time the world stopped whirling Patricia realised they were outside. The rhino had flung itself – and her – through the living-room window, and now it was running – properly running, dragging her off her feet with its incredible strength. She had a bouncing, jolting moment to see Mrs McCarthy's house: the bubble was gone, its destruction revealed, and a woman was standing at the door, her face bright with shock.

A sign gleamed from the shadows behind her. It said POLICE.

'Run,' Patricia whispered. *'Run!'*

*

Feet pounding, hearts hammering, the girl and the rhino ran through Ringsend. They took side streets and alleys, footpaths and shortcuts, any way and anywhere they could not easily be seen. *She was English. She was police. She'll have a car.* They took the footways, slipped into the sunken cinder running track, used the sheds at the Pigeon House generating station as cover, and Patricia's heart climbed her throat every time a car flashed by.

The rhino had put her down, cantering along beside her, its head swaying from side to side, massive as the keel of a boat. Rhinos could run at thirty-five miles an hour. She'd read that. Why wasn't it leaving her behind?

'Go on,' she hissed through clenched teeth. 'I'll be fine. *Go.*'

Still it kept pace beside her, horn gleaming in the light of the stars.

Sandymount Strand was nearly an ocean itself: a vast curve of sand, flat and featureless in beige and delicate grey. She'd never been on it at night-time before. Night-time wasn't when beaches were for, and now it looked eerie and lonely as the surface of the moon.

'The Poolbeg towers building site,' she panted. 'We get there and we can hide. I can forage for you and –'

The rhino was staring up at the stars. She couldn't blame it. Now that the city was keeping its own lights to itself, the stars glittered hugely, close enough to touch.

'Come *on!*' she shouted, and then something blew across them so fast it flung them both on to their faces. *Jet stream,* Patricia thought stupidly, sand filling her mouth and scratching her cheeks. The world swam. Her ears were popping. The rhino was wailing, and that was the sound that made her roll on to her back.

There were lights in the sky. They *moved,* separate and distinct from the stars, and the air became backwash and grit as they began to descend. Patricia staggered to her feet, and saw a machine – a stout cylinder of steel bigger than her house. Icy wind slashed at her face, snowflakes swirling in a sun-bright beam of light that turned the night to day.

The ground shook – actually shook – as the machine landed.

A spaceship. The word rattled around Patricia's ribcage, trapped in orbit round her heart.

And the rhino's back went ramrod straight. Like a nun, or a teacher, it suddenly stood proud and tall, and then stumbled towards the light. Patricia recognised that run. It was the way you ran when you were little, when you didn't care about being able to make yourself stop because you knew someone was going to catch you.

A platform eased from the bottom of the ship. There was a lone figure standing on it. The figure was huge and hulking, and yet when the rhino flung itself into its arms it fell as if toppled. A head the size of a continent turned to the side, horn held aloft like a policeman in a movie holstering his gun, and then its soft cheek nuzzled down.

And the platform lifted them away.

The rhino never looked back, and Patricia's eyes were filled with tears even before the ship's take-off turned the air to dust.

Patricia Kiernan watched the ship rise slowly, jerkily, until all she could see were lights and she didn't know if it was the ship or the stars. She stayed staring upwards even when the crunch of footsteps sounded behind her.

'You missed them,' she said, hating the quaver in her voice. 'They just left.'

'Caring,' the woman said in that odd English accent, 'is the first thing people feel silly for, and the very last thing they should.'

Sometimes it's kindness that makes the tears come. Patricia felt the first sob rise like a seesaw, and she was too small to make it stay down. That was physics. Things just happened. Believing anything else was magic, and this wasn't that sort of world.

'It just left,' she whimpered. 'I can't believe it. After everything I did.'

'The Judoon are mercenaries,' the woman said. She was blonde and had a long coat, and what Patricia had thought was the shock of seeing a rhino jump through a window was actually just her face – a wide-eyed, unashamed amazement, as constant as the ice in the Mother Superior's voice. 'You know what that word means, don't you?'

'Someone who fights for money,' Patricia said, sniffling. 'How do you know I –'

'Because you were confronted with a holo-screen and a young alien half-feral with fear and loneliness, and your response was to look after it. Because I've been alive a very long time and I've never seen a girl try to give a Judoon an encyclopaedia before. You know what words mean. The Judoon are mercenaries. Their whole culture is built around it. Cost and effect. Following the system. Doing what they're told and no more. No compassion. No mercy. "Know your place." '

Patricia was crying again. Hard. The rhino had been grumpy and mean and had mostly cared about satsumas, and yet now it was gone and she might never touch something that big and strange and unknowable again.

'And rhinos can run at thirty-five miles an hour.'

Just for a moment, Patricia felt what it was like to be anyone else in the world listening to her.

'Wh-what?'

'Judoon can run quite a lot faster, actually, because they stand on two feet. He could have left you behind. Standard Judoon Retreat Protocol. You don't have to run the fastest – you just have to run faster than everyone else. And instead he kept pace with you.'

The woman's eyes were very bright.

'There was a fight. A big fight on a world very far from here. And his mother is all alone, and trying to do the best she can, and she had to fight but she didn't want her son caught up in it as well. So she put him in a saviour pod – a machine that would bring him to a world and hide him behind a holo-screen.'

She sighed.

'I offered to babysit, but the Judoon don't like rule-breakers, and that's a bad habit I have. So I decided to check in on the sly, but he already had someone to keep him safe.'

Patricia sniffed. 'Me.'

'You. And, despite the system, despite the way he'd been raised, despite everything his society would tell him to do, he stayed with you. Because you looked after him. And you did it well too – better than most adults, I'd imagine, if a rhino crashed into their neighbour's house.'

'R-really?'

'There are a lot of worlds,' the woman said. 'And a lot of systems. A lot of scared people making cages that keep themselves on the inside and everyone else out.'

That is where she's heading.

Notions.

Songbirds shouldn't look at the sky.

'Why, though?'

'Ignorance. Anger. Fear they'll lose what they have, that there won't be enough room. But things are bigger on the inside.' She smiled innocently. 'Trust me on that.'

Patricia was a practical child, and she knew what question to ask. 'So what do I do? When people tell me what size I'm supposed to be?'

The woman thought for a moment. 'Look them in the eye, and ask them a question.'

'What question?'

The woman looked at her, and in her eyes there was a little anger and a lot of kindness, and deep in their depths Patricia could see herself, bright and small and surrounded by stars.

'Says who?'

THE MASTER

ANYTHING YOU CAN DO

'Let me take you away from all this.'

His hands twirled round each other like escaping doves, the gesture expansive, confident, seeming to take in not just the alleyway in which they stood but the entire planet Earth. The open door of the TARDIS framed him in honey and gold.

'Um,' Faye said, and looked decidedly uncomfortable. 'No.'

The Doctor blinked. 'What?'

'Not that I'm not grateful,' she said hastily. 'Of course I am. God, I've never been so scared as when the – what did you call them?'

'The Caliginosity,' he said, still with that bewildered expression. 'Though that was just a fragment of a fragment of a true Caliginosity. I have no idea what it was doing on this world. They're supposed to be a myth. A bogeyman from the universe's edge.'

'It didn't feel like a myth,' she said, thinking of the way the air had bent round its mandibles, sound and light distorting as if muddled by a paintbrush. 'Everything felt *frayed* around it, as if it was . . .'

'Picking apart reality,' the Doctor said. 'That's what they do. They feast on it. Like moths in a wardrobe, unravelling space from time and swallowing it down. Or so the stories say.' He frowned. 'But that's why you should come! There's a whole universe out there, a whole universe of –'

'Things like that?'

'Oh no,' the Doctor said, grinning. 'Much worse.'

She just looked at him. His smile disappeared.

'No, Doctor. It's a tempting offer. But I have a life here. I have friends and I have family, and I don't want to disappear down an alleyway and have them wondering where I went.'

'Time machine,' the Doctor said, taking a step towards her, his voice almost wheedling. 'I can have you back before they even notice you're gone.'

'But I'll notice, won't I?'

Anger ghosted through his voice, so quick she wasn't sure if she'd even heard it. 'I'm offering you the –' And then his tone changed back to normal, a magician again, with the grin of someone producing something from nothing. 'Come on. What could be here that's better than –'

'Me,' she interrupted, and now she was angry. 'Me, and a whole life that I've built. You've got your life, and I'm sure it's crazy and beautiful and full of adrenaline and . . . and . . . nebulas or whatever, but that's your stuff. Not mine. So thank you, but no.'

He shook his head. 'I'm doing this wrong. I'm doing this wrong.' He rapped a knuckle against the phone box behind him. 'Did I mention it's bigger on the inside?'

'Yeah,' Faye said, turning away and sticking her hands into her jacket pockets. She could still feel the icy burn where the Caliginosity had grazed her skin. 'So are lots of things. Maybe you don't see that as much as you should.'

The Time Lord watched her go, hunched against the Belfast chill, and removed a pen and a scrap of paper from the pocket of his suit. He scratched out a name and sighed.

'All right. Next.'

They'd saved the day. Again.

'We're getting to make a habit of this, Time Lord,' said Cassie Belmont, twenty-three years old, formerly a pilot in the Third Neptunian Airborne and now semi-regular resident of the most incredible ship she'd ever seen. 'What say we make it official?'

'Hmm?' the Doctor said distractedly. He had flung the doors of the TARDIS wide so they could watch the last of the Cyber-ships combust in the atmosphere, roses of gold and red staining the Nu-Parisian sky. Hundreds of metres below, people were emerging shakily from their houses, staggering from the rubble, clinging to their loved ones, and the Doctor stared down at them, a slight smile playing around those sharp, angular features.

'Nothing,' Cassie said, sighing. Funny how he could notice a misalignment in an orbital laser from ground level but ignore what was right in front of his face. 'Just . . . congratulations. You did it. You defeated the Cybermen, and in the nick of time too.'

'A trifle, my dear,' he said, flicking an imaginary spot of dust from his sleeve. 'Cybermen are stubborn, but unimaginative. Their plan to tear away the Earth's atmosphere so they could harvest the suffocated dead was flawed from the start. All I had to do was turn Nu-Paris's weather engines into an atmospheric shield to keep their air in, and then reprogram the Cybermen's electrostatic accelerator to target their own ships, tearing them apart molecule by molecule.'

'Yes,' Cassie said. 'I know. I was standing beside you when you did it.'

He raised an eyebrow at her.

'But it was still really impressive,' she said quickly. 'Nu-Paris is saved.'

He smiled and breathed deeply. 'It is, isn't it? Such a gorgeous dawn.'

Another Cyber-ship exploded, raining down debris on the city.

'Yes,' Cassie said, then cleared her throat uncomfortably. 'Although . . .'

The eyebrow again. 'What is it, Cassie?'

'Nothing,' she said.

The TARDIS continued its slow spin, and Cassie caught a glimpse of what lay beyond Nu-Paris's shields: the airless, icy fields, the blackened sky and floating, frozen dead. 'It's just a pity we couldn't stop them from stealing the rest of the Earth's atmosphere, that's all.'

'Ah,' the Doctor said. 'Yes. Well. Next!'

'I can't tell you how wonderful this has been, Doctor,' said Edwin DuFrane, formerly of the space station *Phaethon's Choice,* and now staring around the TARDIS's control room as if trying to drink in its splendour one last time. The vaulted, soaring ceiling, the dark and sweet-scented wood panelling, the honey-gold lamps a handspan above their heads – so different from the austere corridors of the *Choice*.

In preparation for his return to the space station, he'd dressed in his old plasmic engineer uniform, which was a far cry from the peculiar get-ups their adventures had required. Victorian suits. Deep-sea exploration gear. Even the robes of the Space Pope (though that was entirely by accident and had not impressed the Space Vatican one bit).

It was a wrench, leaving it all behind. But that's what parting company with the Doctor meant.

'Such wonders,' Abeline murmured, lowering her second head in reverence. 'And such terrors.'

'Like the Burning of Madrigar,' Edwin whispered, running a hand through the goatee he had definitely always wanted to grow, and not just because the Doctor had one. 'And the Cruciform Anew. Gosh, we were lucky to survive that one, weren't we, Abeline?'

'I like to think I helped,' the Doctor said, leaning back against the burnished bronze console, and Edwin could only agree. 'The look on the Dalek Emperor's face will keep me warm on long nights to come.'

'But of course, Doctor,' Abeline said, rubbing her forelimbs together with a rasp. 'We'd be dead a hundred times over if not for you. The universe would be, too. And, even though we must return to our own time, it warms my haemolymph to know that you are out there somewhere keeping us all safe.'

The Time Lord smiled that rare, mysterious smile that felt like a victory every time it came to call. 'Well, that is the work I have chosen. Out of all the many worthy pursuits I could have followed, with my genius and many lives, I choose to help. The weak. The less fortunate.' His eyes rested on Edwin for a second. 'The foolish. What could be nobler? And now –' he clapped his hands – 'we have arrived at your time.'

The abruptness didn't surprise Edwin, nor did the way the Doctor's smile vanished as if it had never existed. The Time Lord was famously terrible at goodbyes. So many planets saved, only for the Doctor and his companions to slip away before anyone noticed.

It made other things easier too.

Not being able to save everyone.

Not being able to save anyone, sometimes.

That Edwin was in awe of the Doctor was in no doubt. It was hard not to be. Abeline felt the same. But it was only after those failures, when he and Abeline hid in their room and listened to the Time Lord rage and storm at an uncaring universe, that Edwin was frightened of him as well.

'Abeline,' Edwin said, and now he was an entirely different type of frightened as he realised that this was it: the question he had been practising ever since they'd met. 'There'll be shuttles to your home hive from *Phaethon's Choice* or . . .' This was it. 'Or you could stay. With me.'

Her mouthparts quivered, first in surprise and then in joy. 'I would like that,' she burred. 'I would like that very much.'

'Good.' He had thought the adventures were over, but as she reached out a serrated forelimb Edwin realised they were only just beginning. 'Good.'

The Doctor coughed.

'Sorry,' Edwin said, and grabbed his bag. 'Goodbye, Doctor!'

Abeline reared up and let out the shrill shriek that was the traditional goodbye of her people, and then they stepped out of the TARDIS together and into the corridor of the space station. So enamoured was he of the feel of her chitin against his skin that it took Edwin a couple of seconds to realise that something was wrong.

They were on the *Phaethon's Choice*. There was the logo on the wall – the bright spiralling sunburst – but instead of gleaming white corridors and the ever-present hum of the plasmic harvesters, this passageway was yellowed by age and neglect, the paint peeling back like dead skin.

Abeline's antennae twitched in the stale, dead air. 'Edwin . . .'

He was already running to a wall terminal, its screen faded and flickering, buzzing like a dying fly. It took an eternity to respond to his touch, but finally the date appeared in the patchy light.

'We've arrived five hundred years after I left,' Edwin said. 'The station's been abandoned, left to fall into the gravity well of the sun.' Horror stole over him. It was one thing travelling through time, but yet another to know that time had travelled on without him. Everyone he knew . . . everyone was dead.

'Edwin, I'm so sorry, but at least it is easily fixed.' Abeline rested a comforting claw on his shoulder. 'We can travel back to the right time.' She turned. 'Doctor, I –'

The TARDIS was gone.

'Doctor?'

Luachmhar was a world at war.

War was its natural state. It had been at war with its sun for aeons, gravitational fields and great licks of solar radiation polishing it like a gem in a jeweller's vice. These same forces had put the planet's crust at war with itself in the form of volcanoes and earthquakes, and once the rest of the universe had found out about the rare minerals created by the upheaval, they had brought their own war as well.

Humanity had come for trisonic beryl to power their hyperdrives, and the Atraxi for snowflake diamonds, their eye-ships churning the sky. The Rutans had come for chyism, the Gelth for astonix, and then the Sontarans had shown up to fight everyone because they were upset at being left out.

Ocelot had spent half her life trying to end the Luachmhar War. Originally from a planet that had never known conflict, she'd enlisted on Luachmhar as a medic, patching up leaking Rutans just to learn scraps of their language, risking her life a hundred times to cajole, persuade or downright bully anybody on any side into listening to talk of peace. A one-woman diplomatic task force, but even she had begun to believe it was hopeless. Until the Doctor arrived.

Hopeless was the Doctor's speciality.

'Armies of Luachmhar, please attend carefully.'

He'd parked the TARDIS in a ruined plaza, bombed to oblivion – literally, in this case. It was now a crater so desolate it had been completely forgotten by every side. Beyond the timeship's doors was an empty wasteland of cooked stone and dead dust, but inside was civilisation and honey light.

On the console screens, tacticians, commanders, brood lords and generals from around the planet yelled so quickly in so many languages that the TARDIS's translation circuits could barely keep up. The Doctor just watched, one leg slung over an armrest like an indolent boy king.

'I imagine you are wondering why I hacked into your morning threatening-each-other sessions. Well, after finding the launch codes to all of your carefully hoarded nuclear weapons . . .'

He smiled, slow and wide as a contented cat. Ocelot had seen her share of fearless men. In her experience, they generally made equally fearless corpses. But it was a challenge, that smile. It was a dare, thrown against the entire universe, a grin that said, *I see you. I see what you can do.*

'Are you sure about this?' she said out of the corner of her mouth. 'We should just put them in a room – without weapons, obviously – and make them talk.'

'Big gestures,' he whispered, without taking his eyes from the screens. 'That's what these people like.' He swept suddenly from his seat, glaring at each leader as if trying to tattoo his words on to the inside of their heads.

'There has never been a ceasefire on Luachmhar,' he said. 'Never a moment where you weren't at each other's throats. Until now. Send the word to your troops. If one of you attacks the other – if so much as a single soldier fires a shot – every one of those carefully hoarded warheads ignites.

Nuclear fire will consume the planet. You are here because you know value, and life is the most valuable thing of all. Your own lives, if nothing else. Now. Instead of threatening each other, talk to each other.'

He muted the screens before they could respond.

'Do you think they'll do it?'

That was the question. It was the *only* question.

One of the screens showed Luachmhar from orbit – a beautiful globe glittering with gems and the constant crackle of weapon fire. Ocelot had given half her life to this war and this world, but she had to believe there was a chance. And she did. She believed it because *he* believed it.

'It would go against everything the Sontarans hold dear and every instinct the Rutans have,' the Doctor said contemplatively. 'The Atraxi have no masters but themselves. The Gelth care about nothing but finding a home for their souls. But, at the end of it all, every species in the universe has a little voice in the back of their head that, no matter what, wishes to live. That's who I'm speaking to, Ocelot. That's what unites them.'

'Well,' she said. 'I hope you're right –'

The warheads exploded.

From orbit, they did not look like detonations. They looked like cancer eating a healthy cell – vast, spreading splodges of beige and brick-red that expanded from four separate sites, billowing up into the atmosphere like smoke against glass. It looked distant, like it was happening somewhere else.

The interior of the TARDIS was silent for a very long time.

'Hmm,' the Doctor said eventually.

The splodges were joining up, and new blots were joining them. There was a growing rumble now, not the background hum of the TARDIS but the incandescent roar of approaching flame.

'I think maybe we should go.' He spun to the controls, turning dials and flicking switches, and Ocelot just stared at the screens and at the planet consumed.

'Let me take you away from all this,' the Doctor said, and pulled a lever down.

Eirene was Ocelot's home world, and it had always known peace.

It was nothing like Luachmhar. Luachmhar smelled like cordite and scorched stone, and Eirene like roses and seawater. Luachmhar's sky was burnt orange and veined with missile trails, but Eirene's was so blue it was almost purple, with a gentle, forgiving sun.

Ocelot remembered why she hated it immediately.

'You're upset,' the Doctor said, following her out into the blue meadow. There was a city in the distance of floating orbs, delicate spires. Anything so bright and extravagant on Luachmhar would have been bombed in a heartbeat. 'I've upset you.' Each word was careful, turned over and over like the components of a machine he wasn't sure he understood.

'What do you want me to say?' she snapped. 'You bet a world on a roll of the dice, and it failed. It failed miserably. We should have talked to them. We should have –'

'You did nothing *but* talk to them,' he countered. 'Ocelot, you spent years trying to get those commanders to speak to each other. Did you think none of your messages, your demands, your pleas, got through? They just didn't *care*. It's not a crime to want to cut your losses.'

She whirled on him. '*You* cut our losses. Your gamble. Not mine.' She had to force her fingers to uncurl from fists. 'This is over, Doctor. I know we talked about other voyages, other journeys when the war was over, but I cannot look past this.'

'Ocelot, you will. It fades after a while. You move on.'

'I don't want to move on.'

He looked at her, shock pinching his features, and she shook her head. 'I'm done, Doctor. I'm sorry. This isn't tourism for me. Luachmhar was my life's work and you ended it.'

'What will you do?' he said, already turning away, one hand running down the majestic grandfather clock that was his TARDIS's current form.

'First shuttle out, probably,' she said, the question draining away some of her anger. 'There's a lot of war in the galaxy. Eirene doesn't need me.'

'Oh, but it will.' The Doctor's face was hidden in shadow, pressed against the wooden grain of the clock. 'Not even a hundred years from now. I believe it'll be the Grom. Or perhaps the Roilmind – oh, you'd hate them. Think rats but without the charm. Millions of them, starving millions, descending on this lush, fat world . . .'

'Doctor.' She'd never heard his voice like that. Cold. Dry. Appraising. As if worldwide catastrophe was something faintly of interest. 'What are you –'

'And then there's Mother Agape, and the Witchwood War, and I *was* going to head there to stop them, with you actually, but the thing is . . .' Now he looked at her, and he looked like a stranger. 'It's a big universe. A really big universe. I can't be everywhere at once. And companions help me figure out which places matter most. Keep me focused, that sort of thing. When I find someone else, it'll be their world that gets saved.'

She looked at him with horror. 'Doctor, are you saying what I think you're saying?'

'I'm saying,' he whispered, his eyes gleaming in the light of the perfect, peaceful city, 'that we work well together. And that I saved your life. Everyone on Luachmhar died except for you.'

He snapped his fingers, and the doors to the TARDIS opened wide.

'I'm saying you owe me, Ocelot. This adventure ends when I say it does.'

And so they went to the Galaxy-Trees of the Cheem, and ran afoul of an Auton orchestra in the city-world of Hostus Duum, and duelled with cyborgs above lava pits, and, with the patience of a soldier, Ocelot laughed at jokes and ran down corridors and, above all, watched the Doctor.

Kandahar, the eleventh century. A city on Sol 3 known to its inhabitants as Earth, carved from sandstone, the sky baked blue and hard by the sun. The Doctor had chosen Kandahar because he'd detected a dimensional rift spilling out carnivorous multiforms, and Ocelot had agreed because she'd seen the Doctor's skill with computers and knew that a pre-technology world was the best bet for the plan she had in place.

It was the height of the chaos. The dimensional rift was opening. In the city's main square, the sultan's soldiers were charging the multiforms, and terrible howls mingled with the screams of men. The Doctor was cobbling together some sort of last-ditch solution from cables and wires, and sparks were flying, and in that crucial moment, as the Multi-Queen reared and the Time Lord laughed in the face of death, Ocelot ran.

She turned and ran.

She dodged down an alleyway, slipping between overturned carts and spilled crates of grapes, ducking into a doorway as a multiform slithered past.

Before she knew it, she was streets away. She stole a sheet from a washing line and wrapped it round herself to hide her strange clothes, her mind already racing. *Earth, the eleventh century.* She'd read up on it as soon as the Doctor had mentioned it. It wasn't the most advanced civilisation, but that was no reason to think she couldn't find somewhere to settle down, and frankly she'd had her fill of advanced.

Down streets, head low, making for the city's edge. Behind her, she could still hear the roars and snarls of the multiforms. Occasionally civilians ran by her and she hid her face, ducking into an alleyway whenever she saw soldiers, but Ocelot had spent a lifetime navigating war zones and with a little luck –

That noise. The noise that had, for the shortest of times, brought her hope.

The TARDIS materialised, blocking the mouth of the alleyway, and the Doctor came from it like an oncoming storm.

'You ungrateful child,' he hissed. 'The things I've shown you. The places we've gone. I *liked* you, Ocelot. You were ready to do anything to achieve your goals. That's something I appreciate in an assistant. But this is a betrayal. And all for what? Some pointless, war-torn little planet? We spent too much time there as it was. If I hadn't –'

'If you hadn't what?' Ocelot said, but she already knew the answer. Maybe she always had. 'If you hadn't detonated the weapons yourself? If you hadn't scoured Luachmhar of all life?'

'I did mean what I said,' he responded casually. 'You get used to it. And, really, all this is my fault. I haven't explained myself properly at all. I was trying . . .' He sighed. 'I was trying something different. Trying to be someone I'm not. Someone specific, actually, but I have to say it's turning out to be spectacularly unrewarding. It is nice having an audience, though. Someone to explain things to. I like explaining myself. People get so confused otherwise.'

'Then explain yourself, Doctor,' Ocelot said. There was a knife in her pocket. She'd stolen it at dinner weeks ago. If she could just get close enough . . .

'That's not my name,' he said, and gave her that challenge of a smile. 'And, if you want to make a life here, what kind of friend would I be if I didn't let you go? Goodbye, Ocelot.'

Her brow furrowed with surprise, but he was already inside the TARDIS, and the sound of the door shutting was the most welcome thing she had ever heard. With a creaking wheeze, it dematerialised . . . revealing the insectile, clicking shape of the multiform that had been lurking behind it.

The final casualty of the Luachmhar War sighed, and drew her knife.

It was a new day. Cade had to tell themself that, or they'd go mad.

The ship *Nowhere's Eye* didn't have days or nights or even time, really, beyond the ticking of the onboard chronometer. It didn't have those things because you needed stars for sunrises, and they'd flown *Nowhere's Eye* to a place where there were no stars at all.

The Doctor called it nonespace. Cade had always been fascinated by it. The universe was expanding in every direction every second of every minute of every hour of every day, and nonespace was the vast blankness it was expanding into.

Beyond the universe. Outside everything. If Cade looked out of the portholes at the rear of the ship, they could see it:

distant splotches of light, the hard points of stars. If they looked out of the front, there was just infinite black.

It was a hell of a feeling. Or it had been, for two weeks. Now, Cade didn't feel anything at all.

They rose and dressed quickly, activating the 'morning' routine scans. Every captain and their ship felt a connection, but for Cade it was literal. Wireless linkages connected their brain directly to the ship. Whirring connectors had replaced their fingers. In a way, Cade was the *Eye* and the *Eye* was Cade. They felt the ship's sensors as their own senses, felt the thrum of its plasma core as their own beating heart.

Nowhere's Eye was completely automated. It had to be. It was unsurprisingly difficult to find a crew for a ship willing to trawl out to the edge of everything. Ships' navigation systems failed in nonspace. Scanners broke down. Sensors brought back ghost returns. The engines misfired, failing to catch as if even the laws of physics didn't reach out here. The only reason *Nowhere's Eye* could even venture this far was because it was tethered to an automated buoy by a braided atlasium leash, clinging to the universe like a drowning child to a lifeline.

Just one of the innovations the Doctor had supplied.

He was on the bridge of *Nowhere's Eye* when Cade arrived, pacing the great glass sphere, stepping round the hulking masses of electro-ganglia and gloam-lines. That ever-present expression of disdain he wore when he looked at *Nowhere's Eye* no longer fazed them. They knew the ship was nothing fancy. You had to turn sideways to pass down even the widest of corridors. Every surface was either gummy or grimy, every engine start was accompanied by showers of sparks, and the captain's chair was just a torn couch with its stuffing leaking out.

He can sniff as much as he wants, they thought. He didn't even have a ship, and the battered old grandfather clock that seemed to be his only luggage wasn't going to get him very far.

'Doctor Cade,' he said, folding his arms. There was a jittery, uneven energy to him – like a mongoose or a rat – that had only worsened as the weeks in nonespace went on. Cade had been broke when he found them, their research grant nearly gone and nothing – literally nothing – to show for it. His help had allowed them to penetrate deeper into nonespace than ever before, but that didn't mean they needed to like him.

'How is the tether holding up?'

'Well, we're not tumbling helplessly into the void,' they said wryly. 'So, until you hear me screaming at the top of my lungs, we're generally okay. Though there's one sensor return I'd like to investigate, on a heading of –'

'No,' the Doctor said. 'We stay here.'

'Doctor, I have my own reasons for being out here.'

'That, until one of my cheques bounce, is entirely irrelevant.'

Cade fell silent.

'You'll get your tour of nothingness, Doctor Cade. Be patient. Isn't being out here enough?' He waved a hand expansively. 'Think of it. On one side, a whole universe of motion and life and sound and love, and on the other absolute nothingness, deeper and more perfectly empty than space itself. This is the only place in existence where you can truly say you have your back to the wall.'

'Yeah,' Cade muttered. 'Great. What did you say *your* doctorate was in again?'

'I didn't.' He padded towards them and, as always, they couldn't quite suppress a flinch at that sudden fearful energy. Cade had been of the opinion, ever since the Doctor had hired them, that he was only ever really regarding them with a portion of his attention. They were a little afraid of what would happen if he focused it all.

'In a million years, the universe will have expanded this far and the place will be dreadfully crowded. You should buy property. Get it cheap. But, for now, just enjoy the peace and quiet.'

'You said it yourself, Doctor,' Cade said. 'I'm a person of science. I'd just like some extra data. About you. Why this spot? What's out here? What are you looking for?'

Sometimes, science is just asking the right question at the right time.

'I'm not looking for anything,' he said. 'I'm waiting.'

A phone rang.

Cade knew their ship from ball screw to brake lights. They had repaired and rebuilt it more times than they could count. And, even though there were parts from a dozen alien technologies and twice that many scrapyards, they knew there was nothing on the *Eye* that made the noise of a twentieth-century telephone.

'Ah!' the Doctor said, grinning wide. 'I think it's for me.'

He darted over to the grandfather clock and opened its door. Cade frowned. It must have been deeper than they realised, because the slender man dipped almost his entire body into it before reappearing with a phone on a long cord.

He straightened, and breathed deep. 'Hello?'

'You're using my name.'

Aural insert. Wired senses. Everything that the *Eye* detected, Cade felt. They barely had to strain to hear the speaker on the other end of the line, and the icy rage nearly blew out their circuits.

'I wanted to see what it was like,' the Doctor said. 'And, I have to say, you make it look a lot more fun than it actually is. So much whining and complaining and dying . . . How do you have the patience?'

'You have no idea what I've gone through, putting your messes right. Unpicking what you did to Nu-Paris –'

'I like to think I improved –'

'Rescuing survivors from Luachmhar –'

'There's some of it left? This is what happens when I don't build the weapons.'

'And using my name. Using my *name*.'

'Well, I do technically have one more doctorate than you –'

'*Master*,' the voice on the other end of the line hissed, and Cade's client seemed to stretch at the sound of the name, like a cat testing the reach of its claws. It fit him far better than Doctor. The *smugness* of it. 'Why have you been doing this? Why have you dragged this ship out here? What is this?'

'Oh, Doctor,' the Master sniggered. 'You know what this is. It's a trap.'

Cade had become used to ignoring the sensors because out here there was nothing to sense, but it came through their connection to the *Eye* like the first touch of sun, a rising warmth inside their chest. Cade expanded their senses through the systems of the *Eye*, their modifications and enhancements reading the nonespace as if they were the ship itself.

It was the tether. The tether had begun to glow. Plasmic beacons were revving to life at intervals along its length like perfectly spaced stars, like a line of Christmas lights draped out across the universe's edge.

'I had to be sure you'd come,' the Master said. 'Using your name was the only way. I had to prove it to you.'

'Prove what?'

'That I can master being you.'

And the nonespace opened its eyes.

Cade's father had been an eel farmer. A broke and tired and angry eel farmer who hated his life and hated his kid and hated the slippery, slithering way he made his living. Only once had Cade been brought down to the dingy harbour where their father and the other villagers raked great writhing masses of the horrid things out of the water, and the sight of the swarming threads had made Cade vomit on the spot.

That was what this looked like. Thousands of sets of crimson eyes were opening in the nonespace, like a whole nebula being birthed all in one moment, and yet nothing was showing up on their sensors.

'The Caliginosity,' the Doctor whispered. 'You found a nest.'

'We did always wonder where they came from,' the Master responded. 'I had planned to bring just one to Earth and let it loose, and then I thought bigger. That's your problem, Doctor. Too concerned with the little things. Why would I use one Caliginosity to devour your favourite planet when I could lead a million of them out of the void of nonespace to pick the whole universe apart?'

The tether, Cade realised. They'd thought it was their lifeline back to the universe, but it wasn't.

It was a lure.

'They nested, and they ate, and reality unravelled so much that they couldn't find their way back.' There was a terrible, shining fascination in the Master's eyes, like a child who'd found a new way to bend the limbs of a toy. 'Like ants losing a scent. So I've given it back to them.'

Already Cade could feel the *Eye* straining, as something began to drain it of power. Lights flickered. They could feel parts of their head going numb as systems shorted out or shut down. They reached out to disable the beacons, but pain flung them back on to the captain's chair.

'Oh no you don't,' the Master said, dangling the phone from his hand, as Cade clutched their head and fought a wave of agony that rocked both them and their ship. 'I've had plenty of time to worm my way into your systems, Cade.

Yours and the *Eye*'s. Couldn't have the bait wriggling off the hook.'

Through their senses and the ship's, Cade could sense the Caliginosity swarming the way those eels had whenever their father threw them meat. Lamprey-like mouths affixed themselves to the hull of the *Eye*, so cold they blistered the steel, and Cade shrieked as if it was their own skin.

They were going to die. They were going to die, and the Caliginosity would climb back into the universe and pick it to threads.

'Gotcha,' the Doctor said.

'What?' Cade and the Master said together.

'That's your problem, Master. That's the thing you always get wrong.'

'What?' the Master snapped. 'What did I get wrong?'

The speaker was smiling. Cade could feel it.

'This isn't about us.'

And through faltering senses, through failing scans, Cade saw it: a host of ships, bright and silver against the infinite dark, spinning down upon the swarm. Blinding spears of light lashed out, and one of the plasmic beacons died. The Caliginosity fell back in a confused, teeming mass, and a voice cut through the searing cold, hot enough to light the whole of nonespace itself.

'This is Cassie Belmont and the Third Neptunian Airborne reporting for duty! Targeting these gross worm things now!'

'This is Ocelot of the Luachmhar Retaliation Alliance here, with Sontarans, Rutans, Gelth and humans together to lend a hand. General Stanna, stop firing on the Rutans! For god's sake!'

'Nonono!' the Master snarled, but Cade had pushed themselves to their feet. Their client had somehow got into their systems, rendered them unreliable, overridden their controls, but they could still jettison the tether manually, even if it meant their own death.

They pelted down corridors, seeing through the *Eye*'s sensors as Cassie Belmont and her squadron directed attack after attack on each beacon and an armada of alien ships sought to drive the Caliginosity back with sheer firepower. Panic thrilled through them as they saw that every volley seemed simply to swell the writhing worms more – they seemed to feast on each apocalyptic burst of light, unravelling it to its constituent atoms and swallowing them down.

With the day Cade was having, it was no surprise at all to see two strangers kneeling at a control panel on the second deck.

'Hi,' the man said, rubbing his clean-shaven chin. 'My name's Edwin. Plasmic engineer by trade. We kill all the lights, we might just stop these things.'

The grasshopper lady beside him waved.

'You won't defeat them.'

All the colour left Edwin's face. The insect beside him hissed like a punctured kettle. Cade very slowly turned round.

It was the Master. The glacial disdain with which he had treated Cade and their ship was tattered now and, though he stood tall and grinning as if this was his moment of victory, Cade could see through the mask to the childish madness underneath, the wounded pettiness no amount of affected dignity could hide.

There was a gun in his hand.

'You won't defeat them,' he repeated. 'They're like nothing you've ever faced before. It took me months to understand them, to control them myself, and you just don't have the ti—'

Someone hit him very hard on the back of the head.

The Master fell to his knees, and behind him was a very angry-looking woman with a length of pipe in her hand.

'Except I was standing right beside you when you defeated one, wasn't I?'

'Faye.' The Master gasped. 'Oh, when *he* asks, you come.'

'No, you pillock,' she snapped, and kicked his gun away
to land beside Cade's feet. 'I came for everybody else.
Everyone you're putting in danger. That's why the Doctor's
here too.'

And, between two beats of Cade's heart, a blue box
materialised in the centre of the corridor. It was sleek and
shiny, though they could see that the corners were worn, and
a light shone from its top – a clean and soft light that seemed
the opposite of the teeming darkness outside.

A figure stepped out. In the flickering light of the
passageway, Cade could barely make them out.

'Trying to be me, Master, and yet you missed the most
basic part.' The figure shook their head. 'It's not about me.
It's not about us. It's about them. Their lives. Their choices.
And whatever I can do to help. I care about them, but you
don't. That's what you get wrong. That's why you lose. A
hundred million horrible monsters on your side, and you're
still always going to be outnumbered.'

And suddenly the whole *Eye* lurched to the side. The
pitted metal wall of the chamber bulged under the weight of
long mandibles. Cade screamed at the intrusion. Steel tore,
and a head shoved through – a blind, snapping fist of a snout,
thrashing desperately in its efforts to get at them.

Cade could feel that desperation. That hunger. It had been in the cold for a very long time, and now heat and light were within its grasp.

The Master bolted. He just bolted. He scrambled to his feet, pushing Faye aside as he fled. Cade expected Edwin or Faye to give chase, but instead he just turned back to the plasmic beacon, and Faye was hefting her pipe, and somewhere Cassie was laughing and Ocelot was keeping the peace, and even though there was a monstrosity scrabbling and snapping just metres from them it was the Doctor that Cade turned to for help.

'What do . . . what do we do?'

'Well,' the Doctor said. 'You know this ship better than anyone else, so first we're going to stop the Master, and then we're going to figure out an extremely complicated and *very* last-minute solution that's going to break about four laws of physics but look very good while doing it. That's what we're going to do.'

'Okay,' Cade said. The monster was nearly in with them now, and there were a whole lot more behind. 'But I meant right now.'

'Oh,' said the Doctor, grinning. 'Right now? We run.'

ABOUT THE AUTHOR

Dave Rudden is a former actor, teacher and time-displaced Viking currently living in Dublin. He is the author of the award-winning *Knights of the Borrowed Dark* trilogy, and enjoys cats, adventure and being cruel to fictional children.

ABOUT THE ILLUSTRATOR

Born and raised in Yorkshire, Alexis Snell later moved to
Cardiff, where she completed a degree in printmaking in
2003. She went on to exhibit in and around Wales and Leeds,
and has had two art residencies. Alexis works in lino,
sometimes adding watercolour or gouache to complete the
print. For inspiration, she looks to old matchbox covers,
record sleeves, tea boxes, postcards, explorers, the circus and
films. She has since moved back to Yorkshire, where she
works from her studio.

ALSO AVAILABLE: